Unjust
Cause

Unjust Cause
Tate Hallaway

WIZARD'S TOWER

Wizard's Tower Press
Trowbridge, England

Unjust Cause

First published in Great Britain
by Wizard's Tower Press 2020

Paperback ISBN: 978-1-908039-95-8

http://wizardstowerpress.com/
http://www.lydamorehouse.com/

Contents

This book is dedicated to my wife, Shawn, and our son, Mason, who continued to believe in me.

Praise for Precinct 13

Precinct 13 is a really fun, fast-paced contemporary fantasy that also works well as a police procedural. [...] Hallaway has put together a fascinating scenario, mixing the supernatural and natural worlds in a way that feels fresh, and her characterization is great, especially the voice of the viewpoint character of Alex.

I'm certainly looking forward to more books about both.

Charles De Lint, Fantasy & Science Fiction

Hallaway kicks off a fun new series featuring a young woman who learns that, despite what she has been told, she is not crazy. Hallaway is known for combining the weird and wacky with an element of danger — and this latest offering is no exception. A terrific starting point for a series and a set of characters that promises to be very intriguing.

Romantic Times

I really enjoyed *Precinct 13* and felt it was a great opener to this new series. Everything from the characters to the incredible world felt fresh and unique making *Precinct 13* a stand out in the Urban Fantasy genre. This is one new series you won't want to miss!

KT Clapsadl, A Book Obsession

There's nothing to suggest that a sequel will ever be published, which is a shame, in my opinion. These characters have heaps of potential that could have been turned into a great urban fantasy series, and we're always in need of those.

Maja, The Nocturnal Library

$

Chapter One

I poked Valentine in the chest. "Valentine, we need to talk."

The last few nights had been typical of South Dakota in the summer, hot and muggy, so I hadn't worn much to bed. I was tucked under a thin sheet in nothing more than a pair of Val's castoff cotton boxers. The open window let in a meager breeze that smelled faintly of the dusty scent of wheat.

Valentine cracked open one eye to look at me. When in human form, he was devastatingly handsome. At least to me. I guess other people saw him differently. Where my gaze lingered on regal, strong features, others found the sharp lines of his face full of cold, calculating menace. I'd call his gray eyes smoldering, but they used words like penetrating, intense, and predatory. I was pretty sure we'd all agree, though, that he was long and lean and had wonderfully hard pale skin, a color reminiscent of moonlight, and deep midnight black hair.

At the moment, however, I could sort of understand where other people got their impressions. Silken hair, disheveled by sleep, hid most of his face—except for a singular icy gray eye that stared at me, unblinking, like a lizard's. A growly and deep voice snarled, "Talk? What topic of conversation could possibly be worth disturbing my slumber?"

You know that thing about sleeping dragons?

Yeah.

Anyway, I ignored the menace in his tone. "Do you see anything wrong with me?"

"You're awake." After a moment, he added coolly, "And talking."

"Exactly," I agreed. "Do you know why I'm awake?"

I could tell by the way his lips pressed together he held back a lot of responses that probably began 'because you live to irritate me' or some similar insult. Instead, he finally blinked and sighed, "Perhaps you'll enlighten me?"

8

Sitting up, I showed him the problem. All over my chest, stuck by sweat, were coins. There was a quarter on my shoulder. A dime wedged itself into the hollow between my breasts. Pennies covered my arms. Something large, like a Mexican peso or a half-dollar, poked the inside of my thigh. Peeling a nickel off my neck, I held it out to him. "What is all this?"

He snatched the nickel from my hand and shoved it under his pillow. "Mine," he said simply. He flopped over onto his other side, turning his back to me, like the conversation was over. "I sleep better with it."

"Well, I don't," I said, pulling the coins from my body and dropping them onto his head one-by-one.

My rain of change didn't even make him flinch. In fact, if anything, the soft sound of the coins clinking together lulled him back to sleep.

I nudged him again. "Seriously, Val, you've got a hoarding problem."

"Mmmm, a problem, you say?" he murmured happily. Long-boned fingers picked up a few of the coins from his pillow. He turned them over in his fingers for a moment, doing that thing magicians can do, rolling them somehow along his hand. Lifting his massive frame, he turned around to face me. The bed creaked with the shift of his weight. That alien gaze of his captured my own. Then, he took a quarter in his finger and... licked it.

The way his tongue caressed the metal was sinful.

I was utterly mesmerized. After he finished molesting the money, he stuck it to my arm. He violated another with that long, wicked tongue of his—a penny this time—and pressed it to my stomach. He smiled lazily at me. Crooking his finger, he coaxed me down. Reaching up, he cupped the back of my neck with his hand, pulling me close, my ear to his lips. Valentine's deep voice rumbled against my eardrum, and sent shockwaves of pleasure deep inside, "You're my greatest treasure, Alexandra Conner. Let me lie atop you."

Oh. Yes.

I kissed him. At first, his lips were cool and unyielding, but then he opened to my teasing pressure. My mouth parted hungrily, but Valentine would not be rushed. Maybe it was a cold-blooded dragon thing, but morning sex always began tortuously slow.

Not that I was complaining. As he moved to roll us over, I let myself marvel in the cleverness of his tongue as it finally slid into my mouth, teasing lips and teeth and sending more shivers along my arching back.

In a moment I forgot everything, even the annoying sensation of coins sticking to our hot, sweaty skin.

An hour later, a small fortune clattered to the floor as I left a trail of pennies all the way to the shower.

After I'd showered, dressed, and pulled a dollar thirty-seven out of the drain, I sat down at the breakfast table with our roommate Robert. Technically, Robert owned the house and Valentine and I were lodgers. Robert was an atypical computer programmer—clean-cut, well socialized, and extremely fabulously dressed. This morning he was in a crisply ironed white button-down, and a tie that managed to match his gentle hazel eyes. Robert and I had forged a friendship through an online game and, when things fell apart for me in Chicago, he'd offered me a place to stay until I got back on my feet.

He was a really awesome guy—

—who apparently was as fed up with Valentine's habits as I was starting to be. "It's got to stop, Alex," Robert said, moving aside the seventh set of salt and pepper shakers on the table to give me a stern look. "I think he's got some kind of compulsion. I mean, I love shopping with the man. He's got a real eye for beauty and quality, but... damn. Thank god 'Hoarders' was cancelled years ago, or we'd be the next 'very special episode.'"

"I know," I said miserably.

Robert picked up the silver saltshaker and admired it. Clearly an antique, it glittered alluringly in the early morning light. He set it back down gently, "Plus, I don't know how to say this, but I think... I think maybe he didn't exactly pay for all of this stuff."

Yeah, Valentine's sense of personal property was dubious at the best of times. Dragons were thieves. I'd watched Val casually steal a car because it was 'shiny.'

"And," Robert continued, "This isn't Chicago. There're only thirteen thousand people in this entire town. It's not going to take long before folks figure where all their missing stuff went, Alex."

A raid would be especially awkward since I worked with the police, tangentially anyway, as the county coroner. More importantly, Robert grew up in Pierre. This was his house and his reputation we were ruining. "I know," I murmured again, dejectedly pushing around my soggy cornflakes. "I'll try talking to him."

"Okay," Robert said in a resigned tone that sounded like he knew just what the outcome of that conversation would be—because it would be the same as the last several attempts. Pushing up from the table, Robert took his bowl over to the sink. He rested against the counter and surveyed all the sparkling kitsch occupying every available counter space of his once tidy, streamlined kitchen. "If this keeps up...." Robert's eyes slid from mine to stare at the polished linoleum floor. "I think it might be time for you two to get a place of your own." At my shocked expression, he pasted on a big smile. "Think of it as moving to the next step in your relationship!"

I smiled back, but was thinking: *Next step in our relationship: homelessness. Everyone's favorite, the 'cardboard' anniversary.*

"You could move in with Jack," Robert said. "You're dating him, too, right?"

I was.

I'd say the whole thing was complicated, but it wasn't. When I approached Valentine with the idea, he'd said something about how monogamy was not only a human concept, but a fairly new one. He liked Jack, and, he thought that it was probably healthy for me to have 'one of my own kind.'

The only wrinkle in the whole situation was that I'd been sort of hoping that Valentine would be a tiny bit jealous. He wasn't, not at all.

"I guess I could ask," I told Robert. The hesitation in my voice was due to the fact that Jack lived in an apartment that was jammed full of electronics... which, when I thought about it was not unlike Valentine's silver obsession. Was I just hot for hoarders?

Robert gave me a sympathetic look. "I'm sorry about all this." He set his coffee mug down in the sink next to the dishes I'd intended to wash but hadn't gotten around to. His back was to me, so I couldn't read his expression when he said, "But, if I'm honest, Alex, I'm not sure Valentine is good for you. I'm sure the sex is great and everything, but... he's seriously dangerous." Giving me a nervous glance over his shoulder, he added: "Seriously."

I opened my mouth to defend Valentine, but Robert scurried guiltily out the door before I could. The slam of the door echoed jarringly.

I sat at the table for a long time, staring at the door. Some part of my mind continued to struggle to attempt to defend my lover. Words wouldn't come. Something in my gut tightened, like the coiling of a spring, because, the truth was, Robert wasn't wrong.

After that unnerving conversation, I restlessly tidied the collected silver. I got everything into a pile on the dining room table. As I watched the morning light glint off the various antiques, I sipped the last of my coffee. Who even needed a toast rack? Was this Britain?

No, it was Pierre, South Dakota.

That was a big part of the other, more immediate problem. If Valentine and I got our own place, we'd be committing—to a lot of things, I supposed, but more notably to this place, to Pierre.

Was Pierre big enough for a dragon?

Was it big enough for *me*?

Having grown up in Chicago, I was kind of a big-city girl. Coming to Pierre had been about escaping somewhere else, running from my past, and the people in my life who thought that I was crazy for seeing magic in the world—particularly, my stepmonster, who was probably an actual demon... but that was its own huge problem.

The point was, this place was supposed to be a sojourn, a stopover.

What Robert suggested involved putting down roots. I have to admit that idea terrified me on an intellectual level, but, practically? Where else would I be able to get such a sweet deal?

I could never do my job as coroner anywhere else.

For one, I'd have to relocate to another town with a murder rate of zero... or <u>less</u>, since, technically, Pierre's current murder rate was minus one—the last body on my examination table got up and walked away.

Which was the other thing any new town would need: magic. I was not interested in going back to a place where people locked me up because I could see things they couldn't.

But, having a murder rate of zero was critical, because, frankly, I was vastly unqualified for the job of coroner. In Hughes County, like it is in a horrifying number of places, the position of coroner is an elected one. You can run for it like you can for school board. Also, like all political offices, it's <u>nice </u>if you have relevant experience, but, if enough people vote for you, you can get the job, anyway.

Like I did.

More people voted against the previous guy than voted <u>for</u> me, if you know what I mean. They would have elected Mickey Mouse in a write-in campaign, they hated the other guy so much. It helped that I didn't have a drinking problem and hadn't gotten caught up in a sexual misconduct scandal. Even so, I wasn't anyone's ideal candidate. I barely made the residency requirement and did have that awkward stint in a locked psych ward and a boyfriend who had served time for aggravated assault. Yet, when word got out that I actually had a couple of months of pre-med, I won in a landslide.

Even so, I was pretty sure that the only reason I hadn't been removed from office for incompetence was because of the whole magic thing.

Once that necromancer woke up, pulled his corpse off the slab, and start-ed wandering around town, I'd been recruited—though maybe a better term would be 'adopted'— by a pseudo-law enforcement agency that went by the moniker 'Precinct Thirteen.' Which, knowing Jack, was probably an intentional nerdy reference to TV shows like 'Warehouse 13.'

Thanks to the precinct crew, I discovered that I was a witch who could drop literal f-bombs and that Valentine was more than just a dangerously hot lover with a cold, cold heart—he was an ice dragon, and my familiar.

Just thinking about all this made my shoulders tense. I took a second to un-hunch with a noisy, popping shoulder roll. I let out a big yawn and stood up. After setting my cup in the sink with the other dirty dishes, I headed for the door. I reached into my pocket to make sure I had my keys and felt a random peso or other foreign coin that had come out of the shower drain.

Stepping outside into the heat and humidity felt like walking into a sauna. Worse, it was only 9 am. I squinted up into the too-bright sunlight. I was just contemplating calling in 'sick' so that I could talk to Valentine about Robert's ultimatum, when my phone rang.

"We have a jumper, at a guess," Jack said without any preamble the second I picked up. Good thing I would recognize his lovely little British accent any-where or I'd have thought this was the weirdest telemarketing call ever. "Come down to the big clock tower. You know the one, yeah? The whole team is here."

I held the phone between my chin and my shoulder awkwardly as I fished out the keys to open up my car, which was parked on the street in front of Robert's bungalow. "Tell me what's really going on, Jack. If it's just a suicide jumper, why is our team there?"

"Because?" I could picture Jack's unhappy expression on the other end of the line. It would be his adorable grimace-y sort of frown. "It's a death, love. We don't get many of those. I'm pretty sure the whole city is here. You wouldn't want to miss the social event of the season, would you?"

It was my turn to make a face Jack couldn't see, but which I was sure he'd sense, anyway. I slid onto the hot seat of my car. The vinyl was scorching and the interior must have been twenty degrees higher than it was outside. "Yeah, I'll pass, honestly. I've got a hot game of Solitaire waiting for me at the office." My thighs made a gross sucking sound as I shifted to start up the car, so I add-ed, "Plus, air conditioning."

"Ah, you know there's more to it," he said with a soft chuckle. "Nana Spider woke Spenser up, shouting about how something is eating her people? Not ten minutes later, 'thump!' and it looks like the... victim?... is, er, was, or could have been, homeless, which is, you know, 'her people.'"

Okay, that did seem more up our alley.

13

"'Eating'?"

"Oh, stop dithering and just come see, will you?"

With descriptors like 'thump!' and 'eaten,'" I wasn't sure I wanted to, but, technically, this <u>was</u> my job.

I'd really, really hoped the medical professionals would have dealt with everything by the time I arrived.

No such luck.

Even though I had to park several blocks from the clock tower, Jack met me as I pulled up with a cup of coffee.

Despite the weather, Jack was in his usual nerd gear—black jeans, steel toed boots, and a tee-shirt with an obscure computer joke on it, black, of course. All of this was in stark contrast to floppy, brown curls, and a bit of a baby face.

I had no idea how Jack had found me so quickly me, given that I had only found a free spot by chance, until he waved at me with his phone. Even at a distance, I could tell it was one of his 'mods,' as there were odd bits of exposed tech and wire braided into Celtic knots around the case.

As I stepped out of the car, Jack pointed to it generally with the coffee cup he held in the other hand, "Future GPS. It knows where you're going to be... er, at least fifty-two percent of the time. I'm beginning to believe in multiverses, but, at any rate, I dare say that this one of my better ones. Dead useful."

I beeped my car, which was less of a chirp and more of a multi-layered moan, not unlike a thousand voices harmonizing on some kind of very short, extremely creepy Gregorian chant. That was another of Jack's mods. He always told me it was silly to even bother locking my car in this town, but it was a habit left over from living in Chicago. When I insisted that I was going to do it anyway, he made me this special lock. My car was now armed against regular thieves and... I don't know, maybe ghosts? Definitely gremlins.

Jack handed me the coffee with a smile.

I took a sip, knowing it would be just the way I liked it: black and bitter.

Jack gave me a peck on the cheek. It was still a little awkward, because the whole poly thing was relatively new. We were still working out the rules. We were definitely more than friends, but not exactly full-time lovers. Valentine also liked Jack, and would have been happy to have a threesome rather than a poly grouping, but Jack was still a little uncertain about liking Valentine back in that particular way—probably because Valentine tended to look at Jack like he was something to devour in one gulp, the way a cat looked at a mouse.

But, we made it work.

Mostly.

So far, anyway.

This wasn't the time to be thinking about my complex love life, however. Taking another sip of coffee, I let out a long, steadying breath and tried to focus on what was waiting for us, two blocks ahead. I could see the distinctive clocktower of the courthouse above all the other downtown buildings. Probably one of the oldest buildings still standing, it had distinctive art deco style and a huge stone eagle underneath the clock. "Spoilers first: am I going to barf?"

"Oh, probably," Jack said pleasantly. "I certainly did."

I hated barfing. It made my throat raw and my knees shake. Probably there would also be some crying, if I was honest. This was the worst job, ever. "Why are we here again?"

Jack shrugged. "I guess Spenser is hoping the body will talk to you? Or at the very least Snaky will give you a cuddle?"

Snaky was how Jack referred to the living tattoo on my arm. It constricted in the presence of certain kinds of magic. Apparently, the magical world was divided into some kind of binary: natural and unnatural. It really mattered to some folks which one you were.

By 'some folks' I meant the 'naturals,' of which I was decidedly not one.

We weren't supposed to think about the world in terms of 'natural' equals good and 'unnatural' as automatically evil. But, man, people sure did. Even when reminded that the only distinction was how one used magic—with the flow, or against it—there was always judgement.

So much judgement.

I couldn't help the eye roll as I asked, "What does it matter if they're natural or unnatural? I mean someone is dead either way, right?"

"I suppose," Jack said, as we turned the corner and into sight of the clock tower. "It just narrows down the suspects."

Did it, though? I was beginning to think that the world was more complicated than one or the other.

A small crowd gathered beneath the tower. Even though Pierre was the state capital, it was functionally a small town where not a lot happened, so the downtown cafes, offices, and shops lost their customers to the excitement of a dead body.

The tension in my shoulders drained a little at the sight of an ambulance because it meant that trained emergency medical technicians were wandering around the scene. People who actually knew what they were doing.

I saw a few regular uniformed cops as well, the sort that Spenser called the 'ordinarium,' doing crowd control—a lot of 'move along, nothing to see here,' even though there was obviously something to see.

I pushed through the crowd by holding up my lanyard. I had a very official-looking county employee badge/keycard that had my picture and was clearly labeled 'coroner' in all caps. As I bumped through ranchers and retirees, making accidental contact with arms and hips, 'Snaky' constricted and released.

There were magical people here?

I tried to catch glimpses of faces, but Jack mistook my hesitance as reluctance to deal with the body and pushed me forward. Even so, I might have made more of it, except ever since last spring and the whole necromancer case, more and more people were becoming aware of magic, awakening any latent talents they might have. The whole thing was called "The Tinkerbell Effect," in other words: the more you believed in magic, the more it existed.

Someone had hastily strung up police tape around the perimeter of the crime scene. The plastic had been twisted around lampposts and through the railings of the courthouse stairs. I stood at the edge of the crime scene, trying to decide if I should step over or duck under the waist high barrier. I chose wrong and ended up nearly tripping.

I stumbled onto the open, broad sidewalk where Spenser stood with two other guys in suits—politicians? FBI? --looking down at the body. An EMT crouched next to the corpse, making some kind of assessment or maybe prepping the body to be transported to the morgue. Though, even from here, I could see they were going to need a scraper.

Bones protruded from what remained of arms. My brain registered human hair, but, otherwise, the body looked like roadkill, like someone had run over a deer about a hundred times and stuck a dress on it.

My stomach lurched. Half-digested Frosted Flakes spattered the boulevard grass.

Somehow, I managed to hold onto my coffee cup.

Wow, I am super-good at this job, I thought as I heaved up the last of breakfast.

I felt a hand on my shoulder. I assumed it was Jack, so I gave it a little loving squeeze. The fingers were just a bit too beefy, so I dropped my grip. Turning, I saw Spenser Jones, our special precinct's chief.

You wouldn't know Spenser was half-fairy, because he looked all cop, or at least the cop stereotype: a big-boned white guy with a square jaw, bushy eyebrows, intense gaze. Probably that was part of his glamour: looking so much like what you expected a cop to look like that you didn't even question it.

"They want to take the body to the morgue," Spenser said. "You need to see if she'll talk to you before they do."

Did she even have much of a mouth left?

I nodded anyway and let myself be led closer to the splattered remains.

When I knelt down beside the body, I decided that I really didn't need to look at her, so I didn't. I looked at the sidewalk, trying hard not to notice blood spatter or gore bits. For some reason, I focused on her shoes, which were sparkly Converse. The glitter in the fabric shone in the sunlight, like a disco ball.

When I'd moved in close enough, she did that thing corpses do in my presence. She tried to sit up, which... nope, too many broken bits jangling for my comfort.

Then I heard the voice: **"Forgotten. But I flew."**

⚕

Chapter Two

N o one else ever seemed to notice the corpses moving around and talking, and so the dead woman jittered back into place without fanfare.

Spenser eyed me anxiously. "Well?"

"Better get out your pad," I said, as I pulled myself up to my feet. "It's a strange one. She said, 'Forgotten, but I flew.'"

The EMT shot me a very odd look. Oh crap, I'd forgotten that we were in the presence of normal people! I was about to desperately try to cover my tracks with some lie about random association and lack of caffeine, when he said, "Yeah, you know, that's weird, but I was going to say that this person looks like she fell from higher up than the top of that clock. Much higher."

"Really?" I glanced up at the clock we were beneath. It was by far the tallest thing in this part of downtown, but it couldn't have been more than four or five stories. A large, stone statue of an American eagle, complete with shield in one claw and arrows in the other, glared menacingly down at us. Black lichen streaked down from the talons, like blood.

"What would it take to do this to a body?" Spenser asked the EMT.

The EMT gave my badge a long, meaningful look, as though expecting me to have something wise to say, before shrugging. "I'm no expert, but this kind of impact? Man, I'd want to say low-flying plane."

Spenser glanced up, gave the eagle a suspicious squint, and then crossed something off his pad. "So, it's just luck she ended up under this clock tower?"

The EMT guy shrugged again, and then said in a tone that was clearly meant to make us feel like slackers, "*I'm* not a detective."

"Technically, neither am I at this moment," Spenser said, and for some reason, he glanced over his shoulder at the two guys in suits that I'd noticed earlier. To me, he added, "Infernal Affairs."

At least that's what it sounded like to me, but Spenser must have meant 'Internal Affairs.' Maybe this was a cop joke? Spenser had been suspended pending an investigation after the necromancer case last spring. In fact, he probably wasn't supposed to be part of this crime scene, but did I mention that our little magical department was about seven people, on a good day?

"Since we're done here, I should probably introduce you to my minders." Spenser waved at me to follow him over to the two ominous men in black.

They were dressed so alike that I initially thought the two men were identical. However, the one on the right was Asian and stood taller than the other by several inches. The taller one had what poets would call a regal nose—it was by far his most distinctive feature. Long, straight black hair was pulled back into a tight, neat ponytail that showed off a widow's peak. He had high and classically chiseled cheekbones. Even at a distance, he seemed to stare straight into my soul in an exceedingly intimate and uncomfortable way.

Not unlike Valentine might. Was this guy also a dragon?

Spenser nodded to the men and said, "This is Alex Connor. She's part of our team."

I held out my hand for a shake.

"Nice to meet you, Ms. Connor," the taller one said in crisp English, but he declined my offer of a handshake. Instead, he gave me a slight bow. "I'm Jiroubou..." then he hesitated, as if uncertain of his own surname. Finally, he decided on: "...Tengu."

His partner snorted a little laugh at that for some reason.

When Tengu slid his sunglasses back into place, I felt a strange wave of relief. I turned to his partner with my awkwardly still unshaken hand. He took it unhesitatingly and gave me a firm pump. This one made no move to remove his mirrored shades. Like Tengu, his hair was dark, but slightly more brownish. It was cut short, though long enough to curl at the tips. Like his partner, he was handsome in a 'Man on Street #1' Hollywood actor way.

After releasing my hand, he said one word, "Furfur."

Fur-Fur? Was this some kind of online werewolf name like Moon-Moon?

"What?" Tengu chuckled, "Not going to tell the lady your full title?"

Furfur might have rolled his eyes; it was hard to tell behind the mirror shades. "Go ahead," he sighed. "I know it amuses you."

Tengu's smile was a cold twitch of thin lips. Gesturing dramatically with both hands, as if showing off a prize on a gameshow, he said with a flourish, "This, Ms. Conner, is the Right Honorable Earl Furfur, Commander of the Twenty-Nine Legions of Hell."

"Retired," Furfur added.

19

"Hell?" I sputtered. Had I just been introduced to a demon? I felt the urge to step away, maybe even run. This was the same type of creature as my step-monster, a woman who was responsible for mentally torturing me.

"Yes, Hell," Furfur nodded casually, as if we were discussing the weather. "Mmm, it's lovely. You should visit sometime."

"Um?" Was that a threat? A comment on the state of my soul?

Spenser explained, "Hell is like Faerie. It's an extra-dimensional place. You get there via the Primrose Path."

"So, is there a Heaven, too?" I asked.

Furfur looked a little put out by this conversation. He shoved his hands into the pockets of his trousers. "Hell is just north of the Celestial City—though the exact boundaries are still in dispute."

"'Dispute?' The Right Honorable Earl means <u>war</u>," Tengu said. "Demons and angels have been fighting a horrible, bloody war over territory for centuries."

"Millennia, really," Furfur correctly quietly.

"Right," I said, because I guess I knew that? Only, like everything since coming to Pierre, things were both weirdly familiar and nothing at all the way I thought they were. My throat was raw from vomiting, and I sipped the hot coffee to soothe it. Hot coffee on a hot, muggy day should be gross, but I couldn't stand iced drinks before noon.

"Enough politics," Tengu said somewhat sharply, with a glance at his partner, like maybe this was the sort of thing Furfur could go on about at length. "Can we get back to the business at hand? Is the victim human?"

"I... guess I don't know." I turned to look back at where the EMT was carefully covering the body. It would be delivered to the morgue, my office. I turned back to Spenser. "Is there a test for that?"

Spenser didn't look at me when he answered the question. His attention was entirely on the two agents. "I've got Jack working on it," he said. "We'll know in an hour."

"You should really step back, Jones," Tengu said, his face stony. "We've not yet reinstated you."

Spenser's face tightened. He jerked a thumb at me, "Look, this one is such a newbie that she doesn't even know human from non-human. Jack can only do technical work, Devon's useless—he always has been—and my partner still doesn't entirely remember her own name. The rest of my staff are part-timers, amateur astrologers, tarot or tea-readers, and contract workers, so, unless one of you wants to take over, there isn't anyone else qualified to lead the investigation."

Furfur tipped his sunglasses down, and I could see square, goat-like pupils. "Funny you should mention that.... Your Royal Highness, Spenser Jones, you're hereby relieved of duty. I'll be taking over this investigation."

I held my breath, waiting for an explosive reaction from Spenser. There was so much about what Furfur just said that he would hate, not the least of which was being called out as a faerie prince.

His eyes went hard and he pressed his lips together, but somehow Spenser kept his cool. "What about updates? Can I at least get reports?"

Tengu leaned into his partner and whispered something. I could only catch a few words, something about 'conflict of interest,' but I wasn't sure if he'd said there were some or there weren't.

Crossing his arms in front of his chest, Furfur gave Spenser a long look from behind his mirrored shades. When he spoke, however, it was directed at me: "There are really so few magicals?"

Devon, the vampire-werewolf hybrid, had been AWOL for several days, and it wasn't even the full moon. "Basically," I agreed. "Yeah. I mean, have you seen this place? There's just not a lot of here... well, here."

Furfur exchanged a glance with Tengu but nodded. "Very well, I will keep you 'in the loop.' Understand, that this is strictly a courtesy, Your Highness. We are here because you are suspected of having interfered with an investigation before. My partner insists that we should consider the insular nature of a small town and that there is no reason to assume that, without a personal connection, you would do it again. However, I am suspicious of how you were even alerted of this incident, Your Highness. Who is this Nana Spider to you? What is her connection to Faerie?"

Spenser snarled and grimaced at every use of the royal title. Through clenched teeth he said, "I don't know how many times I have to tell you two, but I don't claim that title. It's just Spenser, or, you know, Mr. Jones."

"Answer the question, Mr. Jones," Tengu prodded.

It looked like Spenser was going to blow his rapidly decreasing cool, so I jumped in: "Everybody knows Nana. She's this nice old homeless lady! We sometimes go to her and she makes weird predictions with ketchup spatters. I think she has a garbage familiar?"

Next to me, Spenser took in several sharp breaths through his nose, but managed to nod. "If she's got any connection to the Realm, it ain't through me. A lot of people with the sight are naturally closer to the Good Neighbors, though, so I wouldn't be surprised if she was known on that side. It's why she called me. Or rather, why whatever numbers she randomly dialed connected to me. The reason I live in South Dakota is because the nearest enclave is thousands of miles away. If my people are anywhere near here, they're usually lost."

"Avoiding your royal duties?" Tengu asked, in a clearly disapproving tone.

"Something like that," Spenser agreed with a shrug.

"Can you arrange for us to interview your mother?" Furfur asked.

Spenser snorted. "I dunno; can you get Lucifer on the line?"

Furfur made a face. "I'm not his bastard son."

"Whoa!" I said, shocked on Spenser's behalf. "I mean, can we say extra-marital or something?"

Spenser lifted his shoulder again. "It's what she calls me, Alex. I'm used to it. And, to answer your question, Right Honorable Earl, no. It doesn't matter that I'm her blood, I can't get her to show up on command. One, I don't know if you've heard about how time works for my mother's people, but 'making an appointment' is not a thing." Spenser frowned deeply and continued, "Secondly, interviewing my mother is inviting madness. I mean, for real, you could go insane trying to get straight answers out of her. Maybe you'd be more immune as a demon, but I wouldn't count on it. Honestly, I might be able to get one of her envoys to come if you're really insistent on this, but that means you need to be ready to talk to a frog and possibly pay in blood or first borns."

"I will handle this," Tengu said, his finger pointing at his nose. "My people, the yokai, are not unlike your faerie. Send the envoy to me, Mr. Jones."

"Your funeral," Spenser said.

"Our investigation," Furfur corrected. "You would do best to cooperate and not make idle threats."

"It's not an—" Spenser started, but I jabbed him in the side with my elbow.

I finished somewhat clumsily for him: "—not a bad idea to have breakfast, huh? Solving crimes sure makes me hungry! Who's with me?"

Which is how I ended up at Big Al's Diner with a demon.

Spenser and Tengu had headed back to Spenser's place, ostensibly to figure out how to get in touch with Spencer's mom, the Queen of Faerie. Meanwhile, the demon and I walked down the block to my favorite greasy spoon breakfast place. Somewhere along the line, I lost Jack. My guess was that he headed off to our main office once the body had been cleared. I'd have to ask him if he was avoiding the 'Infernal Affairs' agents for any particular reason, or just for general purposes.

Not that I blamed him either way.

I wasn't a super-tiny person, but Furfur loomed. Plus, maybe it was his demonic 'presence' but I felt like I was walking in a shadow of slithering darkness. It made me shiver despite the heat. We didn't talk at all during the entire walk, nor any more than what was necessary to be seated once we were at the restaurant.

Finally, I broke when Furfur sat across from me in a cracked patched red vinyl booth and started looking through the menu. His sunglasses were still on. "Furfur? It's a little... I mean, can't I call you something else? Do you have nickname or something?"

"It's already a shortening of the Latin 'Furcifer.'"

I wasn't sure that was any better. "No one calls you anything else?"

Obviously attempting to change the subject, he asked: "What's good here?" Furfur set the menu down in a definitive way and folded his hands on the top of it. He stared at me in a way that implied that he would like to get down to serious business. The business, apparently, of Big Al's heart attack on a plate.

"They do have a steak and eggs thing if you like, you know... blood." I may have waggled my eyebrows unintentionally, but I couldn't help it. How was I supposed to behave? There was an actual demon from Hell sitting in a diner with me.

"I'm not a vampire."

"Oh. Right," I said, though frankly, having met a vampire, I couldn't say that they were a terribly impressive species. I'd been hoping for pale skin and long, sexy black hair, or at the very least, decent fashion sense. From what I could tell, Pierre's resident vampire never changed out of his ratty sweats and collection of food-stained college tee-shirts.

The demons, in comparison, at least had the vaguely sinister corporate haircut and dark black suit, very middle management—a definite evil vibe. I wondered if Spenser's comment about 'Infernal' Affairs meant that only demons populated this particular branch of whatever overarching organization Precinct 13 belonged to or if we were just unlucky to get two of these jerks.

I also kind of wondered if Furfur knew my stepmom.

"So," I said, "Demons eat people-food? I thought you said you were from another dimension."

Behind the shades, I could tell his left eye did a little twitchy-squinting thing. "It's more of a parallel universe thing. Mostly the same, entirely different. You know how it goes."

"No, I really don't."

"Obviously," he said dryly.

"Which, I guess, is weird," I said, staring out at the late morning crowd. "My stepmother is a demon, or so I've been told."

Furfur glanced up at that. "A true demon? One of the Fallen? Or an ifrit?"

I had no idea what the difference was. "Ummm—"

Our waitress was Native, college-aged, and had the look of someone who wanted to be anywhere else but Al's Diner. "What can I get you folks?"

I ordered coffee and a side plate of bacon and another of toast. Furfur gave me a disapproving glare over his menu to which I replied: "What? I'm a simple girl with simple tastes."

Furfur got the granola pancake, surprising us all.

He shrugged helplessly. "I need to cut my cholesterol."

"Bummer," I agreed. "You can totally sneak some of my bacon, if you want."

"How kind of you..." he started sweetly, but finished with a sarcastic, "... to attempt to kill me so soon. I rather thought that would be our second date."

The waitress smiled at that in a way that made me shake my head vehemently. This was definitely not a date, but I don't think she saw my 'nope' expression before she scurried off to put our order in. I suddenly worried that Furfur's pancake was going to end up heart-shaped.

"So," Furfur said, his hands still over his menu. "As your new acting boss, what do I need to know about your division? Who are they? Personalities?"

Boy, where to start.

We'd come to the diner at its busiest hour. A pleasant murmur of conversational noise and clinking silverware blotted out the classic rock radio station that played over the speakers. That particular diner smell—a combination of slightly burnt coffee and whatever oil they used on the industrial grill—filled the air. I collected my thoughts as I played with the sticky paper that held the napkin and utensils in a tight bundle.

"Let's see," I dropped the napkin ring to hold up my fingers to count everyone off. "There's me, Jack, Hannah, Devon, and Spenser."

"Spenser said there were seven of you."

"I think he was counting familiars. Jack and I both come with one."

"I see," Furfur took a sip of water. I tried to see if he had a snake's forked tongue, but then I remembered that his eyes were goat's eyes. I should probably have been looking at his shoes for evidence of hooves.

"And you're all trained police officers?"

I coughed out the water I'd been swallowing. "No, where'd you get that idea? I'm barely trained as a coroner. I think Hannah might be the only other one besides Spenser who went to police academy, but... who knows if she remembers any of it."

Furfur's dark eyebrows came together over the mirrored shades. "That sounds problematic. What's the deal with this Hannah person?"

"Uh, well," I said finally, "Hannah is a golem. She... uh, had an accident where she was kind of erased by a necromancer, but the rabbis mostly put her back together. The thing is, she forgets some stuff. It's super awkward."

"Ah, yes, Hannah Stone, the prince mentioned her as a former partner," Furfur nodded. "She can still do her work?"

"She never forgets any of those details!" I felt myself getting defensive on Hannah's behalf. "The rabbis wrote that into whatever spell they conjured. She's been *directed* to solve crimes in Pierre. She's perfect at her job. Perfect and... tireless. But, it's, you know, the rest of us that drift in and out of her memory. She forgets who she knows and she reintroduces herself. Stuff like that, little things, really—but yeah, no, really big, fucking heartbreaking things. But, other days she's fine."

The waitress returned with the utilitarian, white, chipped and stained mugs, and a thermal pot of hot coffee. I distracted myself by going through the motions of pouring myself a cup.

I didn't like thinking about Hannah. Every time I did, my stomach did a weird tight twist. I'd remember finding a pile of sticks and mud and stone and just knowing that it was her.... Disembodied—no, de-*soul*-ed. The letter for life erased and replaced with death. So simple; so cruel.

Thinking about that also recalled the other big fubar of my life, "And then, there's Devon Fletcher, who is partly blind? Though with his vampire healing, he might be getting better. Anyway, kind of my fault."

"How so?"

"I was never trained as a witch. I didn't know my curses were, you know, curses."

Furfur sat back and gave me a penetrating look from behind his shades. "That's unusually powerful."

"Is it?" I didn't really know any other witches besides Jack, and his magic was completely different from mine.

"You're certain you're nothing more than a magical practitioner?"

"What else would I be?"

Furfur said nothing, but he seemed to be thinking very hard. I thought he was staring at me from behind those mirrored shades. "Your familiar taught you nothing? You know nothing of your craft?"

I rolled my now empty coffee cup around on its edge, self-consciously. The idea that Valentine had failed me by not teaching me witchcraft was something I heard constantly. I didn't want to get into how he'd spent the first few years we were together in prison, and I didn't understand why it was Valentine's responsibility, anyway. Didn't witches learn in covens? I let my coffee cup roll back into place with a sigh. "It's kind of learn as you go? And I don't really have a lot of call for it here?"

Furfur nodded. "I suppose not. I'd heard that this Devon character was particularly useless. The prince seems to think little of him."

"Well, I mean, would you like a guy who tried to kill you? To be fair, Devon might have only been after a snack, but, man, he picked the wrong guy. You know Spenser is a faerie and there's that thing about faerie food... Devon ended up 'Enthralled.'" I didn't make air quotes, but I strongly implied the capital-E.

Furfur pulled a slim smartphone from his inner pocket. He powered-up a notetaking app and started thumbing furiously. "Ah, interesting. The prince keeps a slave, a vampire slave?"

Slave seemed a little harsh, but probably accurate? I found more to quibble with in terms of Devon's 'species' designation. "Devon's not entirely a vampire. The other half is werewolf."

"But you don't disagree that he's a slave?"

"Well, the magic of the thrall means that Spenser can order Devon to do things against his will." That made me plenty squeamish; I'd seen it in action a few times. "I think mostly Devon does whatever he wants, except when Spenser gives him a command." There were nuances here that were probably not necessary to try to distinguish, because, actually, yeah, it was uncomfortable.

My thoughts were interrupted by the roar of motorcycle engines. A horde of them pulled up outside Big Al's. Summer in South Dakota—the home of Sturgis—meant motorcycles were a constant, but this was a larger group than normal.

A few heads glanced up as the cow bells on the door chimed and a half-dozen longhaired, heavily tattooed sorts pushed in. There was a little nervous exchange of glances among the customers when it became obvious that all their jackets matched, and a name was stitched on the back of the jackets: "Lone Wolves."

Furfur glanced over at them and shook his head. "We need to talk about this town and the things Spenser did to it. A werewolf pack? They must have smelled the Tinkerbell Effect a mile away."

Werewolves?

I looked at the group with renewed interest, trying to see if I could determine anything 'wolfish' about them.

That's when I saw the guy we'd just been talking about, Devon.

More accurately, I spotted him for a second, just as he dodged behind the broad shoulders of a burly redhead. It was weird to see Devon in biker gear. He was our local, decidedly unsparkly, not-at-all suave vampire who tended to prefer sweatpants over capes.

The glimpses that I caught of Devon as he tried to dodge my attention surprised me. No ratty college sweatshirts today. He'd dressed head to toe in leather. Biker boots with bandanas wrapped around them, chaps, and a jacket. From what I could tell, Devon had forgotten his shirt, so it was all pale man-flesh visible under the open jacket front. Was that a nipple piercing? A tattoo? Several tattoos?? He looked like a walking strip club advertisement for some-place really skeevy.

Furfur noticed my distraction.

Should I cover for Devon? What had we been talking about? Devon, mostly. Shit! What else? "Uh, yeah, that darn Tinkerbell Effect. Big problem."

Furfur frowned, scanning the group of bikers as they drifted in and took up seats along the counter, buckles and chains jangling. "Some wolf you know over there?"

Devon slipped off for the bathroom. "No?"

"No?"

"No." I said more firmly, though far less convincingly.

My lie was torn asunder when the big burly redhead, whom I, in fact, did not know, came striding over to our booth with intent in his eye. His bright auburn hair was rock-star length, hanging just over the shoulders. To keep the bangs from falling in front of his long, narrow face, he twisted some of it back into a kind of topknot. There was a narrow strip of white at his temple, where hair had come in without color, perhaps after an injury.

Devon, who had been trying to make his way unobtrusively to the bathroom, came running after the big dude. "Just leave it, Mac!"

'Mac' ignored Devon. He stood in front of our booth.

Furfur glanced up at him, a dark eyebrow arched over the rim of his sunglasses, like he was only mildly curious. Yet, at the same time, I could see the way his body tensed for a fight.

Meanwhile, I knew I should feel threatened, but instead I just smiled. Even though the sight of this strange, lumbering, muscular man in denim, leather and chains should have scared the shit out of me, I was fascinated instead. I guessed this was just one of the ways in which I wasn't normal. Things that other people freaked out about seemed kind of hot to me.

Besides, Mac looked like such a wild, untamed thing. The black, geometric lines of stylized tattoos that were visible on his arms below where the sleeves had been cut off his leather jacket only added to the impression that we were being stalked by something.

Smiling disarmingly, Mac nodded at me and offered a huge, calloused hand to shake. "Heya, Alex, is it? You're Devon's witch, right?"

I hesitated. I would never call myself Devon's anything, and also sometimes people got a shock when they touched the hand with my snake tattoo. I gave a little look at Devon, who nodded that it would be okay. I allowed my elbow to be rattled by Mac's enthusiastic pumping. Instead of letting go right away, he turned my palm over so he could admire the 'ink' that encircled my wrist all the way up to my shoulder.

"Whoa," he said, whistling under his breath in admiration, "That's serious work. Who did it for you?"

"A dead necromancer," I said plainly.

Mac nodded, completely unfazed. "Is he all-the-time dead or can you give me his number? That's mighty fine detail on those scales there."

"All-the-time dead," I confirmed. Mac's compliment, however, made my snake tattoo preen.

Mac raised his rust red eyebrows briefly as if he'd sensed it, too. "Oh. Not ink—a spell. Bummer," Mac said.

Letting my hand go, he plunked himself down beside me in the booth like he'd been invited. I had to scoot over to avoid being sat upon. He picked up Furfur's discarded menu. "I'm starving, what's good here?"

Furfur frowned. "Are we friends?"

Devon, who had been standing behind Mac unsure what to do about his force-of-nature friend, sat down next to Furfur. "We are now," Devon said, sounding somewhat miserable about the prospect. "Nice to meet you, I'm Devon Fletcher and this is my... uh, friend, Dunmore McIntosh."

"Mac," Mac said. "Dunmore is just stupid."

"I still don't think we know you this well, Mr. McIntosh," Furfur said, his voice dripping with distain. "Or you, Mr. Fletcher."

Mac waved at a waitress and held up two fingers to indicate the number of extra people at the table who needed service. Off-handedly, he said, "That's fine, 'cuz we aren't here to talk to you, demon. Just the witch."

Was I the only one who noticed the blushing hesitation when Devon introduced Mac as an 'uh, friend'? Where I came from that often meant 'lover.' I'd been glancing between the two men trying to see other signs of a relationship between them when I realized everyone was staring at me. "Uh... so, what can I do for you?"

Furfur resigned to being ignored and sipped his water with a sigh.

"It's time for Devon to rejoin the pack," Mac said. "I'm the alpha now and I need my mate. So, I need you to break the faerie's thrall."

Before I could reply one way or the other, Devon looked me in the eye. His gaze was hard, but the remains of the clouded over haze of his previous blindness were obvious at this distance. "You owe me, Alex."

☥

Chapter Three

I looked helplessly between Mac and Devon. It was true. I did 'owe' Devon. If he didn't have the combined healing factors of a werewolf and a vampire, Devon would be completely blind. It was one hundred percent my fault.

I sipped my coffee miserably and felt my stomach clench in a way that might have been too much caffeine and not enough food, or, more likely, guilt. I glanced up at Furfur and explained, "Devon got caught up in one of my f-bombs."

Furfur sat back against the red vinyl of the booth and crossed his arms in front of his chest. He shook his head. "F-bomb? Ah, yes, the extraordinarily powerful curses you mentioned. You really have no control over them?"

"I try not to swear?"

Furfur frowned.

Mac nodded, "Witch's curses, man. Serious shit."

Furfur scratched the line of his jaw. His frown deepened in Mac's general direction, "I thought the current polite term was 'practitioner.' There's no need to use outdated, bigoted language." To me, he asked, "Despite what the werewolf says, this is not at all typical. You know that, right?"

The waitress returned with a menu for Devon, so I was spared having to answer right away. I wouldn't have known what to say, anyway. No one had been more surprised than I was when an accidental 'fuck' turned into a literal bomb that blew a smoldering crater in the graveyard where we'd had a showdown with the necromancer.

"I thought 'witch' was what you called yourself," Mac said to me. "I didn't mean no offense."

I waved off Mac's apology. "It's fine. I mean, it is? I guess I don't really know what to call myself. This is all still new to me."

"'Magical practitioner' is the current acceptable term," Furfur insisted.

"Can I still call you 'demon'?" Mac asked with a little sneer that made it obvious that he'd be quite happy if that <u>was</u> an insult.

"You can," Furfur said. "Though, I think now that we've made introductions, it's considered good form to use people's given names rather than a species designation, Mr. McIntosh."

"Says the guy who's been calling me 'wolf,'" Mac said. "What was your name again?"

Furfur cleared his throat, clearly unhappy to have to tell. "Furfur."

"That's it? One name?" Devon asked. "Like Cher?"

"He's some kind of count," I added, unhelpfully, but it amused me.

That annoyed eyebrow twitched. "Earl," Furfur corrected. "If we're using titles, I prefer 'Commander.'"

"I bet you do," Mac muttered.

Any argument that might have developed was diverted by the arrival of food.

The late breakfast crowd was in full swing and our waitress was apparently helping customers elsewhere because our food was delivered by a balding, older guy who looked like he was probably a cook or a dishwasher, given the grungy apron he wore. As he set our plates down, he said, "Hell of a thing about that jumper, huh? Seems like every so often some kook takes a dive off that damn building, you know?"

I didn't know, but I nodded politely. I also didn't feel the need to correct the guy that this particular 'kook' was not a suicide—or, at least, not one of the usual sort.

Furfur stared unhappily at his heart-shaped pancake.

Seeing it, Mac smiled, "Oh, is this a date?" Ignoring both Furfur and my emphatic 'no's, Mac said to the waitress, "It's a double-date, then? Make my blueberry pancake like that, would you?"

"Sure thing!" the waitress said, her smile bigger now, like she was pleased that the rough looking biker came with his arm jewelry boyfriend.

When things settled down, Devon cleared his throat. "Can you do it, Alex? Break my thrall?"

I had no idea. "I'll ask Valentine."

Devon nodded, satisfied. But, Mac wanted to know, "Who's Valentine? Another w—practitioner?"

"Her familiar," Devon said. "Ice dragon."

Furfur choked on his heart-shaped pancake.

Mac's eyes went wide, and his face drained of color. He repeated Devon's last word in a kind of horrified whisper, "Dragon?"

I nodded, having forgotten that dragons weren't exactly commonplace, particularly as "familiars."

After clearing his throat, Furfur said, "You're in possession of a dragon? You? You who doesn't know how to harness curse power? Also, it may have escaped your notice, Coroner, but our murder victim just fell out of the sky. Perhaps you should have this ice dragon—Valentine, was it? —stop by the precinct headquarters so that we can rule him out as a suspect. Besides, I wouldn't want to waste the singular opportunity to meet a dragon in person."

"Wait, Valentine's a suspect?" Devon perked up, "There's been a murder?"

I was grateful that Furfur took the opportunity to explain the details to Devon because my mind had frozen at the idea of Valentine being a suspect for a crime... again. The last time Valentine had been brought in for questioning by the police, he'd ended up in prison for aggravated assault—for two years.

For trying to kill my stepmother.

If it were the sort of thing where I could say 'it was all just a misunderstanding,' that would be one thing.

Make no mistake, Valentine was guilty. He never even pleaded otherwise. In fact, he told the court that his singular regret was that he hadn't managed to kill her.

As you might imagine, this did not go over well with the very human, very non-magical judge. I mean, this was in Chicago, at a time in my life, when even I didn't know magic was real. I just thought that my boyfriend and my step-mom didn't get along and that somehow things had gotten violent.

The only mitigating circumstance was the fact that, unbeknownst to me, my step- 'monster,' really <u>was</u> a monster. She was, as it turned out, out to get me, painting me as a paranoid schizophrenic. Worse, she told me that there was no such thing as magic.

None of that was admissible in court, however.

More to the point, even if my stepmonster was quantifiably evil, it's still difficult for me to say that she deserved to be attacked.

Furfur was winding down his explanation of the details of the case. I might not be an expert coroner, but I'd seen enough TV police shows to know that it never went well when you didn't fully disclose criminal pasts to the police. Yet, my previous, real-life interactions with the cops did not fill me with a whole lot of trust. I should say something, right now about my stepmother and Valentine.

I opened my mouth, but I stopped. What were the odds that Furfur, Commander of the Armies of Hell, would accept an attack on one of his countrymen—er, dimension colleagues? —as just cause.

My cellphone beeping made me jump. A notification came in from my office that the body had arrived at the morgue. "I've got to go," I muttered. "Work."

"I'll expect your dragon in my office this afternoon." With a check of his expensive-looking watch, Furfur said, "Say, three o'clock?"

Not trusting myself to speak, I just waved a vague hand and fled the diner.

I walked out into a wall of wet heat.

In the Midwest, there's a saying: "It's not the heat, it's the humidity." Chicago had had days like this, but more often than not, the breeze coming off Lake Michigan offered a fair amount of relief. Here, not so much. If anything, the proximity of the Missouri River just gave the hot, moist air a distinctively fishy smell.

By the time I reached my car, sweat drenched my entire body.

I'd only walked four blocks.

Disarming Jack's multidimensional car alarm, I left the car door open while I cranked the air conditioner.

As I waited for the vents to stop blasting overheated air, I tried to decide what I was going to do about Furfur's demand.

Obviously, Valentine would go in for questioning. He didn't murder that poor woman—at least, I felt fairly certain about that.

I supposed that, technically, Valentine could have slipped out of the house while I showered and done this heinous deed for no good reason, but that would require my dragon boyfriend to have been awake before noon.

Not likely.

More to the point, Valentine would be offended by the idea that he would murder someone indiscriminately and then toss the body somewhere obvious for the police to find. He'd very imperiously remind everyone that he would eat what he killed. He was an intelligent creature, and, as I was sure he'd put it, he'd never be so wasteful.

The air from the car's vents finally felt cool. I shut the car door and buckled myself in. As I drove along the streets to the morgue, however, I couldn't quite shake my feeling of deep unease.

The problem boiled down to the fact Valentine <u>was</u> violent.

I was in court the day that they showed the jury the pictures of what he'd done to my stepmonster. Every woman in that room flinched.

Even me.

He'd chosen to attack my stepmother when I wasn't around. All I'd had to try to understand the events before Valentine's arrest were those evidence photos of fist-shaped bruises, of broken bones. I'm not sure I ever processed them properly, because the next thing I knew he was being sentenced and sent away.

I remembered being shocked, since he never raised a hand to me.

I hadn't thought much about this whole issue since learning that Valentine was a dragon.

My stepmother had shown no signs of being eviscerated or bitten or clawed. All of Valentine's attacks had been constrained by the fact that he'd remained staunchly in human form. Now, I wondered: why? Without me around, the two of them could have had a full-out magical battle. I couldn't imagine that my stepmonster would have held back; had Valentine intentionally hobbled himself? If so, why would he do that?

Clearly, he could do plenty of harm as a human.

Was that what bothered me? Should this roiling in my gut settle better, being reminded that in dragon form he could have dealt far more damage?

Did it matter? Wasn't he just as responsible, no matter what form he was in?

Then again, did we blame a wild animal that killed a person? Perhaps not, but we still tended to put down any beast that got the taste for human blood.

Were there rules about this in the magical world? Would Valentine be in trouble—much bigger trouble—all over again for what he'd done to my stepmonster?

I spent much of the rest of the drive considering ways to evade the questions, to expunge or hide records. As I pulled into the parking space marked "County Coroner," I realized that what I really wished was that Valentine's past didn't exist.

Punching in the code, I swung open the heavy steel door and flicked on the lights. I had an upstairs office, complete with a secretary and a polished wood desk, but I really preferred my hidey-hole in the basement morgue.

It was very, very private. People didn't like to casually drop by a morgue for some reason.

I suspected they were afraid of what they might find laid out on one of the two steel mortician's tables I had. Normally, it was an unreasonable fear. Sure, if you thought too hard about some of the equipment I had—an autopsy hammer and chisel, for instance--it might give a queasy soul some pause, but really, my office wasn't that much different from a doctor's clinic. There were bright lights, polished steel, and concrete floors with floor drains.

Oh, except, I supposed normal clinics didn't have floor drains.

Plus, instead of antiseptic, it often smelled of formaldehyde, which might be a little off-putting for some.

The lights were already on in the exam room when I pushed open the big double doors, which were wide enough to accommodate a hospital gurney and, as I found out once, the corpse of a cow. There was a post-it note stuck to the first table that said "Freezer #3" in fairly legible block printing. I guess, in case I missed that clue, some helpful EMT had stuck another post-it, this one pink, on the third freezer door that simply read, "HERE."

I wasn't sure what I was going to determine by examining the body, but there were procedures that needed following. Plus, I needed to file a report and get a death certificate started.

Pulling out the camera from its usual drawer, I set it on the counter beside the table. I gave the camera a stern look, "No spooky stuff this time, deal?"

Last time I'd used the camera, it was on the body of the necromancer. With every flash of light, the tattoos on his body had shifted. At the end of it all, I'd ended up with the snake that circled my arm. Involuntarily, I glanced at where the serpent's head usually lay against the back of my palm. It had shifted— tucking itself under one of the coils of its body, like it was curled up trying to sleep.

I got the scale and a few other things prepped, and then I pulled out the body, or rather, the bag containing the body. After a previous, embarrassing wrestling of a corpse, I managed to convince the mayor that what he should do with a small part of our budget surplus was buy me a body crane. I pointed out that the last thing he'd want was for a bunch of forensic evidence to get cor-rupted because I'd dropped a body on the floor. Especially if it was someone's daughter.

It was weird how well that always worked.

At any rate, in the long run, a crane was far cheaper than an assistant. You didn't have to pay salary or benefits to a bunch of gears and pulleys.

Technically, I had an assistant, Genevieve, but we didn't really get along. It turned out she preferred sitting in the fancy upstairs office answering phones that never rang and surfing the web. She was far more expensive than helpful, but, honestly, she saved me from having to put in public appearances of the political kind. Genevieve had the kind of polished look that went over well, which meant I could send her in my place to all the annoying social functions. No one really wanted my hedgehog hair to show up and ruin the mayor's fundraiser, anyway.

I got the crane working. As I maneuvered the body bag into place, it was disturbing how saggy it was. There was an unnatural amount of give, like she had no bones... or they were pulverized.

Trying hard not to think about that too much, I let the "routine" of my job take over. Of course, I didn't really do this enough for it to be rote, but I had a list of what needed to be done. Going step by step was its own kind of calming procedure.

Normally, dead people didn't freak me out. I often preferred them to their living counterparts, being generally quieter and less demanding, but I had to admit that I found the state of this particular corpse to be rather grisly. I needed the comfort of busywork.

I weighed the body, subtracting the difference of the bag. Unzipping it, I took pictures. I knew the forensics team had done the same at the scene, but this was for slightly different purposes. After I finished, I carefully removed what I could of her clothes from the back, as the body was face-down. The fabric came away with a gross sticky sound.

Even unbloodied, it was still an ugly dress that didn't suit this woman. She seemed to me to be at the age where she'd have been more comfortable in baggy shorts or jeans and sensible shoes. Probably I was projecting. I really wanted to be one of those old ladies in the purple hats. No way I'd be trying to look half my age in a thrift store sundress.

Unless I had no choice. Spenser had said something about her being one of Nana Spider's clan: homeless.

I folded up the back half of the dress and stuck it in a plastic evidence bag. If I was able to, I'd get the front half later.

The EMTs had left the body in the position she'd fallen for the most part, so I was looking at her back. There were long, regular bruises at her sides that looked like they'd been made by giant hands.

Or talons.

Damn it.

After taking the requisite pictures, I stripped off my gloves and gave Valentine a call. I just needed to hear him say it. He'd barely said hello when I blurted out, "Just tell me you didn't drop an old lady out of the sky today."

"Okay. 'I didn't drop a woman out of the sky today.'"

The way he said it, he was clearly just repeating what I told him to. "No," I insisted. "Seriously, Valentine, I want to know that you weren't out flying around this morning."

I could hear his long-suffering sigh. "I refuse to file a flight plan. That's not the point of a morning stretch of the wings to go in some boring predetermined pattern."

"So, you were out this morning?"

"Of course."

This wasn't helping. "But you didn't drop a homeless lady into downtown, right?"

"Why would I do that?"

His obvious annoyance comforted me. Yes. Why would he? "Besides you'd eat anything you killed, right?"

I'd meant it as a joke. I was looking for a laugh, maybe some kind of self-deprecating remark from Valentine. Instead, I got: "Depends on why I killed it. I find that the taste improves with a fight. The helpless are unappetizing."

Pulling the phone from my ear, I gave it a 'what is wrong with you?' glare.

"Okay," I said flatly when I returned to the conversation. "So, when you were out stretching your wings, you didn't happen to see anything or anyone else flying around, did you? Something with talons, maybe a body hanging on them?"

"I didn't," he said, in his disinterested voice.

"Someone's dead, Valentine," I chided

"Yes," he said in a tone that was more put out than sympathetic. "Does this mean you're working through lunch?"

The abrupt change made me stumble, "I... guess not?"

"Great, I'll be there at the usual time," he said in that authoritative way he had. He hung up then, as if it was all already decided.

Putting away my phone, I thought that I'd better finish up my autopsy. There was no saying 'no' to a hungry dragon.

I rolled the tension out of my shoulders and wiped my hands on my shorts. Maybe if I spent some face-to-face with Valentine, I could get over this strange uneasiness I'd been harboring. Seeing him would remind me that just because he'd been capable of this sort of thing, he wouldn't do it for no good reason.

Yeah, I didn't want to think about that too hard, because when I did my breath did a funny quickening thing almost like—

Well, almost like I was afraid of him.

Never once, in all of the things that happened to us over the years, had I ever been truly afraid of Valentine. I didn't want to start now.

With that resolved, I turned back to my work.

The morgue was quiet except for the hum of machinery. Adding to a forbidding sense of dreary neglect, the concrete walls had a tendency to collect spider webs and dust despite my constant effort to keep them at bay. The janitorial staff refused to do more than a quick, cursory sweep. The rumors about the necromancer's escape hadn't helped matters. No one liked a morgue, but a haunted one was just too much—especially one where bodies got up and walked away.

Several months ago, to try to counter my spooky reputation, I'd tried cheering the place up by taking a cue from my Precinct 13 colleagues. I'd brought in potted plants and stuck brightly colored posters to the concrete blocks with gummy tape.

Even though I'd been secretly proud of the effect, that had lasted exactly one week. I'd taken it all down after my assistant off-handedly snarked that the whole place was one K-pop band away from a freshman college dorm.

So, the morgue remained stubbornly dreary. Professional, but dreary.

Right now, it also felt lonely.

Before returning to the autopsy, I pulled my phone back out and thumbed down my contacts until I saw Jack's name.

He picked up on the second ring. "Moshi, moshi!"

This was apparently some kind of Japanese telephone greeting. Jack was learning Japanese so that he could understand anime without subtitles. Because: nerd—or, I guess, otaku? One was specific to anime and Japanese stuff, I guess, but I didn't really understand the difference. "Huh, yeah, hey, Jack. Can I ask you something?"

"Yes. Sounds serious."

"I guess?" I wasn't sure how to frame the question, so I just stuttered out the words: "Is Valentine... dangerous?"

"Uh...." There was a long, thoughtful beat. Then, Jack wisely surmised: "This is one of those relationship questions, isn't it? Because most sane people wouldn't hesitate to say: 'Dear god, yes! A thousand times, yes!!' but I suspect that's not what you need to hear right now for some reason. What's going on?"

I stared once again, at the claw-like markings on the victim's waist. "Furfur wants to question Valentine, you know, to eliminate him as a suspect."

"Ah."

Neither of us said anything for several moments. I finally let out the breath that I didn't even realize I was holding and said, "That's going to be a disaster, isn't it?"

"Oh, probably. Demons and dragons don't tend to get along as a general rule—er, but I imagine you knew that—uh, anyway, Valentine doesn't always give off the best first... well, I mean, let's go with 'imposing' rather than 'scary,' shall we? But, yes: disaster."

"But not because he's guilty." I really needed confirmation here.

"Wouldn't he eat anything he killed? You know, hide the evidence? Plus, I don't see Valentine finding homeless people particularly tasty."

Was it weird that Jack knew almost exactly what Valentine would say? And yet, I felt strangely reassured. "Do we trust this Furfur guy?"

"I've no idea," Jack admitted. "I'll do a search. Are you worried that he'll try to frame Valentine?"

It had crossed my mind. "It'd wrap up the case pretty quickly."

"But there's no evidence to suggest--"

I cut Jack off. "I found talon marks."

"Ah."

"Plus, there's the conviction and all that stuff with my stepmonster."

"Oh, I could hide all that, if you'd like." Jack sounded surprisingly cheery about offering to commit a crime on my behalf.

Jack's techno-wizardry could easily obfuscate any computer searches on Valentine. I'd thought about asking Jack to do that on the drive over, but I'd dismissed it for a bunch of reasons. Some of them were ethical, but, ultimately, it was because I knew that Spenser already had a printout on file at the station. "It's okay. I mean, we can't get in the business of burying Valentine's bodies for him or we're going to end up doing it for real one day."

"If you're sure?"

I shook my head, because I wasn't sure of anything at the moment. Even so, I said, "I know you're the best at what you do, but if, somehow, it came out that we hid that stuff, it would only make Valentine look guiltier."

"'Guiltier,' as in more guilty?"

"Did I say that?"

"Yes."

I sucked in another breath and said, "I meant more... fierce. Fiercer."

"Right."

I didn't know how it was that British people could agree with you, but sound so disbelieving. "Look, you know I didn't mean that. I'm just... worried."

"Yes, well. Reasonably. I would be too. Er, I am too, since we're kind of all in this together."

If I'd been hoping to be talked off the ledge, Jack wasn't helping. "I should finish this autopsy."

"Oh, fuck," he said softly. "I screwed up the relationship question again, didn't I? I have a tendency to fail these. I'm sorry. Valentine is scary, but he's smart scary and our scary, so that's a good thing."

Not helping one bit. I cut Jack off, "It's fine. I've told you before. I find your honesty charming. Anyway, I didn't really expect you to tell me that Valentine wouldn't hurt a fly."

"Would it help if I said I was certain he never would, so long as the fly was on you?"

No. "Yeah, that's perfect. Thanks."

"Right." This time he managed to pack a lot of relief into that singular word. Then, he added a hopeful: "See you later?"

"Yep. Bye." I slipped my phone back into my pocket dejectedly.

With a sigh, I returned my attention to Jane Doe. Even though the claw-shaped bruises seemed to implicate Valentine, I took several pictures while they were still 'fresh.'

After putting on a pair of gloves, I swabbed the deeper indentations, hoping that the lab would later pick up some very non-dragon-y particles. Maybe, with any sort of luck, they'd find some metal scrapings or other detritus that might point to the bruises having been made by an industrial crane, or something else completely mundane and non-magical like that.

Once all that was bagged and labeled, I wheeled out my mobile x-ray machine from where it usually sat collecting dust in the closet. After a three-minute hunt for a lead apron for myself, which I eventually found in another room in the far back of a supply cabinet, I got as many angles of the entire body as I could.

Given the ruined state of Jane Doe, x-rays were going to be critical for getting decent information about the impact. Plus, film was the sort of thing I could e-mail to people who had expertise that I didn't.

No one had put plastic bags over Jane Doe's hands. Normally that was done if foul play was suspected, so that anything under the fingernails wouldn't be lost. I couldn't imagine trying to fight off something with claws as big as those bruises around her waist... well, only because I never fought Valentine in his dragon form.

40

I got out the kit for taking scrapings. As I worked through each nail, I did notice that her cheap red polish was chipped and peeled. She had several broken and chewed nails. The scraper pulled out a lot of dirt and grime from underneath. I took close-up photos of the broken nails and added a note to my file. The swabs and scrapings I bagged for the lab.

Normally at this point, I'd start removing organs, weighing them, taking slices to send off to the lab, etc., but I wasn't sure what remained intact. In fact, I'd done all of my work so far with the body still lying on the open the bag, which, now that she was warming back up to room temperature, had started collecting a thin puddle of fluid.

Wrestling her over would be a messy job. I decided to save that for last.

In the meantime, I went back to my list and prepped the usual toxicology on other tests. Since I'd decided that the talon marks indicated a possible homicide, I had to check to make sure she hadn't been drunk or drugged.

Finally, it was time to try to turn her over and find out the contents of her stomach and all of the rest of that.

I stared at her for a long time, chewing on my lip. Never in my short medical career—if you could call dropping out of my second year of school a 'career'—had I ever dealt with anything this mangled. It didn't gross me out so much as it stymied me. I felt unusually out of my depth. I wanted help. I wanted a real expert. I didn't want to shoulder the responsibility of untangling this corpse's mysteries all by myself.

Stripping off my gloves and giving them a determined toss in the biohazard bin, I decided this was too much for me. I was damn proud of everything I'd thought to do so far, but I'd reached my limit.

It was a decision I rarely made, but I was going to pack Jane Doe up and ship her off to someone who actually knew what the hell they were doing with a body like this.

My predecessor, who had zero medical training, had outsourced all the autopsies that the county had needed—which hadn't been very many. Thus, most of his job had been to inform next of kin that, yes, in fact, that accident with the harvester had been fatal to uncle Joe. The most medical thing he did was pronounce someone dead and fill out a death certificate. Otherwise, he did what my assistant was currently doing: sitting in a posh office, collecting a salary, doing nothing.

Guilt stabbed me as I zipped up the body bag again. I hated being like that guy. But, as I used the crane to move Jane to a fridge unit, I told myself that, in this particular situation, it was the right call. What if my lack of expertise did more harm than good? Besides, given my connection to Valentine, it was probably better to have someone else put the puzzle of the body together this time.

I left Jane with a little, "I'm sorry," and made my way over to my work desk. Even though I'd let my assistant dictate the look of the morgue proper, my little desk area was partitioned off from the rest of the room by beige fabric-covered cubicle walls. Inside there, I felt free to let my penchant for Impressionist art posters and philodendron run wild. I'd even brought in a ratty throw rug, so my chair wheels didn't sound like they were scraping across some prison floor.

Digging through old files, I found the name of the professionals my predecessor had used in the past. By the time Valentine arrived, I had the University of South Dakota in Vermillion on the line. I waved for Valentine to come in as I finished explaining to the person on the other end, a Dr. Sayegah, "These kinds of cases are so rare here; I would feel better with a second opinion."

I was sure my voice betrayed my embarrassment at not being able to handle it. Dr. Sayegah, on the other hand, acted as though Christmas had come early. She sounded giddy as she asked, "Dropped or fell, you say? Why, yes, that's very unusual. My students will be thrilled!"

I suspected she would be far more excited than they would, but it hardly mattered. "I'm going to transfer you to my assistant who can work out transport and fees and such."

Genevieve, meanwhile, acted as if I'd cancelled her holiday season forever. She complained so long I worried that Dr. Sayegah might have thought I dropped the call. After apologizing to the doctor for the delay, I got Genevieve on the line again. "Listen, you good-for-nothing so-and-so, I never ask for anything ever," I said, losing my patience. "Just do this. There's a file about out-sourcing procedures somewhere in that office. I'm sure you can find it. If you can't.... argh, seriously? Why do I pay you? I will put an ad in the paper today and hire a proper assistant!"

"'Good-for-nothing so-and-so?' My, my, Alex, you sure know how to insult a person." Valentine's voice was a purr in my ear.

I hadn't heard him come in, much less slip beside me. In surprise, I flung my phone halfway across the room. I may also have squeaked in a very undignified way.

"Not exactly the greeting I hoped for," he said.

He went in for a kiss, and I ducked out of the way.

Chapter Four

I tried to act like the reason I dodged his lips was because I needed to find the parts of my phone. The back fell off and the battery skittered in the opposite direction of the case. I could feel Valentine's eyes following me as I kept up constant, nervous chatter, "Jeez, don't go sneaking up on me like that. I just about jumped out of my skin."

"I see that," Valentine noted.

I found the battery beside the file cabinet. It was covered in dust. I took a minute to crouch down on the floor and blow the dust off of it. My back was to Valentine, so I probably took longer than strictly necessary to reassemble my phone. I was trying to get my heart rate back to normal. My hands did not want to cooperate. I put the battery in twice, upside down, before I got it reinstalled properly. I fumbled with the back flap twice as long as it should have taken.

When I had both the phone and myself back in mostly working order, I stood up and turned around.

Valentine watched me with the unblinking gaze of a snake. His face remained impassive, but there was something about his casual posture that seemed anything but.

Despite the weather, he dressed in dark, form-fitting jeans. The white t-shirt was appropriate for the heat, but it also meant that the strength of his upper body and arms were on full display. Normally, I liked that look. A lot. Especially with his long dark hair loose, like it was.

Dark eyebrows drew together. He glanced at the empty examination table and then back to me. "Did your corpse walk off on you again?" When I shook my head, his expression darkened. "You're spooked about something. What?"

I shoved my phone into my shorts' pocket and ran a hand through my hair. "I was just all wound up about Genevieve. I didn't hear you come in."

His expression told me he wasn't buying that was all there was to it, but he shrugged. Perfunctorily, he said, "My apologies."

This wasn't going very well.

I stood half a room away from Valentine. Neither of us moved to close the distance. I knew I should be the one to make the effort. He'd done nothing wrong. I was ninety-nine percent sure that he had not murdered Jane Doe, so, really, it was on me to reassure him that things between us were cool.

Luckily, my job provided the excuse. There were all the various boxes and such that I needed to take up to the mailroom to send off to various labs. "Hey," I said, moving to gather some of them up, "Could you help me take these upstairs?"

Scooping up the lion's share of the packages, he gave me a teasingly withering glance. "So long as you're certain I won't frighten the staff?"

It was clearly meant as a gentle poke but, the truth was, there were some of the government building staff that moved out of the way when Valentine walked through the halls. "They can put up with you..."

"Put up with me," Valentine repeated, thoughtfully, as he followed me out the morgue's door and up the back stairway. "Am I to take it from that phrase, that today is one of those days when you give me an exasperated sigh and tell me that you wish I were a 'normal' boyfriend?"

I hadn't realized that was a thing I did.

Though, I did remember deciding that it would be nice to start up with Jack for those times when Valentine needed to stretch his wings in the metaphorical and literal sense. "Jack is hardly 'normal,'" I pointed out.

"I wasn't actually thinking of Jack at this moment," Valentine said with a little grimace.

Oh, oops.

Time to change the subject. Fast. "I think I met the guy who turned Devon."

We were in the busier section of city hall, so Valentine leaned in closer and dropped his voice. My ploy had clearly worked, because his tone was excitedly conspiratorial. "The master vampire?"

"No, the werewolf," I said. I held on to the rest of the story while we dumped off the boxes with the harried mailroom clerk. I filled out the appropriate POs so that my office would get billed the postage.

Once we were back in the stairwell, Valentine prompted, "I thought I'd smelled werewolf on you." He opened his mouth slightly, the way a cat does to get a scent, and then nodded. "From the scent, a brand-new new alpha."

I ignored the weirdness of that moment. "Yeah, and get this, I think Devon is his mate? They want us to try to break Spenser's thrall so that Devon can ride off with his pack."

"Us?" Valentine mused. "I suspect they mean me. I'm fairly certain the only way to end a spell like that is if the enthraller is dead."

We hit the open sunlight, and I winced from the sudden brightness. After the deep chill of the air conditioning, the heat almost felt good. I turned to look up at Valentine. Was he serious? "You can't murder Spenser."

"Technically, I'm more than capable. However, faerie don't taste terribly good." He shook his head. Smacking his lips together as though finding the memory of something distasteful, he added, "Bitter. Acrid, even. Not worth it. But more importantly, his mother would curse me for all eternity."

I started walking towards my car. "I kind of think the most important thing is that murder is illegal? And, <u>wrong</u>."

"No, trust me," Valentine said, opening the car door for me after I'd de-weaponized it with Jack's beeper, "the single most important thing is not to cross the Queen of Faerie."

I waited until he'd lowered himself into the passenger seat before insisting, "We need to really be clear on the 'murder is wrong' idea."

"Do we?" He paused while strapping himself in to give me a long, hard look. "Alex, you do remember that I'm an apex predator? Murder is called 'dinner.'"

I started the car with a frown. Valentine's tone was light, but it wasn't a joke to me.

Sensing my discomfort, he said, "Listen, I also understand that Spenser is your friend. I really haven't eaten a human being in several centuries. I think the last person I devoured was during the Age of Discovery. As it happened, I didn't really want to be a 'discovery' and they were trespassing. I should've been safely hidden in Siberia, especially with everything going on. Anyway, they were Cossacks."

His tone made it sound like he'd wished he'd eaten more of them. I didn't know what to say. When Valentine talked about the distant past like it was yesterday, I remembered that he was inhuman, a dragon. Those unlucky Cossacks had probably stumbled into Valentine's actual hoard in an ice cave. He'd have probably been in dragon form, sleeping on a pile of gold, snow-white leathery wings and long, spiked tail wrapped around a scaly body.

I'd only ever seen Valentine transform a couple of times. My impressions were: big, very white, sharp teeth, black snake eyes, wings, and not much else. Big, did I mention the 'defies the conservation of matter principle' big? The rest was kind of a blur, however. This was a person I slept with. I don't think my brain really wanted to go there.

After all, this was a <u>man</u> sitting in my car, staring in a desultory fashion out at the maple-lined streets. It was a very human posture he'd adopted, with an elbow braced against the edge of the interior car door and his face pressed into his knuckles.

"Anyway, you needn't worry," Valentine said. "It's not as if I crave it or need to eat human flesh to survive. You could have ended up with a ghoul familiar. That would be awkward at dinner parties. They can't even pretend to be human, like I can."

Pretend to be human.

I needed to remember that phrase. Being human was only a pretense for Valentine. My stomach did a funny little uncoiling thing at that thought.

"You're awfully silent." Lifting his head from his hand, he gave me a look. "What are you thinking?"

Despite the lack of traffic, I kept my eyes on the road. "Our usual lunch place?"

He made a little disagreeing noise. "All this talk of eating has made me hungry for a cow. Any chance we can go to that hipster tavern? You know, the one with the good steaks."

I'd been heading for our favorite Chinese buffet, but I signaled a turn to change direction. "Pierre's Tap."

"Mmmm, that's it," he agreed, returning to stare out the window.

We fell into a silence after that.

Valentine wasn't much of a talker generally, but I tended to fill moments like this with idle chatter about the weather or passing scenery. This drive, however, I was deep in my own thoughts, most of which continued to spiral around the realities of having a boyfriend who was a monster.

I pulled into the restaurant's parking lot. Gravel crunched under the tires.

"Anyway," Valentine sighed, apropos of his own thoughts, "If I was going to eat anyone, it would be Robert. He boxed up my silver. All of it. And put it in the garage. How am I expected to sleep?"

I unbuckled myself. "You slept fine before you bought, er, acquired all that stuff."

"Yes, but now that I have it, it is mine and it is my hoard. You must explain this to him. This is what started dragons eating people, you know. It's a rule." He sounded petulant, but his eyes glittered with a watery silver-gray, dragon-like. "Do not take the things I have hoarded, not one solitary coin, not a single speck of the precious dust that forms from so many jewels rubbing together. None of it. It belongs to me. It is mine."

We got out, and I leaned my full body on the car. My head resting on the roof, listening to Valentine's rant. "I'll talk to Robert."

Valentine shot me the same look Robert had given me earlier. The one that said, 'I'll believe it when I see it.' "Very well. But, mark my words, Alexandra Conner, I will gnaw his bones to pulp if he touches my things again."

We really needed to get our own place, like, yesterday.

Closing my eyes, I thumped my face lightly against the car roof, feeling done with this weird conversation. "Okay."

Other people had roommates that argued over whose turn it was to do the dishes. I wanted to be 'other people' right now.

The bloody steak that Valentine ordered made me think just a little too much of Jane Doe's ruined body. It was a wonder I hadn't turned vegetarian.

The décor of Pierre's Tap had last been updated sometime in the mid-70s. Dark wood paneling covered the walls, mounted deer heads stared blankly-yet-vaguely-accusingly at us, and collectable neon beer signs flickered in the cave-like semi-darkness. The hipster crowd loved this place, declaring it 'authentically kitsch.'

I wanted to know why we didn't go to the Chinese buffet.

"Sushi should not be served in South Dakota," Valentine said.

"Sushi is Japanese."

"Yes, but for reasons unknown to me, they have a sushi bar."

"You could try not eating it? Also, there are these things called 'aero-planes' now that can deliver fresh fish from all over the world in a matter of hours." I said, poking at my salad. I knew I shouldn't have ordered the chicken in a place like this, but I just couldn't do red meat today. "Also, we have this nifty new invention called refrigeration you may have heard of."

"Is that so?" he said mockingly, "What will you clever humans think of next?"

I stuck my tongue out at him.

After all, I suspected the real reason he didn't want to go to the Chinese place was because the older couple that owned the place intuitively knew that Valentine was not in the least bit human. I had to admit that the stares and whispers could get awkward. Still, I would rather have had piping hot, deep fried dumplings than the soggy, wilted salad I was pretty sure had come out of a bag discovered in the far back of some fridge.

"So..." I started, then stopped.

I must have had a serious expression on my face because Valentine looked up from devouring his steak to say, "Is this about my hoard? Because you know it's a natural compulsion of my species. I could, however, be persuaded to relocate some of it to an alternate place. The issue, you understand, is that it must be _me_ that moves it—"

I put up a hand. We'd already been over this, and I did not need to hear the gruesome details of the death suffered by the Mover of the Hoard. "No, I mean, yeah, that's a whole different problem."

His interest piqued, Valentine set his fork down. "What's the current problem?"

"You know how I was asking you about dropping people out of the sky earlier, well, my new boss wants you to go in for questioning—just to rule you out as a suspect, of course."

Deliberately, Valentine folded his hands on the table's edge. His expression was unreadable, but silvery eyes flicked over my face, my body language. A deep crease appeared between his eyebrows. "I sense there's more going on than you're telling me, but what's this about a new boss? What happened to Spenser?"

"He's been taken off the case," I frowned. "It's all this mess with the necromancer case coming back to bite us. Some demons from Internal Affairs showed up."

"Ah, this is what's been bothering you."

I poked at the salad. "Kind of?"

"There's something more. Something to do with me. Oh, I see." He sat very still for several heartbeats, regarding me. Finally, he breathed out a single question: "Why?"

"Why?"

"Why does it bother you so much? The idea of this questioning session?"

There were so many ways I could answer that. 'You're a natural killer' was the first thing that came to mind, but instead I said: "My new boss? He's a demon."

Valentine grimaced a little, but his posture relaxed and he reached for his beer. "I can be persuaded not to disembowel the foul creature on principle," he said, taking a sip. Then, pausing with the glass still in hand, he asked, "Or, is it that you _want_ me to eat him? Rid you of this meddlesome boss, as it were?"

"No!" I said, a little too loudly. Several of the Pierre's Tap patrons turned to give me a curious look. After taking a second to pull myself together with a little cough, I continued. "What I mean is, that would be the worst thing you could do. Just play it cool."

Valentine set his beer glass down on its coaster. He tapped his finger against the rim, three times, before returning his liquid silver gaze to me. "If that is what you wish, I can do that."

I wasn't as sure.

Despite the fact that I never voiced the question that was in my head, Valentine's eyes narrowed as if I had. "Do you doubt me?"

"No," I said automatically.

Valentine fell into a heavy silence, and I didn't know what to do to lighten it. This whole conversation underscored the fact that Valentine sucked at pretending to be human. He wasn't even particularly good at figuring out when to get off a subject.

I pushed away my uneaten salad with a sigh. "I might feel better about this whole thing if I knew why dragons hate demons so much."

Valentine's posture relaxed and he went back to sawing off bloody chunks of his steak. "For one, they smell bad."

I waited for 'the other thing,' but Valentine left it hanging so long, I felt the need to prompt him. "Please tell me that you didn't nearly murder my stepmonster because you didn't like her odor."

"No, although her stink did keep me from you for years. I could have become your familiar a decade earlier had she not blocked your scent from me."

A decade earlier? If Valentine had shown up ten years earlier, I would have been in high school. I sat back in my seat, trying to imagine what that would have looked like. Valentine, what? Hanging around the school yard? Forget assault, Valentine would have been sent away for being a creepy old guy. "Never mind my stepmonster; my dad would have killed you."

"Why?" Valentine said.

The air around him shimmered—or maybe it was more correct to say that it 'smudged,' like I was suddenly looking through glasses in desperate need of cleaning. I rubbed my eyes, trying to clear them, but I couldn't. I squinted into the blur. Though I couldn't make out details, I could sense a change. Valentine was shrinking in mass, becoming more gangly.

When my vision cleared, a teenager sat across from me.

$

Chapter Five

Valentine's face had shifted, too, becoming less filled out, more angular. He'd changed his hairstyle to something straight out of a boy band, a soft sort of undercut, floppy. His eyes seemed larger somehow, yet more world-weary. Just to complete the look, he pulled a phone out of his jacket and started thumbing it.

My phone beeped.

The text read: *It's all smoke and mirrors, my love. The whole thing. I could wear any mask you like.*

I glanced up from the screen at teen-Valentine, who gave me a brief, shy smile over his phone before returning his attention to it.

"Okay. This is weird," I told him. Especially since he nailed 'teen' almost better than he did 'adult.' "So, what are you saying? It would have been like a teen movie where you protected me from bullies?"

The thumbs clacked and my phone read: *If you needed. Who knows? Without the demon's interference, your father might have grown to like me. Perhaps we would still be in Chicago, surrounded by like-minded friends. The magic shines there. I could have made you the Queen.*

He set down the phone and my vision glazed over again. Through the streaked and fuzzy reality, I watched his shape grow and reform. When I was able to see properly again, Valentine had returned to his usual look, fully grown, broad-shouldered, long-haired, with a dangerous smirk.

It was like the teen had never been there.

I re-read his last message. "Queen?"

He lifted a shoulder and finished up the last of his steak. "Larger cities are like realms in a kingdom. A witch with a dragon can rise quickly in such places."

"Would I get a throne full of swords?"

He gave me a withering glance before starting in on the baked potato. "You need to watch less television. Those dragons weren't even real."

"Cool, though."

"I suppose." He inspected the chunk of potato he'd skewered before popping it into his mouth. "I was always a little jealous of the fire breathers. Ice just isn't as dramatic."

I nodded, though I wasn't sure if I'd ever seen Valentine breathing ice. Like so much about him, it didn't seem real.

Except it was.

"It's the elemental thing, I think," Valentine said, as he continued to admire each potato piece before eating it. "Demons and dragons are nearly matched in mastery over them. I suspect that's where the rivalry began. Plus, we're mistaken for them all the time. St. Michael defeating the serpent—bah. It was them he fought, not us."

Vague memories from Sunday school came back to me. "I hadn't thought of that. Lucifer is depicted as a dragon sometimes, isn't he?"

Valentine grimaced. "An angelic smear campaign to usurp us. I hate them all. The lot of them are intruders, foreigners."

A couple of people in the restaurant looked up at Valentine's vehemence.

"Whoa, what's with the xenophobia?"

Valentine stopped his potato appreciation long enough to give me a sarcastically arched eyebrow. "It's not bigotry. I don't mean America, I mean earth. Angels and demons are unearthly. They don't belong to this world."

"Oh, right, the whole other dimension thing." I took a long draught of my own beer. "Have you been to Hell?"

"Only figuratively," he said.

I assumed he meant prison, though he didn't say. He never said. We never, ever talked about the time he did, what it was like, why he didn't just magic himself out of it—none of it.

Valentine might be guilty of the acts of violence, but I felt responsible for them. I never went so far as to ask Valentine to hurt my stepmom. At least, I don't think I did. I'd been taking a lot of antipsychotics at the time, some of which made me feel sort of muzzy. The truth was, I was only on those meds because I'd thrown the first punches. I'd agreed to all the therapy and the drugs because I believed there was something wrong with me. I hated that woman irrationally even then.

The first time that Valentine told me that she was emitting a pheromone that made me feel that way; I laughed. I assumed he was as crazy as I thought I was—some kind of conspiracy theorist who thought that too many wind farms made people gay and overhead wires caused cancer. I slept with him anyway. Our pillow talk was my restless ranting about how she sucked the life from my father, drove me literally insane, and how much I wanted her dead. I hardly talked about anything beyond my burning hatred of her. If the weather was bad, it was her fault. She was the cause of all misery, everywhere. I didn't just want her dead, either. I wanted her mutilated, destroyed. I may never have asked him to do it, but I never hid my desire to see her bleed, suffer.

The law determines guilt not by what you thought about doing, but by what you actually did.

Ever since discovering that Valentine was my familiar, I had wondered what the law would make of that. Had I compelled his actions in some way? I didn't know how I would have done it, but that didn't make it any less possible. After all, I hadn't known that my swear words could turn nuclear, but they did, anyway.

Valentine turned his head, ostensibly watching the bartender serve a group of hunters at the dimly lit bar, but he was clearly lost in his own thoughts.

"Are you happy being my familiar?"

He started at the question and abruptly shifted to face me. "Why do you ask me this now?"

Now? Instead of years ago, when you were sent to prison for making good on my desires? It was my turn to feign interest in another part of the bar. I focused on a group of office workers, mostly women, who were drinking wine and laughing about something. I shrugged and lied, "I'm just curious. It does mean that you're stuck in South Dakota."

Valentine grunted. "This state has its virtues."

I snorted a little laugh and managed to look him in the eye again. "Name one."

"The Badlands," he said.

When I'd moved out here, I'd driven past the turn off to the Badlands. I hadn't gone, however. People told me it was beautiful in an empty, dusty sort of way. Alright, actually, most people just said that first part. "What's so attractive about a bunch of barren rock?"

"Sunlight, heat, colors..." he paused to frown. "Ah. Perhaps you have to be a lizard to fully appreciate the appeal of sunbathing on rocks."

Always, Valentine had to remind me how inhuman he was. Though, to be fair, this time I'd started it with the talk of familiars. "We don't live in the Badlands, though. We're in Pierre."

"It's an easy distance for me," he murmured around a sip of beer. "I make the trip often."

He did? "When?"

"At night, while you sleep."

"Every night?"

"Many nights."

"Last night?"

"Yes," he said. "Last night. The moon was a fine crescent. I sat and watched Draco rise and set from atop a painted peak."

Without me.

I tried and failed not to feel hurt, especially when he continued. "On a clear, dark night, the milky way flows across the sky like a great river. When I fly, it feels as though I could swim in it." Valentine noticed that I'd hardly touched my disgusting salad. "Shall we get dessert elsewhere?"

I checked my phone for the time. It was still hours before Valentine was expected at the precinct. I wasn't feeling dessert any more than I had lunch, but neither did I particularly want to go back to the morgue, especially now that there wasn't much left for me to do. I couldn't even file a death certificate for Jane Doe until I had a better sense of the actual cause of death. Obviously, she'd been dropped, but was she dead before or after the fall? The paperwork would have to wait until I got answers from the university.

I wanted to ask him to take me flying with him, but the one time I'd flown in his claws, I'd hated the sensation. Lifting and plummeting, my stomach dropped out with every beat of the wings. My reaction was probably why he didn't invite me on his midnight flights.

Probably.

More unspooling. At the strange sensation, I touched my belly, curiously. Was my stomach still upset after losing breakfast over Jane Doe earlier? Or, was it that I was feeling so much distance from Valentine?

"Alex?" he prompted. "Ice cream?"

"What about sex?"

Chapter Six

All I had wanted from this lunch date was reassurance. I'd gotten none. If anything, I felt more disconnected. What I wanted more than sex was for Valentine to hold me close, but it felt even stranger to ask for a hug.

I expected Valentine to perk up at the idea. Instead, his brows crinkled. "I fail to see why we couldn't have both."

That, at least, made me smile. "Yes. Both sound good."

We drove to Zesto's, one of those old-fashioned 'outdoor only' ice cream places where you had to walk up to a window and place your order. The free-standing building occupied a corner of the block. A giant neon ice cream cone dominated the rooftop. They had flavors like "blue moon" and "watermelon," and only took cash. From the age of the employees, working a shift at Zesto's was apparently a Pierre high school rite of passage.

In a fit of bravery, I decided to try watermelon. Valentine stuck with a classic: rocky road.

Due to the heat, Zesto's was popular. Even so, I was surprised to see Tengu, the Internal Affairs agent, waving at us. I would have tried to act like I hadn't seen him, except he was sitting next to Hannah Stone.

As we headed over to the picnic table to join them, Valentine leaned into me and asked, "Who's the stork?"

He hadn't lowered his voice, however, and Tengu glanced up. "Ah, if it isn't the 'doragon.'" The last word sounded like a corrupted version of 'dragon.' I got the sense they'd both insulted each other somehow. "Furfur seems quite interested in you."

Valentine lowered himself down on the park bench next to Hannah, though he spoke again to Tengu, "Hmph. Not even an honorific?"

"You started it, doragon-kun," Tengu smirked. "If I'm anything, I'm a bird of prey."

Licking his ice cream, Valentine gave a little 'I guess?' expression and said, "But kites are so _small_."

I stood at the end of the picnic table watching this back and forth posturing with a shake of my head. I caught Hannah's eye as I sat down, "Men, huh?"

"Neither of them is technically a man," Hannah said. The heat had made her perfectly round hair frizzy at the ends, and the sunlight highlighted streaks that looked like the light brown spokes of a wheel, or, if I let myself go there, of a tumbleweed. When Hannah was reformed, the magical rabbis used whatever flora was available to them. "I believe you are the only human at this table, Alex."

"Yeah," I said. "I've been reminded of that all day." I was weirdly warmed that Hannah recalled my name, at least for the moment. However, I had noticed that she was better at remembering who I was when Valentine was with me.

He was giving me a concerned look right now, but I waved off his unspoken question about my complaint with a mouthed: 'later.'

"We were discussing Spenser Jones," Hannah explained.

I shot Tengu a dirty look, "You mean investigating."

He raised thin eyebrows at me, "Which should not come as a surprise to you, of all people, Ms. Conner. You were the one who uncovered his connection to the necromancer."

Spenser's ex-girlfriend might have been the necromancer's sister. There was some slight tampering with evidence, maybe. _Allegedly._

Actually, not so 'allegedly,' but I liked Spenser and the whole investigation had been a bit of a mess from beginning to end. I blew things up. We were lucky we didn't kill more people in the process of solving the crime than the murderer had in the first place.

"I'm not a cop," I reminded Tengu. "I never wanted Spenser to get into trouble."

Valentine yawned, like the whole thing bored him. "What is a yokai doing working for 'the man,' anyway? It's about as foolish as having a faerie as a cop."

"Demons are so often associated with wrongdoing that we have an extraordinary ability to uncover it others. In a lot of cultures, demons are also part of a deeply organized bureaucracy and that also has its advantages," Tengu said.

He seemed to take in a deep, judgement breath before adding, "I, however, can appreciate law and order."

Valentine's chuckle was deep, warm, and friendly. "As can I, but don't you ache to destroy it?"

Shared glances implied a strong 'no.'

"Do you?" Hannah asked.

Valentine finished the last of his ice cream cone before answering. He licked the last crumbs from his fingertips. "Patience is my particular virtue," he said. "Humans change their opinions of nearly everything constantly. What is fashionable one century, is taboo the next. If I am not fond of something, all I have to do is wait. Either it dies or it comes back into fashion."

"Even murder?" Tengu prompted.

Before I could warn Valentine that an honest answer to this would probably not go over very well, he said, "Everyone seems extraordinarily interested in my opinion of murder of late. What makes me so special, I wonder? I'm hardly the only predator here, Tengu."

"How did you know his name?" I asked. They hadn't done introductions, had they?

"Oh, you're going by your species? How... unoriginal." Valentine laughed, as Tengu ducked his head as if hiding a blush. "Perhaps I should start going by Ledyanoy Drakon."

"What's a tengu?" I asked no one in particular, though I was looking at Stone, who shrugged. Clearly, she didn't know either.

"Yokai," Tengu said.

"You just said another word I don't understand," I admitted.

"Yokai are Japanese monsters," Valentine said. "Or do you prefer 'demon'?"

"Neither," Tengu said. "Yokai is actually a catch-all phrase for any number of supernatural creatures. The Kanji characters, being flexible, can be read many ways. I like to think of myself as a calamitous mystery."

"Not an attractive apparition?" Valentine suggested, clearly understanding something about this conversation's topic that I didn't. "Or a bewitching suspicion?"

Tengu gave Valentine a little nod of acknowledgment, "Those would be fine appellations, as well."

I reached across the table and gave Valentine's arm a teasing smack. "Stop flirting."

"Ah, that reminds me," Valentine said, giving me a knowing look, "Alex and I have an appointment we can't miss."

Tengu checked his watch. "You have hours yet."

Valentine was already headed for the car, so I said, hurrying after him, "Sex. He meant sex."

We didn't say much on the drive back to our place. There was a tension between us. I wish I could say that it was mounting excitement, but, for me, at least it was more like an odd sort of trepidation. Would this go alright?

I wasn't used to worrying about sex. Most of the time, Valentine was an exceptional lover, certainly the best I'd ever had. He was attentive, he focused as much on my pleasure, as his own, which... well, maybe previously I had very bad luck, but I could hardly say that came standard with the lovers I'd chosen in the past.

It felt strange to be giving Valentine curious, nervous glances. Despite my earlier awkward proposition, he'd agreed to this. Even so, I asked, "Are you sure this is what you want?"

He startled me with a brisk, "Yes. Just drive."

After that odd exchange, I could tell that we were not off to a good start.

Even though we knew Robert wasn't home, we snuck through the dim house to our bedroom. Valentine held my hand as we tiptoed over the white carpeting, around the antique dining room set, and into our cramped bedroom.

Valentine's hand was cold in mine, but that wasn't unusual. What felt off was that we didn't giggle or make any goofy comments about the situation. Instead, it was almost as though we were making a pretense at being illicit lovers, going through motions, not really feeling it.

I honestly would have called the whole thing off, except for that funny emptiness in my stomach. It felt almost foreboding, a creeping sort of dread that I had convinced myself that only physical contact between us could mend.

I shut the bedroom door behind us.

Our room really wasn't big enough for two people. The white veneer-coated sliding door of the wall-to-wall closet had jumped its track. It hung open at one end. Valentine's clothes spilled out into a pile on the floor, trailing over to the chair in the corner of the room. There were two windows, one on each wall. They were both open to the air, but the curtains were pulled down.

The light was muted and murky, like a cave.

I could see a smattering of coins shimmering in the shag carpeting, but Valentine had changed the sheets. When he sat down on the mattress, coins clinked underneath his weight.

Seeing my curious expression, he smiled, "I thought perhaps they would bother you less under the sheets."

Not a bad compromise.

Valentine took my other hand and pulled me close. He opened his legs for me: I stepped in and stood over him. He looked up at me in the semi-darkness of the curtained room, his eyes glittering.

Leaning down, I kissed him. I used my tongue to try to express the pace I wanted to set—slow and exploratory. He responded more urgently, pushing eagerly until his enthusiasm overwhelmed my direction. I felt him smile against my teeth. A small growl of victory escaped from somewhere deep in his throat.

My knees trembled a little at that sound.

Despite myself, I loved this side of Valentine, the one that didn't take direction well, did whatever he pleased. Yet, all this talk about murder and mayhem made me feel as though I should try to exert control over this beast, this wild creature.

My back was hunched in this position—so I let go of his hands and trailed my fingers up the length of his arms. Through the light short-sleeved shirt he wore, I could feel the steely cords of muscles jumping. I left goose bumps in the wake of my touch.

He sighed contentedly. It was a sexy sound, but I wanted to hear his breath hitch. I wanted him to beg.

I needed to figure out how to get him naked and maybe tied to the bed. Now there was a delicious thought. My kiss faltered sloppily. I wasn't used to multi-tasking like this.

Pulling from our kiss, I tugged at his shirt.

Leaning into me, he nibbled my throat. His hands were on my hips, warm even through the fabric of my shorts. When his teeth grazed my skin, I sucked in a breath, my heart rate jumping. My chest heaved. The space between my legs grew heavy and moist with desire and the sensation of his breath and tongue on my body. Stiffening nipples rubbed against my t-shirt. I groaned. His buttons slipped from my shaking fingers. Forget him; it was me that needed to get naked right now, or my own clothes would distract me too much.

I wished I could do that guy thing and pull my shirt over my head in one sexy move. However, I must have done something right, because Valentine watched my grunting struggle with hungry eyes. In the summer, I rarely wore a bra. My breasts were small enough that I didn't need a lot of support, and there was nothing worse, in my mind, than sweat collecting underneath the swells.

Valentine cupped my breasts the moment they were exposed. His hands were big enough that they completely covered them. Calluses on his palms slid roughly along sensitive flesh, despite his light touch.

I put my hands over his for a moment, stopping his progression. "Calluses? Why do you have calluses? Five minutes ago, you showed me you could be anything, even ten years younger."

"I am the shape of your desire, Alex Conner."

Did I desire someone scary?

Under my hands, his clever thumbs caressed and flicked already aching nipples.

When he moved aside my hands and his mouth covered my nipples, I totally forgot every coherent thought or any plans I might have had to be the one in charge. Attempting to at least make a last-ditch effort, I grabbed fistfuls of his hair, curling my fists tightly.

Despite his full mouth, he laughed. The muffled sound reverberated under my skin. I wanted to be the one to make him whine, instead the sound that came out of my mouth was a whimpering begging noise that only made him laugh harder.

He pulled me down onto the bed and I had a vague sense of being divested of my shorts and underwear by skilled hands.

Worst. Attempt to control him. Ever.

If this was ever going to work, we were going to have to start with him unable to use his hands and that wicked, wicked mouth. Valentine didn't mind my utter failure as he rolled on top of me and licked his way down my body. His tongue left cool trails along my rib cage. When he got to my belly, he pressed his mouth into my stomach and blew a raspberry against my skin. That earned him a smack on the head. He just chuckled again and buried his face between my legs.

Since I failed at dominating, I decided to excel at noise making.

Afterwards, we lay naked, exhausted, and sweaty on the bed.

I stared at the cracks in the plaster ceiling trying to decide if that had worked, if I felt better about the distance that had been stretching between us. It bothered me that I wasn't entirely sure.

What had been missing?

All the satisfying elements had been there, why did I still feel so... alone?

At some point, he'd rolled over, his back to me. I could tell by his breathing that he wasn't asleep. I wanted to roll into him, to spoon up, but there was something about his body language that made me hesitate.

What was wrong with us?

Was he feeling it too?

I was just about to suggest a round two when I heard rustling in the bushes outside.

Valentine heard it, too.

He was up and out of bed so fast that his movements were a blur. "Stay here," he told me, already quietly pushing open the door.

"You're going out naked?" I whispered, though I had to admit that a giant, angry, naked man might scare the crap out of your average South Dakota burglar—especially a guy like Valentine, who could move utterly silently.

He made no reply, just slipped away.

I held my breath and listened intently.

Crouching down behind the bed, I wriggled into my underwear. We'd had a break-in once before. I'd slept through part of it and woken up tied to the bed with Valentine in a very unsexy way. Pulling on my shorts, I fished my cell from my pocket and started dialing 9-1-1, but I stopped at 9-1, my finger over the last digit.

I strained to hear what was going on. Just in case, I started powering up one of my curses. If someone was trying to get the drop on us again, I'd hit them with a 'hell' or maybe a 'goddamn.'

Then I heard a bloodcurdling scream from the front yard, which made me let out a little yelp of my own. I'd just about made the call to the police when I heard Robert shouting, "Good god, Valentine! You scared the shit out of me! Oh my god! Where are your clothes!?"

I was making my own way to the front door, when I heard Valentine ask, "'For rent'? Are we getting new lodgers? Where on earth will they sleep?"

"Oh, um..." Robert said, "I take it Alex hasn't talked to you yet?"

I was tempted to sneak out the back door and even started towards it, but Valentine had already spotted me through the large living room window. He stood in the narrow space between the house and the yews. I could see most of his body, but the lower half was blocked from the street and Robert by the bushes.

Robert held a sign on a narrow strip of wood. In his other hand, he had a rubber mallet.

Valentine's eyes stayed locked on me as he said, "No, she hasn't."

Pierre might be the capitol of South Dakota, but it was a small town at heart. As I stepped out onto the front steps, I noticed that the neighbor next door, a retired schoolteacher, peered out of her lace curtains at where Valentine stood naked in the yew hedge. She had a pair of binoculars around her neck and her cell phone in her hand.

"We should probably go inside," I said, holding the screen door open for them to come back inside.

Robert nodded, though his attention was riveted to the expanse of Valentine's pale skin.

I had to admit, it was hard not to stare at Valentine. He was quite a sight, with the shock of jet back hair hanging in front of his thin, angular face and all those well-toned muscles on full display. No doubt from where Robert stood, he could probably see a tantalizing hint of the little trail of dark curls on Valentine's taut lower abdomen that led to the fuller thatch between his legs. Valentine was otherwise surprisingly hairless for such a masculine man. His underarms were as sparse as his chest, and, from his stubble, I'd always imagined that the best Valentine could hope for in a beard would be a devilish goatee.

Valentine, as usual, had no sense of how to behave like a human being. Utterly shameless, he pushed his way through the hedge. Robert's eyes went as round as coins when Valentine cleared the yew and turned to walk up the steps. Mouth hanging open, Robert looked ready to drool at the sight of Valentine's backside. The neighbor, meanwhile, had the binoculars up for a better view.

The whole scene would have been awkwardly hilarious, if it wasn't for the seriousness in Valentine's expression as he stalked past me into the living room. "You knew you we were being... dislodged?"

I scratched the short hairs at the back of my neck. "Kind of? I mean, I actually didn't expect a for rent sign, but I guess Robert said something about looking for a new place?"

I followed Valentine into the living room. We hadn't switched on any of the lamps when we snuck through to the bedroom. Sunlight streamed in through the windows. Dust motes danced in their beams.

The open floor meant that to my left was the dining room, all heavy wooden antiques with carved legs and dark veneer. The big table was covered in the things Valentine had collected: spoons, salt and pepper shakers, candy dishes, and other antiques covered in silver plating.

The back of the long sofa acted as a kind of divider between the rooms. Two overstuffed chairs had been set at angles to form a conversation nook, or extra seating to watch the TV. The TV was an old-fashioned boxy thing that sat on an entertainment stand just wide enough to support it.

Even without the antiques covering every surface, there was something about the shag carpeting and retro-furniture that made the place feel like we'd been staying at 'grandma's.' Would it be such a bad thing to have a place of our own?

Standing in front of me, Valentine loomed, over six feet tall. I had to crane my neck when we stood this close. "You either knew or you didn't," Valentine said in a tone that made it obvious he thought I had. "Is there some particular reason you chose not to share this information with me?"

"You should get some clothes on," I told Valentine as Robert came through the door.

"Oh, no need to on my account," Robert said in a sing-songy appreciative way. "I mean, really, the view is lovely." Still in the suit and tie he wore for his corporate job, Robert settled himself in one of the overstuffed chairs in the living room as if ready to enjoy the show.

Valentine continued to frown down at me, completely ignoring Robert.

Giving Robert the stink eye around Valentine's hulking, naked form, I asked: "Why are you even home?"

"I thought I should get a jump on renting this place," Robert said. "I bought a sign. I was going to put an ad in the paper tomorrow."

So soon? "I thought you were going to give me another chance to...." I jerked my head in the direction of Valentine, because I didn't want to admit that I'd agreed to try to talk to him about his hoarding problem, "...you know?"

"Yes, I do know. We all know how well that was going to go. He went ballistic over the stuff I put in the garage, and that was only to clear the kitchen." Robert said with a fussy cluck of his tongue. He made a broad gesture to the silver plates and bowls and oddities piled on the coffee table. "A leopard can't change its spots."

The temperature in the room dropped so sharply that I could suddenly see my breath. Valentine slowly turned to focus on Robert, who at least had the sense to look a little nervous. Robert sat up straighter in shock of the sudden chill. He swallowed as if something had gotten stuck in his throat.

"Changing spots," Valentine mused, his voice a low growl. "That's one of those human idioms that makes no sense. I've never understood why the burden to change is on the solitary, far-ranging predator, or why it would be expected to abandon its best defense, its camouflage... and for the convenience of whom, some fool of a man who grows tired of its wild beauty?"

Robert blinked. He looked to me for a translation.

I had nothing to offer Robert, besides a 'don't worry about it' shake of my head. After all, I was sure the comment was squarely aimed at me.

"But, how is hoarding a defense?" I asked him. "What's the evolutionary advantage of sitting on a pile of shiny stuff?"

"It's not just shiny. It's valuable. Therefore, I should think the advantage would be obvious," Valentine said, turning back to me. "I'm never without resources."

"Yeah, but most people don't pay for things in silver and gold anymore," I noted with a look at the silver plates. "And, isn't your nest in Russia?"

Robert blinked and made a choking sound. He shot me a 'Nest, what the fuck??' look.

"Lair," Valentine corrected sharply. "Dragons do not 'nest.'"

"Whatever," I said quickly. "Seriously, what are you hoping to trade for a silver plate? Is there a big call for silver spoons on the black market?"

"Civilizations and economies come and go," Valentine pointed out, "But silver and gold and precious gems rarely devalue entirely."

Robert must have been piecing something together, something that made sense to him anyway, because he said, "Oh, I get it! You're worried about being destitute! You know, my grandmother was like this what with, living through the Depression. She had so much stuff saved, 'just in case.'"

Now it was Valentine's turn to look confused, but, after a moment of consideration, he nodded thoughtfully. "I suppose there are similarities."

"Well, then, what you should do is sell this stuff on eBay for cash and put it in the bank," Robert said happily. "I can help you!"

Valentine's arms unwound and I could feel the room growing slightly warmer. "You're not the first to suggest this," Valentine admitted. "I have several of these bank account things. As it happens, I can't sleep on dividend reports and statements. No matter how many I accumulate. I've tried. It doesn't work."

Valentine had a pile of bank statements? We were going to have to talk about that later.

In the meantime, I had a compromise. "I don't think Robert would care if we kept some coins in the bed. When they're between the mattress and the sheet, it'd bother me less."

"Um, sure?" Robert seemed a little stunned by the weirdness of this whole conversation.

"I see," Valentine said, looking between us. "And if these changes are made, we could continue to stay here?"

"Well..." Robert couldn't meet my eyes, "I still think you two should consider getting a place of your own at some point, but..." he looked up then, and gave Valentine and me a wan smile. "If you can really get rid of this stuff, I could be patient, I guess."

"Is there some other problem?" Valentine asked pointedly.

Robert took in a deep breath, looking vaguely guilty again. Finally, he blurted out, "It's really hard to bring someone home with you two here all the time."

"You have a lover." The way Valentine said it, it sounded like a statement of fact, but Robert was shaking his head.

"I wish!"

"Ah." This was something Valentine understood immediately. "Of course," he said suddenly. Turning for the bedroom, he said: "We'll leave as soon as possible."

Robert and I watched him go. After the door to our bedroom shut, Robert looked at me. "That's it? All I had to say was 'Hey, Valentine, you're cramping my sex life'?"

I shrugged. "I guess so."

I slumped back against the backside of the couch.

"So... um... is Valentine one of those 'otherkin'?" Robert asked.

"Otherkin? What's that?" I asked.

"I heard him call himself a dragon," Robert said, his voice dropping so as not to be overheard. "Is he one of those people who believe they have non-human souls?" When I continued to stare at him blankly, Robert continued. "You remember 'Fairyl' from the game? I got to DMing them one time, and they told me that they were otherkin. They said they were a fairy in a past life." Robert shook his head. "I had no idea what to think of that, but I looked it up on Google and I guess it's a thing."

"Oh..." I started, not sure what to say. I wanted to explain the truth about Valentine, but Robert had no reason to believe in magic. Clearly, during the whole conversation about lairs and hordes and such, he'd kind of rolled with it and even came up with his whole 'otherkin' theory.

Thanks to our living in his house, he'd had a run in with the necromancer's sister, but from his perspective that'd been a routine break-in. Even so, I didn't want to lie to Robert. He was being a bit of a jerk about this moving out stuff, but he'd come through for me when I needed a friend. "Yeah, you could say Valentine has a dragon's soul."

It wasn't really a lie, was it?

Robert nodded. "I thought so. But, that's kind of weird, though, isn't it?"

"Uh..." I was spared having to answer by a knock on the door. I glanced over, half-expecting it to be our neighbor, or possibly the police, but instead it was Jack.

Seeing me, he waved through the door window. A brown mess of curls hung over his ears and, despite the warm weather, he wore black jeans and a t-shirt with some Anime character on it holding a comically large sword. A necklace made of coaxial cable and stripped copper wiring hung around his neck. He had a similar thick bracelet on his wrist. He'd apparently needed a costume change from this morning. "Hiya," he said, opening the door. "Spenser—er, the new one, Fun Times, is it? —sent me. We've got another jumper."

‡

Chapter Seven

I left Robert and Jack staring uncomfortably at one another in the living room and dashed off to change into something more work appropriate, since I was basically in my underwear still.

Standing in front of our overflowing closet, I considered the scene I was likely to encounter. I picked my least favorite pair of 'someday these will fit better' jeans and jammed myself into them. I chose a worn shirt with a tiny Chicago Cubs logo over my left breast. If the scene was as ugly as the others, at least this was something I wouldn't care about if it got covered in blood.

I grabbed a pair of socks and my black Converse and pushed the door open to the living room/dining room.

The men all stood around not talking. Robert remained in the living room chair he'd first sat down in. He'd pulled out his phone and busily swiped at things—knowing him, he was probably playing some game or other.

Or maybe looking for that new boyfriend.

Still stark naked, Valentine rested a hip against the back of the couch. His arms were crossed, and he frowned at the pile of silver-plated items that crowded the dining room table.

Jack had closed the door on himself and stood on our stoop, his face turned toward his vintage VW bug parked at the curb, as if wondering if he should just go hide and wait for me there. It wasn't a huge surprise that Jack put a screen door between himself and Valentine. Their relationship could be summed up thusly: Valentine had a tendency to call Jack "rabbit;" Jack had a similarly unfortunate tendency to squeak in Valentine's presence.

Plus, it was kind of obvious that Valentine and I had just had sex, and that made Jack uncomfortable, even though we were all supposed to be open and okay with it.

At my arrival at the door, fully dressed and ready to go, Jack smiled happily and hopped down the stairs towards his car, not bothering to see how closely I followed behind.

As I went out the door, I told Robert, "I hope we can talk more about this. We're not ready to move right away."

"I won't throw you in the streets," Robert said with a little chagrined smile. "I just think the sooner we start this process the better."

"Agreed," Valentine growled in a way that made me pause halfway out the door. I could only see part of his face. His dark, shapely eyebrows crumbled into a deep frown as he continued to glare at the silver.

I glanced back at Robert. I wanted to tell him to be careful. It was clear he'd angered the dragon. Before I could formulate a way to say that that didn't sound silly and 'otherkin'-y, Jack tapped the horn.

"Try to be good," I said on my way out—though I was not sure if I meant that for Robert or Valentine.

As I made my way to Jack's car, I felt almost giddy with relief. If there was another body there was absolutely no way Valentine was guilty. I could call Furfur and tell him where to shove it.

Even with the windows rolled down, the interior of Jack's car felt like an oven.

"You know they make new ones of these," I grumbled as I tried not to burn my fingers on a seat belt buckle that probably hadn't come standard on this antique, either. As we pulled out from the curb, I watched my car disappearing behind us and made grabby hands at it. "Or we could have taken mine."

Jack said nothing. Normally chipper and chatty, he watched the road intently, like a model of drivers' safety.

"Are you taking lessons from Spenser?" I finally asked.

"Erm, what?"

Jack blinked at me from under a mop of unruly curls.

"I said, is the reason your eyes haven't left the road because you're taking driving lessons from Mr. By-the-Book Jones?"

"No," he said simply, his eyes dutifully returning to the road. "I'm not looking at you because you have a huge hickey on your neck and, frankly, I'm feeling left out."

"Oh."

"Can we have a date Friday?"

I tried to remember what might be on my calendar, but when I noticed that my hesitation had made his frown deeper, I said, "I don't see why not."

"I think I'm terrible at this poly thing. I want to have jealous, angry sex."

If I was honest, that sounded weirdly fun. "That could work."

He finally took his eyes off the road to blink at me. "Really?"

"It's worth a try, right?"

The tension left his shoulders. "Yeah. Okay. Good."

"So," I said, changing the subject. "Tell me about the new body. Who found it?"

Jack's hand left the steering wheel briefly to pull at the nose stud in his nostril thoughtfully. "Werewolves."

I suspected that meant Mac and his motorcycle gang. "Did they see what dropped it?"

"Oh, good heavens, no," Jack said. When I gave him a curious eyebrow quirk, he explained, "Let's just say this particular body has been around a while longer... at least we think so from the state of it."

Oh. Yuck.

And, so much for my hope that I'd be Valentine's alibi.

I thought about this as I hung my arm out the window to try to catch some relief from the stifling heat of the car. The interior smelled of hot dusty upholstery. Jack had a magpie figurine made out of computer parts hanging from the rearview mirror that swung back and forth at every bump and turn. The ceramic circuit beads and solder flashed in the green motherboard wings and long, signature tail.

We turned onto a county highway. Fields of sunflowers flanked either side of the road. Bright yellow heads as far as the eye could see, all tilting in the direction of the sun. In vast numbers, they had a distinct earthy smell—nothing flowery, more like the scent of broad leaves drying in the sun.

"Why do they think this is related to our other victim?" I asked.

"Obviously, we can't be sure," Jack said. "To be fair, the werewolves thought the guy had been run over by a semi. I guess he looks like roadkill."

"Oh, that's just wonderful," I noted, already feeling a little queasy. Why did I have to decide to be the county coroner again?

"But, it occurred to the demon—BeelzeBob, is it? —that he could have been dropped, so he called me to fetch you."

"Furfur," I said.

"Sorry, what?"

"The demon. His name is Furfur."

Jack shook his head. "That's just silly. I'm never going to remember it."

Seemed fair, and I was about to say so when a ping came from somewhere among all the electronic doodads on Jack's dashboard, followed by a pleasant robotic voice. "Accessing, Wikipedia, Furfur, demon. 'In demonology, Furfur (other spellings include Furtur, Ferther) is a powerful great earl of hell, being the ruler of twenty-nine legions of demons. He is depicted as a hart or winged hart, and also as an angel.'"

"Stop, Love," Jack said.

"You have some kind of Alexa in your car?" I wasn't sure why I seemed so surprised. This was his wizardry after all.

"Modified," he nodded proudly

"Naturally," I nodded. I wanted to ask how bad the body looked, but then I decided that I didn't want to know. I glanced again over at Jack who seemed to have suddenly become unhappy at the sight of the blank, flat expanse of county road.

I noticed that there was no coffee at the ready this time. "Are you mad at me? Like, from before the sex thing?"

"What? Why do you think that?"

I didn't have a good answer so, instead, I asked again, "Are you?"

He sucked in a breath, but then shook his head. "I just... sometimes it's hard being the second to an actual... I'm just rather thrown. I'm not sure I've seen Valentine naked before and I'm feeling a bit inadequate. And, I don't just mean in the manly department, although, yes, also that, but, really, I should probably renew my gym membership, holy shit."

Thinking about it, I noted, "I don't think I've ever seen Valentine actually working out. And, um, to be fair, I think he looks the way he looks because he's magically trying to look like what I find hot?"

I could almost see the all-caps of Jack's: "That's not helping!"

I had to swallow back a chuckle as I tried to think of something more comforting to say. "So, Friday seemed specific. Are you taking me somewhere?"

"Um, well, I'd wanted to invite you over to watch that new anime I was telling you about, but now I feel like maybe I should suggest burlesque or something more risqué."

"I wouldn't know what to do at a burlesque show," I admitted honestly. "Cuddling in front of the TV sounds amazingly... human."

That last part sort of slipped out, unintentionally. Jack looked over to find me staring at him longingly. I didn't think Jack would take it the right way if I said out loud just how... exhausting it could be to be with someone so alien, so non-human as Valentine all the time. His body was perfect because it was an illusion, he'd reminded me of that today. Jack was real. What I saw was what I got, and I craved that with every fiber of my being right now.

Especially right now.

Jack gave me a helpless look like he could tell what I was feeling, but, of course, we'd arrived. I could see the flashing lights of a squad car ahead.

The body—no, more accurately, the remains—could have easily been mistaken for a deer carcass if not for the shoes. As I knelt on the side of the road near the ditch to inspect the body, I pulled on a pair of latex gloves that Spenser had handed me. For some reason, out of every horrible fly-and-maggot infested detail, the thing that stood out to me was that the body was wearing black Converses, just like mine.

When we'd first pulled up behind Spenser's cruiser, I'd noticed two 'Lone Wolves' leather jackets among the police uniforms. A woman with nearly white blond hair that fell to the back of her knees in a thick, ropey braid crouched down beside me. She had pseudo-Japanese full-color sleeve tattoos on both arms. "The shoes, am I right?"

"What?" Blinking away from the horrible mess, I looked at her. She had one of those broad handsome faces that had gone a bit leathery with age and too much sun and cigarettes. Her eyes reminded me of Mac's: unnaturally intense. It was like her blue eyes sparkled with a kind of electricity I could feel thrumming deep inside my chest.

"I nearly skidded into the ditch when I saw those shoes," she said again. Then she held out her hand for me to shake, which I took, after quickly stripping off my latex gloves. "Vonda."

"Alex," I said, while my hand was so vigorously pumped I felt my teeth rattle. I expected a jolt from my snake tattoo, but apparently the necromancer's gift was cool with werewolves.

"Ain't never known deer to wear Converses," Vonda continued. "Centaur, neither. Then I got a whiff of him, and I knew he was human... or, was."

Jack, who'd gone into the drainage ditch to throw up, came back up out of the tall grasses, only to turn and rush back down. I was kind of surprised I hadn't done the same, but I'd been keeping myself busy taking notes and snapping pictures with my phone. Even if the EMT crew couldn't do anything more than scrape the remains into a bag, I wasn't sure I was allowed to bring so many bugs into the lab. I knew enough to know that there was a way to tell time of death by the life cycle of all the gross critters on the body, so I made sure to document everything I saw, the best I could.

Spenser, who was leaning against the hood of his cruiser, asked, "Can you tell if he was dropped or run over?"

"Out of my pay grade," I admitted with a shake of my head. "Way out of my pay grade."

Furfur stood next to Spenser, all tall and thin where Spenser was square and squat. "The werewolves have been more helpful than you, Coroner."

And after we'd shared breakfast and everything.

I shrugged. "I'm an elected official."

"Ah," he said, giving me a measuring glance over the mirrored shades. "That explains everything."

"When Jack is recovered, he and I are going to ask the neighboring farmers if they remember seeing anything strange in the sky."

"Actually, you're doing noth—" Furfur started.

I cut him off. "You might want to check air traffic control, too," Standing up, I stripped off the other glove and stuck both of them into a biohazard bag that Spenser handed me. "Maybe the airport noticed a blip."

"Y'all saying this was done by an alien?" Vonda asked with an incredulous glance up at the clear, blue sky.

I hadn't considered that possibility, so I glanced at Spenser, "Are there aliens?"

Spenser stuffed the biohazard baggie into a larger red one that he'd gotten from the trunk of the cop car. "Who can say? I guess Stephen Hawking thought there could be."

"He was certainly correct about multiverses," Furfur said dryly.

"Oh, there are definitely aliens," Jack said, pulling himself up out of the ditch by hanging on to fists full of weeds. He kept his eyes pointedly away from the remains on the side of the road. "But, are they the sort who do anal probes and zip about in flying saucers? Doubtful."

"There's a relief," said Vonda. Wiping her hands on her jeans, she stood up.

A semi blasted past us. The size of the semi's haul cast us in a deep shadow and, for a brief second, it sounded like we were in a wind tunnel. The truck's wake pushed the cloud of flies and gnats from the body and kicked up a cloud of road grit. Once the semi was gone, the flies lazily made their way back.

71

Overhead on the telephone wires was a gang of crows... no, magpies, by their tails and white markings.

I waved up at them, "Hiya, Sarah Jane!"

One of the magpies cawed at me. I assumed it was Sarah Jane, Jack's familiar, but I really had no idea. Jack gave me a hard time for it, but damned if I could tell one magpie from another. Many times, Jack patiently pointed out marking differences and personality traits, but, really, all I knew was that Sarah Jane had been bird-banded, while the rest of her gang hadn't.

After Sarah Jane said hello, the rest of the birds on the wire dipped their heads and cawed, too. Natural bird behavior, sure, but it appeared as though they were all bowing and saying 'hello.'

Vonda looked at Spenser, "Can we get out of here now?"

Spenser shrugged. "I guess so. Thanks for calling this in."

A black woman with close-cropped hair nodded to Spenser. I hadn't noticed her sitting on the back of a sleek, fast-looking motorcycle parked on the side of the road. Vonda straddled the bike and the other woman waved goodbye to us as the motorcycle started up with a snarl.

The engine noise must have covered the corpse's first attempt to talk to me. I felt something snag at my socks. A rotted hand, with white bone visible through gnawed tendons, grasped at me like a claw. The flies by the remains of the ruined mouth buzzed loudly.... rhythmically.

It was trying to talk to me. The ruins of the corpse's mouth moved as though trying to form words. White enamel of exposed teeth and blackened tendons gaped and gulped horrifically. Maggots bubbled from its throat. Flies swarmed near the mouth and buzzed angrily.

No, I realized as I crouched down to get a better listen, the buzzing noises were the words.

"...Juzzzduzz..."

WTF. Had this body really roused itself from the dead just to say: "Jazz dance?"

If a skull with little more than ant-infested pits for eyeballs could shoot an 'are you a complete moron?' glare at me, this one did. It tried again to send its message from Beyond. The buzzing took on an exasperated sound. Irritation didn't make its words any clearer, however: "Juzzzzzzzzzzzzzduzz."

With that, the corpse let out a disgusting belching sigh that stank of rotting meat, and then spoke no more.

I sat back on my heels and tried to parse out any meaning to of all this. "Juzzduzz," I repeated. I said it a few more times, faster, "Juzzduzz-juzz-duzz-juzzzzzzduzz," until I finally heard, "Justice."

Both Spenser and Jack stood over me. Spenser adopted that classic cop pose, with one thumb hooked into a loop of his khaki pants. The other held on to the rim of his cap, as though shading his eyes to the sun. Of course, this would be more impressive if he were still in uniform. Instead, he wore the closest thing, trousers and a short-sleeved button-up shirt. The ball cap even advertised the policeman's union.

He did not look like a guy who was not working this case.

Jack had his thin, pale arms wrapped around his stomach, which kind of made it look like he was giving the anime character on his shirt a hug. His eyes watched me intently. "I felt a magical ripple. He said something to you, didn't he?"

"'Justice,' I think." I said, pulling myself to my feet.

Spenser and Jack exchanged a look. Spenser's hand dropped from his cap to rub his chin. "What's that mean?"

"Like I know? The dead tended to be cryptic, like this, or worse just plain incomprehensible. Once, one talked to me and all I got was 'moo.'" Seriously. A dead cow reanimated long enough to bellow at me. I had a stupid superpower. Just once it would be nice if the dead would send nice, obvious messages, like the name and address of their murderer. My magic was determined to remain useless and cryptic.

"You think that's a sign that this was, in fact, foul play?" Jack asked, releasing the stranglehold on his gut a bit and inching a step closer. "That the corpse is demanding justice for his death?"

"Or maybe that his death served justice," Spenser mused.

Sometimes it was obvious that Spenser wasn't entirely human.

Jack seemed to be thinking the same thing. "You really think a person would struggle all the way back from the Other Side just to say 'yippee, my death was meaningful'?"

Spenser shrugged. "I would."

Jack and I shared a silent, 'yeah, he would.' "The cow just said moo," I said. "It could be totally random."

Another semi rushed by, blasting us with heat and diesel. Its passing flushed a flock of pheasants from the sunflower fields. The magpies on the wires above hopped into the air and resettled, as well.

"The cow turned into a critical bit of evidence, if I recall," Jack said, starting to look at the body, and then quickly changing his mind.

Spenser, I noticed, flinched a little at the memory.

"Maybe," I agreed, watching Spenser trying to remain casual as we talked about the case that had landed in him in such hot water with Infernal Affairs. "I guess the fact that this corpse animated itself to talk to me could be seen as evidence that the two cases are connected. The position of the body is different this time, though." The passing semis made me nervous, so I stood up and moved further off the road to stand next to Jack in the ditch. The sweet smell of clover was a welcome change from the stench of death. "This one is face up."

I didn't mention that one way I would be able to tell if the two victims were related was if there were talon marks around the ribs. Not that it would necessarily be easy to tell with this body. Regardless, it would come out in my report. I didn't need everyone thinking of Valentine right away.

Not that my omission stopped Spenser, "Could just be the way they got nabbed. People aren't like mice. We walk upright. So, depending which way the creature swooped in—" he made a scooping claw motion in one direction and then the other.

"Did I miss something?" Jack asked. "We're looking for something that scoops things up? Does it bop them on the head as well?"

"The perp is not Little Bunny Foo-Foo," Spenser said.

"I wouldn't have thought you'd know about Bunny Foo-Foo," I said to Spenser.

He lifted a shoulder, "I saw the meme. I had to look it up."

"Meme?" Jack quirked a smile, "You do memes now, Spenser?"

"The picture of the bunny.... Ah, never mind," Spenser sighed. "Just say I learned it from the Interwebs."

"Can we go now?" Jack asked Spenser. "I mean, we're not expecting Alex to take that back to the lab, are we?"

Spenser took one long, frowning glance at the body. "We can't leave him here. I'm sort of hoping that the EMT will uncover a wallet or some other ID. Otherwise, that's two J. Does in one day. I don't like it."

Furfur decided to leave his spot by the car to come join us. "Nor do I."

Especially in a town this size. It wasn't so small that everyone knew everyone's business, but it was small enough that strangers were noticed. I'd thought our first Jane Doe might have been homeless. I said so now.

Adjusting his hat, Spenser nodded, "Nana Spider called me this morning. You know she only breathes into existence when she's needed, so that seemed ominous."

Did we know that?

Jack seemed to, because he nodded, "Like an ever-moving spider's web."

"What did she say, exactly?" I asked.

"'Expect morning showers,'" Spenser said.

I glanced at Jack to see if he'd gotten more out of that than I had. I shook my head. Turning back to Spenser, Jack asked, "Um, so how did you get from that to knowing that there'd be a body?"

"I didn't," Spenser admitted, frowning down at the corpse. "Nana Spider doesn't reach out to me unless it's got something to do with her people."

"She said 'showers,'" I noted. "That's plural. Do you think she meant these two... ?" I glanced up at the clear blue sky warily, "...or do you think more are coming?"

Jack made a face. "Let's hope this is it for now at least."

I couldn't have agreed more.

⚕

Chapter Eight

Jack offered to take me back to precinct headquarters. I could have waited around with Spenser and Furfur for an air-conditioned ride, but I wanted to gossip.

"I meant to ask you before," I said, once we were down the road a way. "What do you think of the Internal Affairs goons?"

"Goons?" Jack repeated, giving me a sidelong glance and a little smile. "Not biased, are we?"

"They're scary," I said. Hanging my arm out the window, I let the sixty-mile-an-hour wind push it around, like a kid. "One of them is a demon."

"Both are, really," Jack corrected. "Tengu are Japanese bird-like demons... sort of, anyway, you could classify them that way if you wanted to."

"He thinks he's an Elegant Danger or something like that but, regardless, you're making my point," I said with a smile. "What I want to know is: have you talked to them?"

Jack chewed on his lip. Sarah Jane, who had flown into the backseat when I opened the door, made a sharp caw that only made Jack look more miserable.

I looked over my shoulder at Sarah Jane, who bobbed up and down in a very nodding way that made me say, "So, you did? Was it a formal interview?"

Jack's mouth screwed up unhappily and he moved his head from side to side. It was clear he didn't want to talk about it. Then he let out a long, slow breath. "I probably got Spenser in trouble. What've you said?"

"That I didn't want to narc."

"Oh, well, that's straight forward. I should have tried that one."

The grassy horizon stretched on forever on either side of us. I could see a cluster of brown beef cattle nosing around, like they do. Despite having lived in

South Dakota for over a year now, I still felt the need to point them out when I saw them, "Cow."

"Oh, yes, lovely, thanks, we never see those, do we?"

Of course, as we turned left at the county road intersection, there was another completely separate herd on the other side of the road. I held back mentioning that I'd spotted them.

I'd rather keep pointing out the obvious than think about how guilty Spenser probably was. It was more than the fact that Spenser dated the necromancer's sister, it was that he'd kept that information from the rest of us. He'd dragged his feet a lot, too. I'd warmed up to Spenser to the point of thinking of him as a friend, but... like him or not, he was probably guilty of obstructing justice.

"I'd hate to think that something I've said might get Spence suspended, though," Jack was saying. "He's a cantankerous old fart, but basically a good guy. I mean, I know that what he did was wrong, but we caught the bad guys. Should count for something, shouldn't it?"

I didn't know. My experience with the magical police's Internal Affairs unit was nil. Maybe they were sticklers for details, but they could just as likely be a good ol' boys network of cover-ups and free passes for the son of the Faerie Queen. "You'd know better than I would. What are these guys' reputations; you've checked in with the aether, right?"

He frowned at the highway and the flat, expansive South Dakota horizon. "I have, and the signs... confuse me."

"How so?"

Jack slowed as we approached an old-fashioned farmhouse, its white paint peeling in the summer heat. Behind it stood a classic red barn and the obligatory rusting farm machinery. There was even a windmill creaking as it lazily spun in the breeze. He turned into the gravel driveway, and said, "Furfur is a former commander in Hell, which makes him one of the Fallen. It's a special order of soldiers, you know, like Special Ops would be here. Those are pretty big guns for what is really a penny ante case. I get the sense that someone is after Spenser, hoping to bring him down, but I get no sense of who or why. The vibrations of the web aren't at all clear."

Pulling onto the grass beside an old Ford truck with a broken tailgate, Jack stopped the car.

I looked at the farmhouse. "A friend of yours?"

"Oh, sorry, no. I just thought we should do a little footwork while we were out here. You know, ask the locals if they saw anything fly over in the past few days... or, erm, longer," Jack said, looking a little queasy again. Unbuckling, he added, "You can stay in the car, if you like."

Without a/c or even a working radio? No, thanks. "I'll tag along."

"Lovely," he said.

If I had to guess, the two-story house had been built in the early 1900s. It wasn't fancy enough to be a Victorian, but there were nice details that made it look like a house that had been built to last. Large windows with lace curtains looked out onto an open porch. There was a swinging bench hung from the ceiling with a brightly colored patchwork quilt as a cushion. A white wicker table had been set up on the other side of the door, and two mismatched plastic chairs—one olive green, the other a faded yellow--sat around it. The foundation sagged dangerously in places, but the house gave the impression of being worn, but well-loved.

Not finding a doorbell, Jack knocked on the screen door loudly. Peering into the interior, he shouted, "Hullo? Anyone home?"

I could hear noises from the kitchen—pots banging and a radio playing big band music. "They can't hear you," I said. "Try knocking louder."

Jack did. Still no answer.

Just when we considered going around the house to see if there was a side door we could try, the radio switched off. A wavering, old man's voice demanded: "Someone there?"

"Yes!" Jack said, cheerfully. "Police. We want to ask you a few questions."

A nearly bald head, with wisps of pure white hair and large droopy ears peered around the door. The man looked ancient to me, which could mean he was anywhere between seventy and a hundred and three. Or younger, since he still seemed to be running this farm on his own. "Hold your horses," he said, as he made his slow way to us. He shuffled in that old man way. "Police, you say?" Peering through the screen, he gave Jack's anime character a hard look. Then, he locked the door. "Bullshit."

Slamming the heavier door in our faces, I heard him say, "Fucking kids these days."

Jack looked down at his shirt. "Nerds get no respect."

"You should have had your badge out."

"Oh, right," Jack said. "I always forget to carry it."

I laughed a little as we turned back toward his car. Neither of us looked much like police officers. Of course, I wasn't one, but Jack... well, actually, I had no idea what Jack was.

"Are you even a real cop?" I asked him.

The gravel crunched under our sneakers. Cicadas buzzed in the heat. Jack gave me a funny, crooked smile. "Are you asking if I've a license to kill?"

I shook my head at his suggestive eyebrow waggle. "No, I mean, really, are you a cop or a detective or what?" I was honestly curious, especially since I'd never seen Jack wear anything other than his usual gear. "Did you take an oath to protect and serve Pierre? Do you even own a uniform? Have you ever carried a gun?"

The door to the VW bug came open with a creak. "Oh, heaven's no. Guns make me nervous."

I opened my side. Immediately, a wave of heat hit me in the face. "You're avoiding the question," I noticed. "Are you embarrassed?"

"A little," Jack admitted finally, pulling a ring of keys from his pocket before sliding into the driver's seat. More charms than keys hung off the small metal ring. Many of them were plastic characters with wide, anime eyes. "I took some courses in police procedure at university, but never finished a degree."

I cranked down the window, thinking about my own unfinished medical degree. "That makes two of us," I said, since I could see the beginnings of a blush coloring the tips of his ears and I wanted him to know he wasn't alone in his 'fail.'

A soft smile graced Jack's lips as he started up the engine.

"Spenser better not lose his job," I mused. "He's the only one of us actually qualified for anything."

"Sad, isn't it? Especially given that he graduated from the police academy in the 1930s or something like that," Jack said casually.

The nineteen—what now?

I fumbled with the hot buckle. "Are you serious? Wouldn't that make him eighty?"

"At least," Jack nodded, backing around onto the grass to get us pointed toward the highway again. We bounced on the uneven ground. "Could even have been earlier than that, I can't rightly remember. Point is, he's been a copper a long time."

"Longer than I've been alive," I noted.

"Longer than both our lives combined," Jack said.

Our tires kicked up beige dust as we bumped down the gravel driveway to the highway.

It was hard to believe Spenser was that old; I supposed his slow aging had something to do with his faerie blood. Regardless, that was a long time to be a police officer, which made me wonder, "That's a long time to be 'on the job,' as they say. I mean, maybe the rules used to be looser, but you'd think if he was prone to obstructing justice, he'd have been drummed out long ago. Has Spenser ever been investigated before?"

"Not that I know of," Jack said, as we waited at the end of the drive as a pair of motorcycles zoomed by. "Of course, the cold hard truth is that we never had that much magical crime until recently. It's the Tinkerbell Effect, I'm afraid."

I always forgot that the Tinkerbell Effect was basically a new phenomenon. The last big bad we'd fought had tried to push the envelope so far as to cause a kind of magical meltdown, a Tinkerbell singularity of sorts.

The VW Bug sputtered along the highway. The heat poured through the cloudless blue sky relentlessly. The green fields stretched out flat and wide as far as the eye could see. Occasionally, we passed a windbreak of scrubby oaks. And cows; there were always cows.

"If the Tinkerbell Effect is new, why did this nowhere town even have a magical department? And why is the Prince of Faerie its chief? For that matter, why did you come here?"

Sarah Jane made a fluttering honk from the back seat.

I gave her a smile. She never let Jack get away with any secrets. "It's a good story, I'm guessing?"

"Erm, well, remember how I said I never quite finished police training? Well, it was more that I got kicked out."

Before I could get the story, a huge shadow passed in front of the sun. Twisting around, I glanced through the windshield in time to see a white shape soaring overhead. Its bat-like, leathery wings spread wide, soaring on the thermals. Long, serpentine body twisting like a kite on the wind.

"Valentine?"

Jack pulled the car onto the shoulder. I jumped out and stood on the side of the road watching the dragon flying away. It carried something in its front claws, some kind of bundle that I couldn't quite see at this distance.

I looked over the rounded roof of the car at Jack. Could he tell what it was Valentine carried? "Do you have binoculars or something?"

"Better," Jack pointed at the group of birds in the sky.

Darting out the open car door, Sarah Jane let out a caw.

$

Chapter Nine

I spent an anxious ten minutes kicking pebbles into a drainage ditch on the side of the road. Tall stalks of field mustard and leggy clover grew wild among the grasses. White cabbage butterflies fluttered lazily from flower to flower. The smell of manure drifted in the hot air.

Sarah Jane fluttered down to perch on the overhead wire. Jack looked up at her and said, "Well?"

There was a lot of cawing and whistling and magpie-talk, I guess. I watched their back and forth anxiously, only to have Jack turn to me and say, "Inconclusive. She says she couldn't get close enough to really see anything more than a lumpy burlap bundle."

"But it was Valentine?"

Sarah Jane nodded to me and then, as if trying to make sure I understood, let out a loud caw.

"None of the other victims were in burlap," I told Jack.

"Uh..." his mouth hung open for a while. He blinked at me for several seconds before adding, "So, we were still worried that Valentine was our body dumper?"

I kicked at another bit of gravel, feeling like a bad girlfriend. "No?"

Cicadas buzzed. Jack lay back against the hood of his antique of a car, patiently waiting for me to tell the truth.

After a few seconds, Sarah Jane yelled at me.

"Okay, all right," I fumed. "A little?"

Jack's frown was sympathetic. "What aren't you telling me?"

I hesitated, but even if I never reported the claw marks on this morning's body, the autopsy from the university's lab would note them. "Jane Doe had been pierced by something with talons."

81

After glancing up at the clear blue sky in the direction of Valentine's flight, Jack turned back to me. "Could there be another white dragon?"

"There could be anything." Walking over to where Jack leaned on the car, I rested my backside against the hood beside him. "You're more of an expert in this stuff than I am. Valentine assures me that he doesn't find helpless things tasty, and, as weird as it sounds, I believe him?" I looked over at Jack, who nodded in wary agreement. After a moment of chewing on my lower lip in thought, I added: "What else would eat people?"

"Well, whatever this is, isn't actually eating people. It's throwing them from the sky."

"Good point—if ghastly," I said.

We both stared out at the cows in the field. "Valentine has no particular hatred of the homeless, does he?" Jack asked.

I shrugged. We were about to be kicked out of our house, but he didn't know that until after the first body had dropped. Anyway, I'd have thought that would make him more sympathetic than less.

"What about Nana Spider?" Jack asked, "Any bad blood there?"

With Valentine, it was always possible that there were vendettas that I didn't know about or history he'd neglected to tell me. Truth was, I didn't know him that well. We'd had a whirlwind affair when we first met. Then, it was just as suddenly over, and Valentine was in jail.

Even now he kept secrets, like his stargazing trips to the badlands.

"I suppose we have to report this," I said with a long sigh.

Jack's eyes were on the ditch. "With Internal Affairs around? I imagine that would be best."

A little too quickly, I offered: "I think maybe *I* should be the one to tell."

He must have heard the slight edge in the tone of my voice, because he caught my eye and slowly shook his head. Pushing off from the car, he made his way to the drivers' side. "We should do it <u>together</u>, Alex. We have to do this right, if for no other reason than that people are watching. Weren't you the one who insisted that it'd go better for him if we were upfront? No hiding history and all that? I did offer, remember? Besides, we should trust Valentine. There could be a completely innocent explanation for it all."

Innocent was not a word often associated with Valentine. Weakly, I collapsed back into my seat in the car.

As we buckled in, Jack watched me thoughtfully. "You're having doubts? I mean, yeah, you are. Obviously. That's why you called, before."

I found I couldn't meet Jack's gaze. Trying to untangle my feelings, I busied myself with unrolling the window with the ancient crank mechanism. "I guess? I don't like how it feels, though."

Jack started up the car, the engine grumbled unhappily. "You feel like it's a betrayal. Not trusting him."

Still unable to really look at Jack, I stared at my knees.

"This is a problem with having a shape-shifting familiar," Jack said. "I mean, I never have to feel responsible when Sarah Jane eats someone's pet gecko or tarantula."

I chuckled a little at the difference in scale. "True."

After a beat, he added much more seriously: "And, even if Sarah Jane were able to become human, I'd never sleep with her."

I'd never heard this before. "Why not?"

"For one, she'd be a magpie in human form, not a human who turns into a bird. And, well, I don't know what you know about bird sex, but it can be quite weird. Crows, which are related to magpies, of course, have... um, been observed engaging in necrophilia. You know I'm up for a lot of things, but I have a few hard nos and fucking the dead is one of them."

"There go my plans," I teased, but I was thinking about the distinction Jack had laid out and how it applied to me: Valentine was a dragon who could become a human, not a human who could become a dragon.

I'd literally never wondered about dragon sex before.

Now it was all I could think about.

"Then, there's the power dynamic," Jack continued, shooting me a little side-eye. "I'm not interested in sex with someone I could bend to my will. You could Compel him, you know."

"I could?"

Jack stared at the road a little uncertainly. "Technically? It's possible?" Jack said after another long pause. "I mean, this is why people don't normally have dragon familiars. A hamster might have been better, love."

"I don't remember having any choice in the matter."

As we pulled up in front of the abandoned looking storefront, Jack shook his head. Quietly, he said, "No, you don't. None of us do."

I stared out the window at the door to the precinct. It didn't look like much, of course. It was nothing more than a dusty 'opening soon' storefront, an illusion to keep the regular public from wandering in, but what I saw as I frowned at it was the worst parts of my history repeating itself.

A stabbing flash of a memory of Valentine fighting the police who had come to arrest him that night cut through my mind. With a shudder and a pounding heart, I recalled the sound of bones cracking, screaming, and the deep-down, sickening sense that Valentine had been holding back the whole time. I could see it in his eyes when the police finally forced him to the floor. That look that said, 'I only bow my head because you ask me to.' Maybe I'd Compelled him at that moment? I certainly had a sense that, if I'd wanted, they would have been like nothing to him, he would have left lifeless bodies on the floor in a flash, and we could have escaped.

As Jack started to unbuckle, I put a hand over his, stopping him. I wasn't sure I wanted to say, if anything. I think more than anything I just didn't want to face Valentine at this moment.

Of course, that was when Valentine leaned his head into the driver's side window of the car and asked innocently, "Am I on time?"

Jack squeaked. Or maybe that high-pitched terrified noise came from both of us. I certainly jumped again, like a cornered mouse.

Valentine chose to ignore our bizarre response and added, "Only I had an errand, and I'm not good at this whole time-keeping thing that you humans insist on."

"So, it was you? Flying?" Jack managed, while fumbling his way through finishing unbuckling. "Earlier? We saw? West of here?"

Valentine stepped back so that Jack could open the door. As I made my own way out of the car, I heard Valentine mutter, "I don't really want to confirm that. It will ruin the surprise."

"'Surprise! I'm a murderer'?" Jack offered with a little bit of hysterical warbling.

Valentine looked to me as I joined them on the sidewalk, his tone like ice: "Is there no one who isn't convinced I murder for pleasure?"

I tried not to visibly flinch, but, internally, I winced at the hurt tone in his voice. "It's this case," I reassured him. "Bodies are falling from the sky, so, of course, we think of the people we know who can fly."

"Of course," he repeated, his expression closing off instantly. "So," he turned to Jack, his voice clipped and brusque. "When are they questioning you?"

"I... er, what?"

"Jack doesn't—" I started.

"He's a witch, is he not?" Valentine cut me off. "He flies. Don't you, Jack?"

"Oh, well, um, I mean, I <u>can</u>..." Jack gave me a helpless look, "With the right equipment."

84

This was news to me. All witches could fly? Our suspect list just expanded exponentially. My mouth was hanging open at the possibilities, as I stepped through the door Valentine held open for me.

Behind me, Jack hesitated to step inside, since it would involve passing beside Valentine who still dutifully held the door. Jack apparently made a decision to dart through.

Valentine did nothing, only caught my eye meaningfully as he closed the door behind him, deliberately, gently.

I felt bad. Jack was right. I'd betrayed Valentine by even considering him guilty for a second. I should be more trusting.

The interior of the precinct was oddly quiet. Spenser wasn't lying when he said that we were a small operation, but, even during our slow times, our office was a hangout for the local... well, oddballs, I supposed. Everyone from serious astrologers to the wide-eyed 'cryptid' hunters liked to get involved in whatever cases we might be working on. So, it was strange to see so few of the desks occupied. It looked like even the Bigfoot enthusiasts had cancelled their afternoon card game session.

Spenser tried to make the place look like the police stations you see on TV, where the detectives all had small desks crammed together, overflowing with case files, but all the cases we ever worked on—solved and unsolved—were in chronological order, neatly shelved on the bookcase outside of his glass-windowed office. The desks were there, jammed in tightly, but mostly they held potted plants, collections of crystals, and the occasional tarot spread laid out on top of the weekly crossword puzzle. I swore that there were days when Spenser made the place look busier by artfully placing "abandoned" coffee mugs in strategic places. No one had taken down the case notes from the whiteboard from the last big job—finding Mrs. Johnson's cat, which, admittedly, had turned out to be a shapeshifter that we'd discovered in Rapid City at a casino.

The point was, without Spenser on the job, no one was as invested in keeping up appearances.

Furfur, who'd taken over Spenser's office, looked up when we entered. He stepped out into the main room, his eyes riveted to Valentine.

Business-like, he strode over to us and held out a hand. "The dragon, I presume."

Valentine sneered. I wasn't sure if it was at the offer to shake, Furfur's attire, or his entire presence. The only acknowledgment he gave was a slight nod, and, "Fallen."

"I prefer the term 'demon,'" Furfur said, pulling his hand back, annoyed.

"As you wish," Valentine said.

Jack watched this exchange with wide eyes. "Fallen? Is that true?" Jack asked Furfur. "Are you a turncoat? Were you once an—"

The fierceness of the growl that escaped Furfur's throat shocked Jack into sudden silence. The sound was not only threatening, but it was profoundly... *primordial*. It was so anciently triggering that, although I'd never been Catholic in my life, I considered making the sign of the cross.

"Demons fly," Valentine remarked dryly. "And, we all know that angels have wings."

That broke the mood.

Jack, to his credit, said, "You're making a lot of valid points, Valentine."

Valentine tipped his head to Jack, but his eyes watched me.

I looked away guiltily.

I wasn't the only one who had thought Valentine capable. Furfur pulled himself back together with a straightening of his jacket and adjusted his shades. "Alex, would you allow me to take your familiar into interview room two? You're welcome to watch, of course, but I need to know you're not exerting your Influence and I have been assured that that room is equipped to nullify that bond."

Valentine frowned slightly. "Witchbane?"

"Yes, rue. Worked into the concrete, apparently," Furfur nodded in answer to Valentine's question. His gaze, however, had never left me. "Do I have your permission, Alex? Will you temporarily release your familiar to me?"

There was something about the formality of the word 'release' that I didn't like, but when I glanced at Jack, he shrugged. If there was something to be wary of here, he didn't know what it was either. Reluctantly, I said, "I guess?"

Furfur seemed somewhat unhappy with that reply. Finally, looking at Valentine, he let out an exasperated sigh, "Will that work?"

Valentine crossed his arms in front of his chest. I was happy to see that he had several inches on Furfur and could look down his nose at the demon. "The room is warded with witchbane, what more do you need, demon?"

"I would like assurances," Furfur said.

Trying to make up for my earlier blunders, I said, "Valentine will cooperate. He's got nothing to hide."

"Fine," Furfur said, clearly disappointed. To Jack, Furfur said, "You'll run the recording equipment?"

"Uh, sure, but I should probably tell you that I'm in a relationship with... erm, both of these people."

Furfur blinked. He blinked at Jack for a long time. Then, he blinked at me and then at Valentine, and then back and forth several times between the three of us. "All together? Currently? As in, right now?"

Jack and I nodded.

"Demon," Valentine drew out that word playfully. "You're awfully shocked. Surely a life-long demon such as yourself isn't scandalized by something as commonplace as polyamory?"

Furfur cleared his throat and then did that jacket straightening thing again to pull himself together. Ignoring Valentine's jibe, he said, "All right, I'll get Carol to do the actual recording. She's in the back." He paused and gave us all a look, "You're not sleeping with her as well, are you?"

Carol was the precinct's favorite astrologer. I wasn't surprised she was around; the only place deader than the precinct was her New Age shop on Main Street. "Besides," I said. "She has a crush on Hannah, not us."

"Which is a shame, really," Jack noted off-handedly. At my look, he added, "What? I think she's attractive. I like all those flowy, mirrored skirts."

Valentine chuckled darkly, "And Sarah Jane is the magpie?"

"There's a reason she's my familiar," Jack said. "Likes attract."

"But no actual relationship with Carol?" Furfur asked, making sure.

"No, no, I haven't ever even asked," Jack said. "I mean, I don't want to step on Hannah's potential action... I don't even know if Carol is bi."

With that settled, Furfur disappeared to the backroom to hunt up Carol.

Apparently Carol had been organizing the supply cabinet with Hannah, so Hannah joined Jack and me in the interview recording room. I cannot say how disappointed I was that the precinct was not cool enough to have one of those one-way mirror deals in the interview rooms. To be fair, interview room number one, which I had been in before, was a weird green space with a koi pond. Apparently, this is psychologically advantageous against 'unnatural' sorts, which included me. I can't say I felt especially uncomfortable in it, though I did find it weird.

Hannah, despite having seen me at ice cream not hours earlier, introduced herself. "Hannah Stone," she said.

I took the hand she offered, despite the fact that I knew she'd get a small shock from the tattoo. Nothing spelled lawful good like a golem made for the express purpose of fighting crime. The little zap surprised her, so I said, "Must be dry in here. I'm Alex, Alex Conner."

Jack just held out his hand next, "Jack."

Hannah frowned at him. "You do this every time, Jack. I know who you are."

"Right, sorry, just going with the flow!" Jack laughed, unconvincingly.

Carol gave us all pitying looks, but was the only one brave enough to say, "You know you have memory troubles, Hannah. They're just trying to be polite."

Hannah looked chagrined. She tapped the side of her head, "Sticks and stones. They got put back together in a hurry, I'm told. Sorry, if I seemed snappish, Jack."

"No worries, love," Jack murmured.

Under Carol's ministrations, the video equipment snapped and hummed to life. Carol sat in front of a control console that looked like it would be at home at a rock concert. After removing her big, dangly earrings, she slipped the headphones over her long, straight red hair that I was pretty sure she dyed. I might be wrong, but the color was just a touch more vibrant than I would expect to occur naturally. The earrings and the skirts were clearly part of Carol's astrologer 'costume.' I was pretty sure she adopted the fashion because she liked it, but she didn't follow it up with the overdone makeup or the long, polished nails.

There were several banks of TV screens, all of them recording different angles of the room that Valentine and Furfur entered.

Carol pressed a button and said into a stand-up mic, "Go ahead. We're set."

After listing off the precise date and time, Furfur began, "Agent Furfur of Internal Affairs acting as chief of Precinct Thirteen, Area Forty-Seven, is interviewing the ice dragon familiar of Alexandra Conner..." Furfur's professional patter died awkwardly. "Uh, what are you going by? Anything beyond 'Valentine'?"

Valentine had taken the seat offered to him in front of a small microphone. Deliberately, he leaned into it to say, "Let the record show that Alexander Conner's familiar refuses to offer their Magical Name to Agent Furfur."

My fingers pinched the bridge of my nose. I had to hold back a small swear as I muttered, "C'mon, Valentine, don't be like this."

Jack reached out and gave my hand a little squeeze. We stood together behind where Carol and Hannah sat in front of the equipment.

Meanwhile, Carol twisted to give me a questioning look. "Has Valentine always used the they/them pronoun? I'm so sorry! I think I've been misgendering h—them."

"Uh," was all I had time to say because Furfur was continuing the interview.

"Not feeling cooperative, are you, Valentine?" Furfur asked. After several seconds of unnerving silence from Valentine, Furfur said, "Can I at least call you Valentine during this interview?"

To my surprise, Valentine said, "That is Alex's name for me. You may call me that, if you wish."

Hannah and Carol turned to look at me to see if I was shocked to discover that maybe I didn't know Valentine's real name either.

I was.

Meanwhile, Jack was unfazed and apparently unaware of the expression on my face. "This is standard stuff," Jack said. "I would never use Sarah Jane's True Name in public, either. It doesn't mean she doesn't know it." Sensing something in everyone's reaction, Jack finally turned to look at me. "You do know it, right? You wouldn't send Valentine into a warded circle without knowing his True Name, would you?"

A sense of panic swelled in my throat. "Is that bad?"

Jack went white as a sheet, but he said, "You're fine. I'm sure you're fine. I mean, no one would take 'I guess?' as binding would they?"

"What do you mean?" The panic was making my voice crack. "I was looking at you, Jack. You know I don't know any of this witchy stuff."

"I thought we were sharing a 'WTF' look!" Jack admitted nervously.

"What are you two yammering about?" Hannah asked.

I looked to Jack for an answer as well. "Uh, it's just that Furfur used contract language to try to get Alex to release her claim on Valentine. I mean, it's meaningless if the familiar bond has been sealed with the exchange of names, which is why I found it so strange. Maybe Valentine never offered that part?"

I shook my head.

"Shhh!" Carol warned, pointing at the screen.

In the interview room, Furfur had stood up to move behind where Valentine sat. Putting his hands on either side of the back of the chair, Furfur leaned into say into Valentine's ear: "She doesn't know, does she?"

Valentine said nothing.

"I could smell it," Furfur said. "The incomplete bond. Its odor is like rotting leaves. Hanging in the air between you, the stink is at once attractive and the scent of decay. I will admit it caused me to be tempted to take you from her. But, I'm curious, The-One-Alex-Calls-Valentine, why wouldn't you commit? Is it because she's human and so short-lived? Or are you unhappy with fate's choices? Do you not like the witch you've been bound to?" When Valentine

89

continued his silent act, Furfur moved back to the seat across from him. "You do realize how this makes you look."

I found myself moving closer to the screen, trying to read Valentine's face.

"There wasn't time," Valentine said at long last.

Furfur tapped a finger on the thickly stuffed folder on the table, "Because of your arrest?"

Valentine nodded. There was a small glance at the camera. Instinctively, he honed in on the very one I was looking at, and our eyes met. "I would have not awoken had Alex not known my name already, somewhere deep inside. That unconscious bond was enough that I felt a strong pull to obey her, even without the Exchange. I let them take me away because it was as she wanted." His eyes left the camera, and he turned his attention to Furfur. "You're a fool if you think I would risk such a thing again."

"How long were you in prison? Did you make any friends there, or enemies, perhaps?"

I held my breath.

Valentine let one out, his shoulders slumping a little. "I don't remember."

"You don't remember two years in prison?"

His shoulder lifted slightly. "I went into hibernation. The body moved, went through required motions. I did only necessary things, my mind elsewhere."

Furfur said what I was thinking, "You sound bitter."

Valentine's lips thinned, but he said nothing. He dropped his gaze, his eyes hooded in the harsh overhead lights of the interrogation room.

"Are you resentful? Is that why, now that you're free, you've never entered into the Exchange?"

I could feel everyone's eyes on me in the recording studio. My heart thudded dully in my ear, ticking off each second of Valentine's silence.

"You did luck out. Your witch is either too unschooled or too stupid to know the difference. How much longer until the bond erodes completely, The-One-Alex-Calls-Valentine?" Furfur asked. "And when it does, will you seek a new master?"

"I will not," Valentine said sharply.

"Oh, now we've hit it, haven't we?" Fufur purred. "You can't stand being owned, can you?"

Owned? The word echoed in my mind. What, like a cat?

My eyes stayed glued to the screen I hunched inches in front of. I watched Valentine's face anxiously. I wasn't sure what I was looking for, maybe a sense that he didn't completely hate me, that our time together hadn't been a lie. It couldn't be, could it? Did he stay with me because he <u>had</u> to?

"What does demon-kind think of witches?" Valentine asked, his tone flat and matter-of-fact, "Your sort have been made into familiars, as well. Some taken by force."

I glanced over my shoulder at Jack to confirm. He nodded.

"I'm not the one who might be taking my anger out on the fine citizens of South Dakota." Furfur reminded Valentine.

Valentine laughed, darkly. "Nor am I. You and I both know that this 'interview' is a ruse. You've already said that you think Alex is too naïve to possess me. That's why you tried to use the devil's power of contract to have her release me temporarily. That's why you were nearly salivating at the thought of a room laced with rue that would further weaken our bond. The real question is, have you already laid a transfer spell down, or are you still hoping I will leave her of my own free will?"

Furfur leaned back in this chair, but his expression betrayed no sense of shock at Valentine's accusation.

"He wouldn't try something like that with all of us watching, would he?" Jack asked no one in particular.

My throat was dry. "Try what?"

All of a sudden, Furfur stood up. He snapped his fingers and runes of some sort illuminated the walls of the interrogation room. With a shout of something in Latin, the screens went black.

$
\text{\Large ⚕}
$

Chapter Ten

Throwing open the door of the recording studio, I dashed across the hall to the interview room. I nearly wrenched my shoulder out of its socket trying the door. "It's locked!" I shouted in panic. "Someone get a key! Is there a key?"

Jack, who had stumbled out of the room after me, nodded. He took off down the hall in the direction of Spencer's office. His feet pounded on the nubby carpeted halls.

I banged on the door with a fist. "Valentine!"

Getting no response, I pressed my ear to the door to try to hear what was going on. Just barely, I could hear an odd incantation. Light pulsed through the small slit at the bottom of the door.

Frantically, I used both fists to whale on the door now. "Valentine! Can you hear me? I'm so sorry! I should never have—" what though? I found my fist hesitating mid-air, because what I wanted to say was that I should never have sent him away, but, if I hadn't made him stop short of killing that day, what would we have done then? Gone on the run? Forever?

Muffled laughter had me pressing my ear against the door again. I could make out a smattering of words, "...see? ...selfish. Doesn't even know... sorry for."

I stepped back from the door in defeat.

I had been selfish. I'd been willing to use Valentine's strength, his inhumanity, that day, but I'd shrunk away from the responsibility of owning the choice. I made him bloody his hands, and then I sent him away to somewhere horrible to be punished for doing what I'd asked.

That strange unspooling I'd been feeling all day intensified, making me feel almost sick.

Maybe Furfur was right. I didn't deserve Valentine.

That's when something snapped inside me. Almost like a bone break, except the sensation was deep in my gut. I doubled over from the sudden, intense pain.

Valentine's roar shook the building.

Somebody swore. It might have been me, but it was difficult to know if it was my hissed 'shit,' or Valentine's cry that flung the door outward from its hinges. The walls around the door exploded. I would have been pummeled by the rain of debris, except that I'd collapsed to my knees and, by chance, the door had fallen forward in a way that protected me. Plaster dust filled the air.

Crawling out from under the door, I shakily pulled myself upright. Coughing, I wiped the stream of tears and plaster from my eyes. "Valentine!"

Though the gaping hole that was once a wall, I could see runes glowing in the air. Whatever illuminated them sparkled in the dusty air. In the center of the circle they formed, Furfur stood. He'd transformed. No longer entirely human, the shape of him was the same, but his naked body shimmered with the same brilliance as the glyphs. Snow-white wings had unfurled at his back.

Hannah stood in the doorway of the studio, her arms wide, no doubt to use her body as a literal shield to protect Carol. Seeing Furfur, she whispered something guttural, probably in Hebrew, "Mal'akh."

Furfur turned at the word. His body appeared as sexless as a Ken doll. Goat pupils disappeared, only to be replaced by something more terrifying—a starry void of darkness. "Not quite," he said in response to Hannah. "I am an angel no more."

Steadying myself on the door, I scanned the wreckage of the room for Valentine.

Unlike Furfur, Valentine fully retained his human form. A swirling tornado of red light encircled him. The tendrils of it slashed around him, pulling at locks of his black hair. The fabric of his clothes rippled in the magical tempest. More solid streaks of light snaked around his arms, as if trying to secure or capture his hands. Valentine easily repelled the efforts with little flicks of his wrists. Despite the desperation in his earlier roar, his expression was more warily amused than upset.

When I caught his eye, my mouth opened to say, 'thank god you're okay.' The look he shot me made me swallow the words back, however. I felt another deep stab in my gut.

Jack came stumbling into the hallway holding a heavy keychain. For a comical second, he stood there holding the now useless keys as his triumphant smile faded to horror. Then, he saw me. Dropping them, he ran towards me— or at least hurried around the various bits of debris, "Alex, are you alright?"

I shook my head. Tears welled in the corner of my eyes. So many words and feelings bubbled up, but the only ones that made any sense were the simplest. "I... broke it. I think I lost him."

"Oh." Jack looked first at Valentine and then back to me. "This is bad."

I moved towards Valentine, thinking maybe, as I'd tried earlier, a touch might help us reconnect. Before I could reach the glowing glyphs, however, Jack grabbed my arm. Jerking me back violently, he pointed to characters I couldn't read.

"That's keyed to you," Jack said. "I have no idea what would happen if you touched them, but I think it would definitely be the end of your bond. For good."

"So, there is at least one clever witch among you," Furfur drawled. Turning to Valentine he asked, "Is it clever enough to be a threat, do you suppose?"

"Clever enough, without a doubt," Valentine said. "Brave enough? Uncertain."

"Oi!" Jack started, but we were interrupted by the sound of the flutter of wings coming from the opposite hallway. I turned, expecting to see Sarah Jane and her gang of magpies, but it was a raptor of some sort. What was it doing here? Was it lost? How did it get in the building? I hadn't destroyed any outside walls.

The image of the bird turned inside out, as a human form crawled out of it. My brain baulked at something large emerging from such a significantly smaller bird-form, but it was done in a second, and, suddenly, Tengu stood beside me. He took in the shattered wall, his naked, winged partner, and the whirlwind that encased Valentine in a single glance. "You finally broke."

Furfur's laugh was more of a chuckle than maniacal, villainous laughter, but the vibe was the same. "An ice dragon," Furfur said, pointing at Valentine. "The weapon to win the war."

"There is no winning that war of yours," Tengu tsked his tongue disapprovingly.

A weapon? That is what Furfur wanted? To make Valentine fight demons— or angels? I wasn't entirely sure which side he was on.

Moving towards Jack and me and the largest opening in the wall, Tengu hopped lightly on the various broken bits of concrete. He moved like he was skipping through a playground. He gave a little bow to Hannah as he passed her.

Confused, she nodded back.

Once Tengu stood beside Jack and me, he took a longer look at the situation inside what had once been the interview room. "Despite your bluster, Commander, you're not actually holding the dragon all that well."

I turned back to try to see what Tengu did.

Valentine had that little smirk on his face again, as he continued to lazily bat away the red swirls of wind.

I leaned into Jack. Putting my hand on his shoulder, I drew his ear closer to my lips. "This is good, right?"

He made a 'not so sure' face. "I mean, yes? It's just... well, do we know whose side Valentine is on, if he's not bonded to you?"

Furfur, meanwhile, had straightened his shoulders and fluffed out his wings. "Tell me your name, Beast-That-Alex-Calls-Valentine."

"Mmmm," Valentine cocked his head as though considering it. "No."

A stirring in my gut sprouted near that place where everything had broken. It was a comforting, familiar warmth. I glanced up to see Valentine looking back at me. My lips started moving, as if trying to form a half-remembered word.

Furfur must have sensed what passed between us, because he swung around to glare angrily at me. "The witch knows after all."

Valentine watched me from beyond the red wind veil. I couldn't tell if his expression was hopeful or doubting. I lay a hand over the spot where I felt the warmth emanating on my stomach. I had a sense that if I closed my eyes and opened my mouth, something would come out.

If I did that, Valentine would be bound as my familiar, at least in some way. Did I want that? Especially since he still hadn't offered his name to me of his own free will. I took in a breath and started to open my mouth. That's when I noticed Furfur staring at me hungrily.

He wanted this.

As usual, I had no idea exactly what was going on, magically-speaking, but my instincts said that if I spoke whatever was bubbling up in my gut I was playing right into his hands... and trapping Valentine against his will.

Looking Furfur hard in those creepy, bottomless eyes of his, I quite intentionally said: "Fuck this."

The power of the curse slammed against Furfur like a gale-force wind.

Unfortunately, it hit everyone else the same way.

I watched it happen as though in a horrible slow motion.

It'd been several months since I let loose a real, intentional curse, and so the magic in me blew open like a pressure valve in need of release. Power radiated outward in every direction with my body at the epicenter. It manifested like a surge of wind, almost like an atomic blast, but with sparks of electricity forming the forefront of the surge.

Jack was thrown like a ragdoll from my side. He would have collided against the opposite wall, had Stone not reached out a hand to catch him by the arm. I was pretty certain from sounds I could hear over the roaring release of my own magic that she had dislocated his shoulder for him. Even so, I imagined that was better than being flung, full-on, into the masonry. I prayed that was the only damage I'd done to him.

On my other side, Tengu went tumbling through the air, like a bird caught in an unexpected updraft. I thought he might smash in the wall in that direction, but before he could, he suddenly transformed into a hawk. In that form he was able to wrestle against the surge and stay in the air.

The target of my ire, Furfur, stood his ground against the assault. All my destructive force did to him was ruffle his hair.

I'd have been devastated to know that I'd only managed to hurt friends and allies with my curse, except for one thing. The swirling tornado that had imprisoned Valentine was gone. He shook off the last of the crimson wisps with a shrug.

I smiled. Now we'd show Furfur a thing or two!

Except Valentine didn't return my smile. He frowned, a hand absently rubbed at his abdomen in the same spot I'd been feeling that strange uncoiling all day. When he finally met my eye, I was shocked at what I saw there.

It was a goodbye.

Crouching down, Valentine jumped.

Instead of coming down, his body changed the second his feet left the ground. Elongating and shimmering white, he lengthened into a sleek, slender creature of scales and wings.

The building shuddered as Valentine broke through ceilings on his way out. Pipes burst. The electricity went out with a deafening pop.

By the time I'd finished calling his name, he was gone.

Chapter Eleven

My power dissipated, I collapsed to my knees.

Time returned to its normal operations with a rush of noise and clatter. Over the pulsing wail of the fire alarm, Stone shouted at me to 'cease and desist.' Water rushed down into the interview room from the shattered pipes above. Tengu returned to his human guise with a flutter and a squawk of, "You are a danger!"

I assumed that he meant his partner until he grabbed me by the elbow and hauled me to my feet. His grip was like iron. He began to drag me away, but he took time to admonish Furfur, "Get yourself together, Furfur. This obsession with the war must stop."

The blare of the fire alarm cut and was replaced by anxious blinking lights. They strobed in the gloom of the darkened hallway.

In the blink of an eye, Furfur was back in his off-the-rack suit and sunglasses. He ran a hand through his hair. Plaster dust drifted onto the shoulders of his dark suit like dander. Casually, he sighed, "Well, it was worth a shot."

"You tried to steal Valentine!"

"I do believe we just proved he isn't exactly yours to command," Fufur said, pushing aside one of the chairs that had been tipped in one of the various explosions, despite the water gushing from the ceiling and the chaotic lights flashing. "More importantly, you behaved extremely irresponsibly. Twice, you let loose curses without any idea what might happen. You could have killed us all."

My mouth hung open. This was what we were talking about? I tried again, "Okay, but you tried to steal Valentine!"

Beside me, Tengu made a little disagreeing noise. "Arguably, the Right Honorable Earl was merely attempting to pick up what was lying on the ground, unclaimed."

I sputtered in frustration. "He lured Valentine here under false pretenses! He separated us on purpose!"

Furfur noticed dust on his suit and brushed it off. "Partly true. There was no lurid 'luring.' I merely took advantage of the opportunity. It may be in poor form, but that's not really a crime. What is a crime, however, is the blatant misuse of power that you displayed not only once, but twice."

"I...?" I shook my head. "How did this become about me?"

"You'd better come with me," Tengu insisted, tightening his already vice-like grip on my arm.

Furfur snapped his finger, and I felt something tighten in my throat. "No more curses from you for a while."

My hand went to my throat. "What did you just do?"

"A muzzling spell—well, technically, when I do it it's a...." He coughed uncomfortably and looked away to mutter almost inaudibly, "...miracle." That said, his voice returned to a normal volume, "but basically the same thing."

Tengu explained, "You won't be able to curse for—?" he glanced at his partner to finish the thought.

"Twenty-four hours."

Tengu frowned, "That's a bit excessive. Aren't you starting to impinge on rights? It's a witch's power you're curtailing. I'd have thought an hour or two would have been more appropriate."

Furfur shrugged in a way that had me wondering if he was lying as he said, "It was the shortest time period I had available."

Furfur moved in to flank me.; Tengu moved us down the hall.

"Where are you taking me?"

"Holding cell," Tengu said.

As we passed Hannah, I looked to her for help. I was surprised by her stern expression and dark nod. "I will make sure the humans get to the hospital."

Hospital?

"Wait, is Jack alright?" I struggled against Tengu's grip only to discover that Furfur had grasped my other arm. Dragging my feet, I tried to slow them down. "I thought it was just a dislocation. Did something more happen? Wait! If it's serious, I want to go with him! I have to know if he's okay! Is he okay?"

Hannah didn't even look at me when she said, "We shall see."

I wanted to swear but found that I couldn't. Hanging my head in defeat, I allowed myself to be taken away.

Tengu and Fufur brought me down a flight of stairs that led to a strange, wide hallway. The walls were brick and mortar. Above us, exposed pipes and ductwork snaked along the ceiling. Without electricity, I could barely see. I'd have tripped on the uneven floor, if the two agents weren't holding me so tightly. We passed a series of doors—some were wooden, some stone, still others polished metals of all varieties. All of them were different, and each had been marked with a special rune or symbol or... something.

"What is this?" I asked, "Where are we?"

"These are holding cells," Tengu said. "Have you never been down here?"

I shook my head. They finally stopped in front of a forbidding black door made of polished gemstone, which, instead of reflecting the light of the overhead bulbs, swallowed it whole.

In the center of the door glistened a blood-red glyph, the edges of which was drooling and ragged, like it had been spray painted by an angry, inexperienced tagger.

Never had a simple door made me more uncomfortable in my life. I shrank back against the agents' solidity and asked, "You're not putting me in there?"

"We have no choice," Furfur said. "Nothing else could hold a dragon."

"But, Valentine left!" I growled at Furfur, "Because of you, I might add."

"It's not that one who is a danger," Tengu said. "Besides, if this is the right cell for you, it will open. If not, we will try the next one."

As if on cue, the door swung open on its own. The hinges made a hollow, empty creak that echoed in the hall, reverberating against my very bones.

With a shove, I fell into a dark, gaping maw.

The darkness wasn't as complete as I first thought.

My eyes slowly adjusted. A murky, ghostly light emanated from the strange black gemstone walls. The floor that I'd been so unceremoniously dumped onto appeared to be made of gold. My fingernails dug into the soft metal, a sensation that triggered an odd sense of comfort and hominess.

What was this place? How had I ended up here?

I was aware of the sequence of events, but none of them made sense. How was I the one behind bars and not Furfur? I knew that something bad had happened to the bond I shared with Valentine, but had he left me for good, or just for now? Why hadn't he done this Exchange thing with me?

I tried to think back on our relationship for signs that Valentine wasn't committed to it. I was missing a critical piece, but this room made it hard to form coherent thoughts. The only things that came to me were moments when I asked for distance or space, like the day that I asked if we could expand our relationship so that I could have some human companionship in Jack. Valentine hadn't appeared bothered by that, but maybe he had been relieved?

My head felt heavy, and I struggled to keep my eyes open.

Was this even important? I was such a terrible witch. I'd never learned a single spell or how to control my cursing, I probably didn't deserve a familiar as powerful as Valentine. How different was having a familiar to what Spenser did with Devon, keeping him as a lackey or a slave? I didn't really want to burden Valentine that way, did I? Maybe it was best to let him go.

What was that thing they said about what you should do if you loved something...? Would that work with a dragon?

It didn't matter. After all, people who stayed close to me got hurt. Maybe that was why I ended up attracted to creatures who were more than human.

I yawned, letting my head fall back on the soft blanket of rich gold. Safe inside a cavern made of gems, snuggled deep in my precious gold, I thought, yes, sleep would be nice.

There was something I should be panicking about, but the moment my head hit the gold, it drifted far, far away.

I'd been dreaming of flying when the scrabble of wire and metal woke me. I cracked one eye open to see what disturbed my slumber. Birds argued just outside my heavy prison door with bossy, irritated caws. Then, the scratching started afresh.

Curiosity won over my bone-tiredness, and I managed to pull myself up out of the deep, warmth of the soft gold.

The door shifted. A series of runes flashed down its length like a magical neon advertisement—one symbol, then the next, on and off, colored a deep blood-red that was only barely brighter than the darkness that surrounded me.

A click signaled the last tumbler turning.

My prison door swung open.

A bright stab of light nearly blinded me. I expected to see someone standing there, but instead a gang of magpies swooped in and mobbed me.

$

Chapter Twelve

The magpies fluttered and hopped. Beaks and talons reached for my clothes, snagging the cloth. With effort, they pulled, pushed, and cajoled me upright, flapping mightily, and shouting at me. I could almost understand them, they seemed to be saying: "Come! Come!"

With their help, I stumbled over the threshold of my prison and out the door. It was harder than I thought it ought to be to leave behind my hoard of gold and gems, but their incessant shouting and tugging kept me from turning around and going back to sleep.

Once out in the hallway, the magpies continued to herd me toward an exit sign. My eyes watered from the brightness, but I let them blindly push me along the corridor.

They tried to be quieter now, though with limited success. One would shout excitedly, and the others would shush the offending bird, growing louder and louder in their own protests for everyone to be sneakier.

Something about their antics made me pause. "Wait," I said, resisting them momentarily. "Is this a jailbreak?"

There must have been a dozen birds. In my daze, I could barely distinguish one from the other in the jumble of black and white feathers and beady, insistent eyes, but, at my question, they all nodded: _Yes, yes, they were breaking me out of jail._

"Come! Come!" they shouted again anxiously.

"Right, right," I said. Now that my prison was further behind, the cobwebs began to fall from my mind. I followed the lead magpie that hop-fluttered a few steps in front of me. "But," I asked them, "Aren't you mad at me? I mean, I hurt Jack—"

I had, hadn't I?

"No! No!" they all yelled, even as the image of Jack flying backward flashed into my mind and threatened to cause me to stumble. Their cries pulled me onward: "Come! Come!"

I picked up my pace as they led me up another flight of stairs that ended in a door marked 'maintenance only.' The lead bird stopped, landing in front of the door. It turned its black, fathomless eye to me. I didn't get what it wanted until it stretched out one of its wings and made a half-turning motion.

Right, I was the one with opposable thumbs. Turn the knob, monkey.

But, when I tried, it didn't move. "Locked," I explained.

The lead bird, who must have been Sarah Jane, landed on my shoulder with sharp claws. She peered around my body as though looking for something. Were we being pursued? I glanced behind me just in time to see a magpie flutter over my head. It held something shiny in its mouth. It perched awkwardly on the doorknob. Hanging upside down, it poked something into the keyhole. Around the flurry of feathers that struggled to keep balance on the knob, I thought I saw a paperclip that had been bent into a tool.

When I heard a familiar tumbling click, I laughed joyfully. "You're lock pickers, too?" Of course, they had to have been. How else could they have sprung me from jail? I beamed at the whole flock, "You're awesome!"

They puffed out their breasts at my compliment, but Sarah Jane made the motion with her wing again. This time I knew my part. Turning the knob, I pushed the door open, and we all slipped through into what looked like a loading dock.

There was a small flight of concrete stairs that led down to a large open bay, big enough to back a semi into, that smelled of oil and diesel fumes. Piles of cardboard boxes lined the wall. A metal cage surrounded a crude wooden desk and a rickety office chair. I passed an old-fashioned timecard punch clock and a rack of cards on my way toward the garage doors. The magpies flew around in the larger space, taking up perches where they could find them.

Beside the garage doors was a regular, human-sized door. The birds seemed to be waiting for me to exit. I still didn't know why they'd rescued me. I glanced around at their avian faces. "Just... I thought you'd be angry with me. Why are you helping me?" Then, it finally occurred to me to wonder, "Are you helping me?"

A number of them nodded 'Yes.'

I supposed it could be some convoluted kind of revenge to break me out of jail, since now I was on the lam.

"Why?"

"Fly! Fly!" they all said in unison. I didn't know if that was the reason or a command to get out before anyone caught us. Either way, I took it as my cue to exit.

As I opened the door to freedom, I waved goodbye, "Thanks!"

They flew one direction; I ran in the other.

I didn't think I could go home.

Once Furfur and Tengu figured out that I was missing, they'd have someone watching my place right away. That meant the morgue and my favorite coffee shop were out, too, as were any of my usual hangouts.

Scanning the skyline, I tried to decide which direction to head. My eyes lingered on the clocktower. The noon sun cast deep shadows on the carved stone eagle. The stylized 'v's of its wings were dark slashes, its eyes deeply hooded.

Just as I turned in the direction of the public library, I saw a homeless person hunched over the garbage pails in the alleyway. As if sensing my eyes on her, Nana Spider's frizzy white hair popped up. "Oh dearie me, the dragon's broken free."

It was a weird way to talk about the broken bond between me and Valentine, but I nodded sadly in agreement.

Nana Spider regarded me with bulbous, watery eyes. Of all the things to have settled on, she chose to be dressed in a long patchwork skirt that hung all the way to her ankles—or maybe it was an actual quilt, wrapped around her hips and held up with a thick rope/belt. Over that, she wore a man's button-down office shirt that looked two-sizes too big for her slender, almost emaciated frame. On her feet were flip-flops of different colors. Chunky costume jewelry adorned her wrists and ankles.

The wind tossed two 'fun-sized' potato chip bags behind her shoulders. One would pop up, then the other, then they'd drop, and, a moment later, do it again, almost as if they were hopping up to get a better look at me over her shoulders. I couldn't say why, but it felt like the dancing bags watched my every move even more closely than Nana did. It didn't help that the way the wind played with them their tops opened and closed like laughing mouths.

"The demons will be cross to discover their loss," she hummed to herself. The bags joined in to crinkle musically.

"Since when do you talk in rhymes?"

When I first met Nana Spider, she'd performed an elaborate ritual that Spenser had hoped would give us a clue to solving the necromancer's murder. It had involved fast food ketchup packages, which was weird enough, but I'd been super disappointed that she didn't talk like a proper witch, no rhyming iambic pentameters. It struck me as odd that she would now.

"The rhyming Witch took a fall, now the burden is on us all."

"Fall? Wait, are you talking about the woman from this morning? The one we found at the base of the clocktower?"

"Not today, you've slept the night away." Nana said.

"Oh," I said, shocked to discover that I'd lost so much time. "Uh, okay, well, so the lady from <u>yesterday</u> was a witch?"

Nana nodded, shuffling down the alleyway. With a claw-like hand, she beckoned me to follow.

I glanced behind at where the gang of magpies perched on the telephone wire over the precinct's loading dock. They nodded, their black heads bobbing, as if to say it was okay, there was nothing to fear. Even though I felt far too much like Alice going down the rabbit hole, I followed Nana Spider. The chip bags slid across the ground as if to sniff at my shoes. A bit of wind sent the bags back into the air to circle both Nana and me, crackling joyfully.

Nana reached for my arm, as though for support. I offered it to her, and she leaned heavily on me. "Ymir was a witch like me," Nana said. She shook her head violently, and managed, "Not like you."

"Hey," I noted. "No rhyme this time."

"Ha," she smiled, her teeth a gnarled mess of yellow and gaps. Her claw-like finger tapped my shoulder. "That's because you took up the burden. With luck, someone else has it now. Ugh, I'll miss Ymir. Kept the powers happy with all that rhymy-whimy silliness. Makes them feel important, doesn't it?"

She stopped suddenly and glanced up. We'd come to the end of the alley. On the overhead streetlamp someone had thrown a pair of shoes that dangled by their laces. A rush of wind blew from behind us, and the pair of bags circled up the lamppost. When they got to the top it was like the wind cut out, and they paused midair momentarily. After hanging there for a moment, they fell back, drifting down as if they'd fainted.

Nana watched the bags settle on the street. They looked flattened, like something had sucked the life from them.

Nana toed the now lifeless bags. "Hmmm, maybe not that way."

"Yeah," I agreed. Even though the alley led back to the precinct headquarters where I was pretty sure the demon agents would be, it was hard to argue with dead bags.

Nana surprised me, by blinking up into my face and asking, "What do you think? You have a dragon's heart, what does it tell you?" Before I could even formulate an answer, she said, "Also, an invisibility spell would be nice right about... now."

Right in front of us, two uniformed police came running down the sidewalk. Wow, the demons had been fast calling that APB. They must have had a better working relationship with the ordinarium than Spenser did.

I held my breath, praying that somehow, despite our proximity, they wouldn't see us. *Be invisible*, I thought.

"I'm pretty sure she went this way!" shouted one, not seeing us as he dashed right past the alley's opening. The other split off right under the hanging shoes and yelled, "I'll check this side."

I winced in sympathy as the second cop stepped right on one of the bags of chips. But, instead of hurting it, the kick of the officer's heel sent the bag scooting back into the air.

Once the police were some distance away, Nana patted my arm, "Thank you, dearie."

"For what?"

"The invisibility, of course," she said, as if I were stupid.

"But... I didn't do anything."

She turned down the alley again. Clucking her tongue, she said, "Well, it couldn't have been me. I can only read the signs. Anyway, to turn the eye is a skill for those who fly." Her face crumpled up and she put a hand over her mouth. Lifting her fingers, she muttered, "Oh, fiddle-dee-dee, it's back to me."

I felt bad that she got cursed with the rhyming already again, so I gave her knuckles a sympathetic pat where they were still wrapped around my elbow. "You know, when you say it like that, you make it sound like I'm not human."

She gave me a funny look, her lips pursed together. "That's a secret that's not mine to tell, ask the one who knows you well."

"Valentine?"

Nana snorted, "No, you fool, your father!" Then she smiled. "Ha! Gone again! I swear to fate, I'm not going to speak for a week! Oh, listen to that. Is it back or was that an accident? Oh! Seems gone. Good!" To me, she added, "You should buy me a cup of coffee, dear heart. This was very exhausting. I don't know how Ymir could stand talking like that—so cryptic! No one ever understands a word you're saying. How the hell did she ever find the lady's room?"

Despite saying I owed her coffee, Nana wandered off shouting to herself. The one recovered bag stuttered along behind her.

I stood in the alley behind the precinct building for a long time, wondering what to do. I really wanted Valentine, but he'd flown off somewhere, possibly leaving me forever. Jack was injured, possibly still in the hospital even now. Robert wanted me to move out... never mind that I was on the run from my own friends, or, at the very least, a double-crossing pair of demons.

Nana told me to talk to my dad and, given how alone and lost I felt, that was starting to seem like a good idea.

I fished out my cell, which was, remarkably, still shoved into the front pocket of my jeans. I suppose the agents hadn't really been too worried that I'd make an unauthorized phone call in the gold-lined, gem-encrusted cell they'd tossed me into. The gold had put me to sleep and, anyway, reception was probably crap.

The gold had put me to sleep. Now that I finally had time to think about it all, that struck me as very... weird. Then there was Nana Spider telling me that I'd been the one to cause the cops not to see us and that invisibility was a kind of magic that belonged to those who fly.

What? Was I a dragon?

I didn't think so, because, you know, baby pictures. Back home, in Chicago, I'd seen the albums full of photographs. There was the classic naked in the bathtub shot, the zonked out with teddy bear one, and... mom? Why did I not remember seeing any pictures of my mother?

I let my shoulders fall back against the rough brick of the alley wall.

My mother was dead, I knew that—I mean, I feel I could tell anyone who asked about how I'd felt when I'd gotten the news, except... how old was I? Grade school, maybe?

What did she look like? My dad always said I had her eyes. But what was her name? Did she have curly hair or straight, was it blond, brunette, black? I had no clear memory.

You know what this reminded me of? It reminded me of when I used to try to think back to my first meeting of Valentine.

Was my mother a dragon? Was that even possible?

I'd been staring at the face of my phone this whole time. Swiping it open and putting in my password, I dialed my father's number. My hand shook as I raised the receiver to my ear and listened to the rings.

How the hell did I even ask this question? Hi, Dad, I know you haven't heard from me in years, but, hey, was Mom a dragon?

A woman's voice answered after the third ring. "You left your cellphone here again, hon. Do you want me to drop it by the library on my way to work?"

The stepmonster.

I'd gone silent in shock. "Daniel?" she asked. She must have pulled the cell away from her ear to finally check to see what number had called, because her voice hardened with ice when she returned. "Alexandra. This is certainly unexpected. To what do we owe this... pleasure?"

Despite the summer heat, cold shivered down my spine. She terrified me. I took in a steadying, if shuddering breath, and tried to remind myself that the power she had over me was gone. I knew now, for a fact, that magic was real. The things I saw weren't delusions; there really were faerie and trolls and vampires and golems.

"My friends want to know if you're a true demon, an ifrit, or one of the Fallen," I said, as steadily as I could manage—which, admittedly, involved a bit of stuttering and a squeak.

"Ifrit?" She spat, as though I'd insulted her. "Do your new little friends think an ifrit could befuddle and trap a dragon, or did you not tell them of that humiliating experience?"

Okay, so she wasn't denying any of it. This was new. Normally, she'd already have on her lawyer voice and be patiently explained to anyone listening that I was insane, obviously, given the nonsense I was spouting. "They know about all that. They're cops," I said. "And witches."

"How nice for you," she sneered.

Here's where things got awkward—well, more so, because with a normal person, I'd be able to say something like, "So, how's Dad?" or ask after the cats or her job or something. Instead, I just listened to the silence on the other end, wondering what the hell was my life and if Dad was okay. The worst part of this whole conversation had been how it started. She'd sounded so very... well, like a wife, worrying after an absent-minded husband. I kind of hated that. Because then she was at least somewhat innocent and just in love with my dad, and I didn't know how to feel about that.

Was it possible that my dad and I shared the same taste in lovers?

Monsters.

If that were the case, then I might have to learn to get along with her—or worse, I might have to feel guilty that I sicced Valentine on her, nearly killing her.

I had to remind myself that she had tried to put me into a mental hospital for good, keys thrown away and all. She'd also kept Valentine away from me with whatever magics she possessed. She wasn't blameless in this.

It was really cruel to convince a young woman she was insane and, worse, to turn her father against her. Especially since magic was real and, as a demon, my stepmonster knew that full well.

"Why did you do it?" I asked her. "Why didn't you just let me be?" I wanted to say, but couldn't quite: why didn't you just let us be a proper family, the three of us?

There was a little huff of a laugh on the other end. "It's my nature. I am the Destroyer of Worlds."

With that, she hung up.

Chapter Thirteen

'**I** am the Destroyer of Worlds.'

The words my stepmother said echoed in my head over and over as I stared at the 'call ended' message on my cell. What the hell did that even mean? It was a famous quote or something, wasn't it? Or, maybe, it was something from scripture? More importantly, given all the magic in my life, was my stepmother being metaphorical when she said that... or literal?

Because: that didn't sound good.

Sirens wailed, startling me out of my reverie. Shoving my phone into my pocket, I blinked away my thoughts and tried to get my bearings. Even though I was shielded from the main road by a large dumpster, I hadn't made it more than a half a block from the precinct headquarters.

When my phone rang, I nearly jumped. Frantically, I fished it out of my pocket only to see that it was Spenser calling. Ah, shit. I was the worst fugitive ever. I needed to dump this phone,

and—

"Caw!"

A bird-banded magpie swooped onto the lid of the dumpster. As it flapped around for balance, its wings nearly brushed my head. Finally finding a good perch, it gave me a beady glare. With the band it could only be Sarah Jane.

My phone continued to ring.

The magpie nodded at the phone.

I glanced at my cell and then at Sarah Jane. "You want me to give you my phone?"

She bobbed her whole body in a fair approximation of 'yes.' Right, because probably the cops could use the little tracker thing-y inside to trace me. A bird could take the phone anywhere and make it look like I was on the move.

"You're smart," I told Sarah Jane. For good measure I added, "Thank you. I think I owe you some cracked corn or something."

The bird preened and nodded again.

Not sure how this was going to work I held my cell out to the magpie. Deftly, she snatched it out of my hand as it took to flight. Off she went down the alley, laughing "Ha, ha, ha," and disappearing from sight.

Of course, there went my communication to the outside world, too. I sure hoped I was right about who she was and I wasn't just conned by some random thief-of-a-bird looking to score the latest Android technology.

I needed to figure out where I should go.

Trusting that maybe somehow I was still 'invisible,' I started down the alley in the direction of 'away' from the precinct. I walked without hurrying, which was hard because I felt a thousand eyes on my back. The sun was hot, but a cold sweat prickled under my arms. Unlike Chicago, there were no huge crowds to blend into, no train to hop on, no bridges to hide under. I walked along the streets of Pierre trying to project a sense of confidence and belonging, while feeling like what I really wanted to do was bolt and run like a rabbit.

If Spenser was calling my cell phone, he already had Robert's house surrounded. With a grim chuckle, I imagined that was going to be the last straw. Robert was probably chucking our stuff out into the street even now. Well, that was the least of my worries. Right now, I needed to figure out where I could go that would be a safe place to regroup and plan my next move.

That's when I heard the growl of a Harley.

Please let it be Devon or Mac, I prayed to whatever gods might be listening. Or any of the friendly Lone Wolves.

As the motorcycle roared into view, I caught a glimpse of auburn hair and tiger-stripe tattoos. "Mac!"

He shouldn't have been able to hear me over the sound of his engine, but his head turned, spotting me immediately. Rounding the corner, he pulled his bike into an empty parking spot and waved me over. I jogged up the street gratefully, a huge smile on my face. "You're a lifesaver!" I told him.

Mac's grin was toothy, "I think you mean 'aider and abettor'."

"You heard already?"

He patted the backseat in a gesture for me to hop on. "Not a lot happens in this town. A jailbreak is big news."

I straddled the bike and gripped his waist, which felt awfully intimate with a guy I barely knew. I kind of wanted a helmet, too, but this was a case of 'fugitives can't be choosers.' "Are you sure you want to help me?"

He laughed and revved the engine. "You're going to free Devon from the faerie prince for me, remember? Consider it part of the payment."

I didn't know if I had the ability to anything of that magnitude now that Valentine had left me, but I wasn't going to point that out until we were safely away.

This was my first time on the back of a motorcycle. I clung on tightly, burying my face in Mac's broad back, smelling leather and sweat, and closing my eyes to the sun and the wind. Turns terrified me, especially at speeds, but I just held my breath and trusted.

At some point, I got used to the sensation enough to sort of look around. We traveled along the hills of the Missouri River Valley. The gentle slopes were dotted with the grassy expanses of cattle farms.

Mac slowed, turning down toward a huge lake. The sign we passed said Lake Oahe Recreational Park. The parking lot we entered was full of RVs, campers, and... a whole row of motorcycles. We pulled up beside them.

Switching off his engine, Mac explained what I'd already guessed, "A bunch of the pack decided to go fishing today." He got off and offered me a hand to help dismount. "No one's going to look for you here."

Yeah, no one was. This was not the normal place for a fugitive to run to—it was basically a park. Under the shade of tall elms and cottonwoods, there was a scattering of picnic benches and barbeque stands. Signs directed visitors to a boat landing and reminded them of fishing rules and regulations. The air smelled of lake and grass. A large placard attached to a boulder explained that, by volume, Lake Oahe was the fourth largest man-made reservoir in the United States.

Mac led me along a gravel path, following the signs that pointed to campgrounds. We wound our way deeper into the park, and pretty soon I could smell wood smoke and hear the sounds of raucous laughter.

Tents came into view. Scattered here and there, of all sizes, shapes and colors, the majority of them encircled a fire pit. Even though it was afternoon, the fire blazed like a bonfire. Camp chairs were set up, and longhaired, bearded bikers in leather and denim drank beer from cans and roasted fish in cast-iron pans. We were greeted with a chorus of 'hey!' and 'hello' and 'Look what the pup dragged in!'

I was offered a beer, a bag of potato chips, and a spot on the picnic table. Shoving the salty goodness of the chips into my starving mouth, I decided I was already in love with all these people.

With a jangle of buckles, Mac plopped himself on the table's top, facing me, his booted feet on the seat. "You good?"

Having inhaled the chips, I glanced mournfully at the empty bag. I crumpled it up and tucked it under my butt, intending to toss it in the garbage when I next got up. "Yeah," I said, letting out a long, relieved breath. "Thanks for the rescue."

"You can stay here as long as you like... uh, well, actually until next week Tuesday at about 8:10 p.m."

"Full moon?"

Mac touched the side of his nose and gave me a broad grin. "Got it in one. Because, trust me, you don't want to be around a full pack at moonrise."

I imagined not. Though I would love to be a fly on the wall, as it were, to see what that was even like. Maybe it was rude to ask, but I blurted out, "So... do you become actual wolves or like man-wolf things?"

The guy next to me nearly snorted beer out his nose. "Jesus, Mac, where'd you pick up this stray?"

"Alex ain't one of my strays," Mac corrected, because apparently, he had a history of picking up strangers and bringing them home? Oh, right, Devon.

The big bearded guy rolled his eyes like he didn't believe that for a second.

"I'm serious, Joe," Mac insisted. "Alex is just hiding out with us from the cops for a while."

Joe, who couldn't have looked more like your stereotypical biker dude if he tried, scratched a meaty hand in his bushy beard. "Oh, you're the jailbird?"

Did everyone already know all my secrets? "How did the news get all the way up here so fast?"

"It's all the birds have been talking about," Joe said, like it was completely normal to understand the language of birds. "You dragons are part of some rogue magpie gang, right?"

"I... guess?" Because what the hell did you even say to that? Plus, I still wasn't sure why the magpies had gone to such lengths to save me, especially since I'd accidentally injured Jack. Still, it didn't feel right to deny my association with them. I owed them my freedom. "But, I'm not a dragon, I'm just... er, formerly associated with one."

Joe squinted at me. "You sure?"

I opened my mouth to say that I was, but closed it remembering that I hadn't had a chance to talk to my father about any of it. "I guess not?"

"There you go then," Joe pronounced sagely and went back to swigging his beer.

Under the dappled shade of the oak trees the temperature was several degrees cooler. I wasn't entirely sure why anyone would bother with a fire on a day like today, except that some people were cooking fish and other campfire fare.

Devon wandered over and slouched next to me.

Still dressed in his biker gear, lots of leather and not much else, and he seemed much more at ease here among the werewolves than he ever had in Spenser's presence.

"Did I tell you that some of the guys saw one of the 'hitchers?'"

"I don't think I know what a 'hitcher' is in this context, so, no," I said, taking another beer someone offered me. Even though I didn't really drink much, I figured it was bad form not to accept the offerings of werewolves. It was, at least, cold and felt good in my hand.

"A hitcher is a kind of urban legend ghost. Usually, you see them on the highway with their thumbs out. If you stop for them, they'll ride with you for a while and then disappear. In a country song, it'll end up being the ghost of Hank Williams, but in real life they're usually people who were killed either on the road or while hitchhiking."

"Sounds grim," I said, taking a tentative sip of the beer. It smelled and tasted very hoppy, which is not a favorite flavor of mine. I looked at the label, but I'm just not a connoisseur. It was probably expensive and fancy. The good stuff was always wasted on me. "I'm not sure why you're telling me, though."

Mac shifted to sit next to Devon. He started up a conversation with Joe, but his back rested against Devon's shoulder, lovingly.

"Well, it's probably nothing," Devon agreed. "It's just that with the bodies falling from the sky, I figure any uptick in supernatural activity could be significant."

"I'm kind of on the run from the precinct right now," I said.

"And I'm AWOL," he said. "Doesn't mean I'm not interested in the case. I figured you would be, too."

It was an interesting assumption. I was still trying to process the fact that I'd been thrown into jail, broken out by magpies, and was very likely no longer in any kind of relationship with Valentine, despite everyone calling me a dragon.

Thinking about the case was a nice distraction, at least. "So, what did this hitcher look like? Did they say?"

"I'm not sure anyone picked him up," Devon said. "But someone said he looked like a soldier, I think."

"Huh," I said, trying to hide my disappointment. I was hoping Devon would say 'homeless,' because at least then there was a stronger chance at a connection. "Oh, I ran into Nana Spider. She said she caught the rhymes from our first victim. Apparently, she was a witch."

"Oh, so this wasn't a homicide? Just some kind of flying accident?"

"Witches can fly?"

"Can't they?"

"Shouldn't we have found a broom, then?" I asked.

"I think brooms are metaphors," Devon said.

"For what?"

"Drugs, I always figured, but I'm not a witch."

I started to open my mouth to complain, once again, about how Valentine hadn't exactly caught me up on all this magical stuff, but another thought derailed that. "You mean, like something I could detect? An actual drug that would come back in a toxicology report?"

"I'm even more out of my depth there," he said, "But, maybe? Would that solve the case?"

I shrugged. "Maybe, although we had another body out on County 27. That one had been there for some time, however. I'm not sure what we'll get out of that one."

"Well, if it's to do with witches, we'll have a third victim. Threes, you know."

I didn't know. Of course, I didn't know. I was getting really, really tired of not knowing. "Okay, what's the three thing?"

Devon gave me that vaguely shocked 'you don't know!' look, but it faded at the sight of my obvious ire. He raised his hands in surrender. "Sorry, I forget that dragons aren't exactly the best familiars. The three thing comes from the faces of the goddess: maiden, mother, crone. When witches are involved, things tend to come in threes."

I wondered if Furfur was expecting a third victim, or if he even really cared about this case. "Furfur tried to steal Valentine from me."

"No shit?"

"Seriously," I confirmed. "There's apparently a room with witch's bane in the walls and he laid out all these runes and a red tornado. It was crazy. I think... I mean, I know it worked to break our bond, but also Valentine never made the exchange of names?"

Devon took in this jumble thoughtfully. "Wow."

"This is bad, isn't it? I can tell it's bad."

Devon tried to reassure me with a pat, but it was a very awkward shoulder slap. "I don't know, Alex. Valentine rarely shows you his true face, why would he be any different about his name."

Definitely not helpful.

At least Devon realized his mistake, as he quickly added, "You should talk to Jett. She's our resident witch." He stood up and leaned in to add, "And former alpha, but don't bring that up."

As if conjured by her name, a woman stepped into the clearing. The crowd parted as she pushed her way toward our table. Tall and slender, her long black hair fell behind her back like an inky curtain that nearly brushed her knees. She wore a black leather vest, zipped up tight to contain her ample breasts, jeans with leather chaps over the top, engineer boots, and those fingerless riding gloves that were popular in the early 80s. Not that I would have breathed a word of that last bit out loud ever in a million years, because the lava-black gaze she caught me in was fierce and I had no doubt she could and would tear me to bits.

Her voice was hard, like a hammer hitting steel. The question she snarled sounded more like an admonishment. "You brought that dragon here, Mac, to us?"

There it was again, someone calling me 'dragon.'

Beside me, Mac shrugged easily, "Yeah, hey, Jett. I want you to meet my friend Alex. Alex, meet our pack witch, Jett."

"Uh... charmed?" I gulped.

Jett was super-unimpressed with both of us. "Walk with me." She turned back to the forest she'd come out of. She went three steps without anyone following her. When it became clear that neither Mac nor I knew which one she meant, she sighed and said, "Both of you."

"Oh, right," I said.

"Yeah, fine," Mac agreed, sliding off the picnic bench. He paused long enough to give Devon a quick goodbye peck on his cheek.

Jett walked down an asphalt path toward the lake, clearly expecting us to hustle and catch up to her.

Mac fell into step about a pace behind her, like a well-trained honor guard. I flanked her other side, because I had no idea what else I should do, and I figured I'd rather be able to exchange glances with Mac without having to be obvious about it. We walked along a path, under the shaded canopy of tall cottonwoods for awhile, in silence. Leaves rustled in the breeze and our shoes crunched on the gravel.

Finally, Jett said, "You've got a problem with strays, Mac."

"Hey now," he said, "I don't see how Alex counts as one of my problems. It's not like she's signing up to ride with us."

"No, but you are expecting us to protect her," Jett pointed out. She stopped and turned around to pin us both under her fierce, obsidian gaze, "From the police."

Mac's hands went up in a very submissive, surrendering pose. "Well, it's really more of 'hiding out from' than 'protection,' but... yeah, kind of?"

Jett swung her attention to me. "I would think a dragon could protect herself just fine."

"I'm not a..." I started, and then stopped. "Okay, you know what? The precinct has a gold cell with my name on it," I pointed out. "Which, I didn't even know would work on me until... it did. I'm thinking the cops know a lot more about me than I do. And... no one told me, even though they're supposed to be my friends. I mean Jack had me thinking I was a witch—" I petered out when I realized I needed to take a breath, and that this was devolving into a full-on whine fest. "Look, the point is, I just need a place I can think about all this in peace for a while. If the agents actually track me all the way out here, you have my permission to throw me to the—" I was going to say, ' to the wolves,' but, well that was awkward,"--uh, that is, you can hand me over. No hard feelings."

Jett listened to all of this with her arms crossed. "Very well. I suppose it would not harm the pack to have a dragon who owes us a favor."

I didn't know why everyone was calling me a dragon, especially since I'd just lost Valentine.

"Right," I said with a confident nod, like we'd made some kind of bargain I had any hope of making good on. And so, when she offered her hand, I shook it: deal sealed.

Mac let out a breath. "Yeah, that was my take. And, you know, I am the alpha now."

Jett growled.

The two of them stared at each other for so long that I considered leaving them there to fight it out or whatever werewolves did to establish dominance. Just when I was starting to take a step back, Jett sighed and broke eye contact.

"Fine," Jett said, and turned and stalked away.

Mac shook his head at her retreating form. Turning to me, he said, "You are welcome, you know. I mean, it'd be nice if you'd consider breaking Devon's thrall sometime before you get arrested again. I'm holding you to it, regardless."

Now it was my turn to be the victim of that wolf-like intense stare. Since I didn't have a good answer for him, I decided to divert him. "Why does everyone keep calling me a dragon? You know that I'm just a witch, right? One who probably just lost her familiar, no less, so I'm not sure what that makes me, honestly."

Mac glanced in the direction that Jett had gone. "We don't always get along, Jett and me, but she's got good instincts when it comes to magic. That's how she first became our pack leader, and I haven't got her nose for it, so if we need magical leadership again, there's going to be another fight." He returned that animal gaze to me, "I guess what I'm saying is that, if she's calling you a dragon, maybe you ought to do a little self-examination. She probably sees something you're avoiding. And, maybe, it's because your familiar is away that people are seeing more of you, you know?"

I frowned, because that last part hit uncomfortably close to something that felt true. "Wouldn't I know this? Do people just discover that they're dragons half-way through their lives?"

Mac let out a little huff of a laugh. He put a hand on my shoulder and squeezed it. "Hon, if you're a dragon, this ain't nowhere near half your life."

Well, that was a cool thought, I supposed. "Okay, but... my question still stands. I would have thought that dragons hatch out of eggs. Wouldn't that be kind of memorable?"

"I have no memory of my birth. I have to take my mother's word for it," Mac pointed out. "Why don't you ask your mama this stuff?"

"I don't remember my mother."

Mac gave me a look that said 'see, there's a clue.' Then, he patted my shoulder again, paternally. As he walked away, I was left alone in the woods with my thoughts.

Instead of heading back toward the campground, I continued down the path toward the lake. I felt the urge to sink my toes in warm sand and watch waves lapping on the shore. Honestly, I couldn't cope with too many other people right now. Just like I told Jett, what I really needed was some quiet thinking time.

I reached the beach. It really wasn't much more than a sandy strip, but I found a spot without too many burrs and sat down. Picking up a flat rock, I flicked my wrist and gave it a toss. It bounced once on the water's surface, but then made a loud kerplunk. I tried skipping rocks a few more times, with the same limited success.

I couldn't suddenly just be a dragon, could I? That just didn't seem right. Wouldn't people have noticed before, or was there something about having broken the familiar bond with Valentine that caused all of this to surface somehow?

How did I feel about it? Did I want to be a dragon?

I had to admit that the idea of living a longer-than-normal lifespan appealed. Like most people I knew, I never felt like there were enough hours in the day to do all the things I wanted to do. If I had an extra couple hundred years, I might take up snorkeling or belly dancing or any number of other hobbies I never felt like I had the time to learn.

I didn't like flying when I was clutched in Valentine's talons, but the idea of being able to pick up and go anywhere I wanted without having to worry about money was also kind of cool. If I could sprout wings, could I fly all the way to Hawaii, I wondered? What about places where I'd normally need a passport? Europe? South America? China?

Becoming a dragon had some perks, perhaps, but didn't it also represent the loss of my humanity? All the things I'd been finding so off-putting about Valentine lately—the coldness, the tendency towards homicide—was that what I would become too?

Who was I kidding? Honestly, that should be the real clue that I was a dragon. I hurt people without thinking.

At least Valentine's violence was a precision strike, as intentional as it was devastating.

I sighed.

If I started hoarding, too, we'd definitely need a place of our own.

I grunted at that thought and revised it: *my own*.

Valentine was gone.

Watching the sunlight dance on the waves, I pulled my knees up against my chest and hugged them. The summer air was still muggy, but the breeze coming off the lake brought a cool relief.

Letting my head fall against my knees, I closed my eyes. How did everything end up this crazy? When I woke up yesterday morning, the only worry I had was sticky coins... and maybe Robert's ultimatum and a dead body. Okay, that was probably a lot for most people, but I never expected Valentine to leave me. I thought he was the one constant in my life. I believed him when he said that if I ever needed him, I could call, and he would come.

"Well, I need you now, Valentine—or whatever your real name is."

Instantly, a shadow passed in front of the sun.

I glanced up to see a pair of white wings, soaring over the lake. As high up as he was, he looked like a shimmering silver ribbon against the bright blue clouds. After circling like a lazy hawk several times, he dove deep into the lake.

Chapter Fourteen

As Valentine emerged from the lake, I was reminded of that famous painting of Venus on a half-shell... if only because of the white caps and the fact Valentine was completely naked.

Despite the hazy summer sun, there weren't a lot of fishermen out on the lake. Even so, I did have to wonder how many people noticed the snow-white dragon circle and then dive deep into the lake. Maybe, since the Tinkerbell Effect was lower around these parts, they just mistook dragon-Valentine as a fast-moving cloud.

Making his way to the shore, Valentine gave a nod in the direction of the main park. "I didn't expect to find you in the company of wolves."

"Then you shouldn't have left me to them," I grumped, not looking at him. I didn't want to be distracted by his beauty right now. "You did leave me, didn't you? I mean, we're not together right now, are we?"

"I came when you called, didn't I?"

He had—like, immediately. I couldn't be angry at that.

"Sit down, would you? I can't talk to you like this." With a frustrated wave to indicate his nakedness, I lowered myself back down into the spot I'd been sitting.

He chuckled but complied. "I've been away for less than a day. What could possibly have happened in my absence?"

"Okay, let's see, since you left," I ticked off all the events on my fingers, "I got arrested maybe for cursing, but really I have no idea; tossed into a prison clearly built for you: discovered gold and jewels make me sleepy; got rescued by a gang of magpies; spooked by Nana Spider; called my stepmonster; and started hanging out with a werewolf biker gang!" I was nearly out of breath and fingers, but I added very sarcastic and exasperated: "Typical day, really! You??"

Valentine considered this for a long moment, his gaze focused on the sparkle of the waves in the sun. "So..." he said, finally. "If I filled our bed with pure gold you would complain less?"

I smacked the top of his head. The bop was just a tap, really, no real force behind it beyond my frustration with him. "That's not the point!"

Dodging a second blow, he asked, "What, pray tell, was the 'take away' I was meant to have gathered from your laundry list of woes?"

Giving up trying to pummel him, I let out a strangled cry of frustration and flopped back onto the sand. Staring up at the blue sky dotted with clouds, I said, "I don't know, I'm not sure myself. Everything got really weird once Furfur tried to steal you."

"He can't steal me. I don't belong to anyone."

"And, isn't that a problem? What about the whole exchange of names?"

"Ah," he said. For a maddening moment, I thought he was going to leave it there and say no more. Then, he unwound to lay back on the sand with me. Propping his head up on one elbow, he looked down at me. He smoothed the hair away from my face with his other hand. As always after transforming, his touch was cold, almost icy. In the heat of the day, it felt good. "I can't exchange names with someone who doesn't know their own, now can I?"

His smile was patient, as if willing me to catch up to him. My remaining irritation sputtered in confusion. I had a magical name, too? Was he saying that, all this time, Valentine wasn't holding something back out of malice or because he didn't love me enough to want to be bound to me? "You would tell me your true name, if I had one of my own to exchange with you?"

He made a long, drawn-out thoughtful noise, then said: "No."

My anger came roaring back with a vengeance. "What!?"

"Could you really be happy if you knew I only followed orders because I was compelled by magic to do so?"

"You mean you've never been compelled to obey? If that's true, why did you attack my stepmother?"

Rolling onto his back, Valentine stared up at the sky. His body was long enough, that waves sloshed at his toes. Folding long-boned hands over broad, hairless chest, he said, "She was denying you your birthright. The question isn't why I attacked her, but why I didn't kill her when I had the opportunity?"

"Okay," I said, slowly, almost uncertain if I really wanted to know the answer. "How about that one, then?"

"She had me trapped, in a way. You were the lynchpin. You didn't really believe I was a dragon. You still sometimes don't, which is why you have hazy memories of our first meeting."

"I don't believe...?" I sputtered, starting to defend myself. I stopped because it was true. They say seeing is believing, but minds are tricky things. Several times recently, I'd witnessed Valentine as a dragon. Even though one of them was literally minutes ago, it didn't seem entirely real. Maybe... maybe because I didn't want to believe.

This was all tied up in how I felt about Valentine's penchant for violence. If I truly admitted that Valentine was inhuman at his core, then I had to accept that part of his nature—the predator.

Predators were sexy from a distance. Tigers were all sinew and liquid grace. We infantilized the claws, called them 'murder needles' and talked about 'the beans' like they wouldn't rip us to shreds if hungry enough.

I slept with this tiger. I assumed I was safe because he was my familiar, but now I knew that nothing held him back. I never had any hope to control him or stop him.

Except, I supposed, trust.

I pulled myself up on my elbows. Valentine lay on his back, sand clinging wetly to his skin. Long ropes of wet hair were dotted with it, as well. That alone made him inhuman. How could he stand having so much sand getting into his hair?

When he glanced up me, I decided that what I needed to do was clear the air, see if I could trust him. "Jack and I saw you in your dragon form, carrying something in a burlap sack. What was it?"

He rolled all the way over onto his stomach, completely covering himself in sand. His elbow pressed against my shoulder wetly. "Ah, the surprise. Yes, I moved much of my hoard to a place in the Badlands. I thought it might help me not murder Robert."

I laughed. It was from relief, but also for the irony. Only Valentine would prove his innocence by threatening to kill someone else.

"You thought I was carrying a body, didn't you?"

It wasn't really an accusation, but it stabbed me right in the gut—that same place where I'd felt our bond unwinding. I didn't want to admit it, but I did. "Yeah."

"I see," he said.

Water dripped from the tips of the dark hair that hung in front of his pale, angular face.

I wanted to reach out and brush the sand from wet strands, but I hesitated. Did he even feel the discomfort, given that this body wasn't even real to him? Did it bother him to spend so much time as an illusion for my comfort?

As if sensing my thoughts, he asked, "Will you ever accept me for what I am, I wonder?"

"I guess I'm trying to reconcile everything," I said, sitting back up to hug my knees again. I took a second to formulate my thoughts and stare out at the lake, watching a pelican dip and soar along the shore, its beak pouch inflated. "It felt weird to be in love with someone who is basically another species, and..." I gave him a little side glance, "I always thought I was human."

"Ah," he sucked in an excited breath. "Could it be true? Did the gold awaken you that much?"

"That, and everyone telling me I'm a dragon?" I said, with a little self-deprecating chuckle. "I still don't think it's real, okay? You think I'm having trouble believing you? I'm really having trouble with this. If it's true, why didn't you tell me?"

Valentine pulled himself around so that he sat behind me; his legs stretched out to envelope me. His sandy hands rubbed the tension from my shoulders. "Nothing is truly learned by telling," he said into my ear, his voice a deep rumble that reverberated somewhere deep inside my soul. "More importantly, you are what you say you are. Humans—even part-humans—have the ability—a dark, deep, ancient magic—to name things into being. The Hebrew text speaks of this. 'Adam' named all the things, and, by naming, that is what they became. Your will creates."

I leaned back into his touch. Closing my eyes, I let Valentine's words roll over me, into me. "What are you saying? I'm only a dragon if I believe I am?"

"You have to believe it and name it," he said. "And then be named so by others."

This reminded me of something. I had half-formed memories of Robert and I texting back and forth on the vent Discord channel of our gaming guild about his coming out process. He told me how important it was to start telling people and to have his identity acknowledged. "Like coming out?"

"Humans are in a constant state of 'coming out,'" Valentine agreed. "You are human, Alex—at least in part. Had you decided that being human was the sum of your total, it would be so. I could never tell you differently. But dragon magic is slippery. Storytellers, the namers, defined us early as mythical and magical, so we remain outside of simple categorization. We are myth. We are magic. There's a reason no one could ever define you.'"

It all sounded very abstract, but some part of me understood. There is power in naming things. Saying who you are, out loud, makes it real, valid.

I decided to try it out, a little. "I'm..." I faltered a little, because the word 'dragon' felt too heavy. It was too much to take on, "...<u>more</u> than a witch."

Valentine made an encouraging murmur. "You <u>are</u> more than a witch."

All he'd done was echo what I'd said with more confidence, but I felt it. A warmth of the truth spread through me, lifting me up, somehow. I was more than a witch.

Much more.

"How did this even happen?" I asked as Valentine continued to rub my back comfortingly. "Is my mom a dragon or something? How did she and my dad hook up?"

Valentine chuckled darkly. "Dragons have the same needs as any. As you should well know." His fingers dug pleasantly into the knots in my neck, popping out the tension, as he continued. "I doubt, however, that your mother was a full dragon. We're not so common as that, and you would be a shifter, like me, which you aren't. I suspect your great-great-great-great grandmother was—or even further back. You're of dragon kind, Alex. You carry dragon-blood."

Twisting to try to see his face, I asked, "And you couldn't tell me because naming me would... what again?"

"Humans name things into being," Valentine reminded me, resting his chin against my shoulder. "I couldn't tell you because only you can name yourself. That's not for anyone else to do."

I frowned. "But, then, where does this whole True Name thing come from? Wasn't I named by fate?"

Valentine chuckled. "Your True Name is the name you give yourself. The one you become by naming."

Leaning back into Valentine's body, I closed my eyes to the sun and listened to the sound of the wind lapping the waves against the sandy shore. His naked, muscular arms grasped my stomach lightly. Surrounded by his strength, I felt grounded.

"So, when I'm ready to say what I am, out loud to other people, I'll also know my True Name?"

"Yes," he said. "It is the way with all magical creatures."

"I'm a magical creature," I whispered, hopeful, the wind nearly swallowing the words.

"You_are a magical creature," he agreed, again more firmly than I'd dared.

If I understood Valentine correctly, I had dragon blood in my veins. My dragonkind status was a power I didn't entirely understand, though I imagined my ability to 'curse' was related to it. If I said something was fucked, then it was, often in an 'oops-I-hadn't-meant-to-level-the-town-like-a-nuclear-bomb' kind of way.

Valentine's nose nuzzled the short spikes of my hairs and his arms tightened around me. Where they'd been wet, sand stuck to his legs.

"What do we do now?" I wondered.

"What do you want to do?"

I honestly felt like I could sit like this, wrapped in his arms, forever. As much as I wanted that, there were other pressing concerns. "Are we in danger from Furfur, do you think?"

"That turncoat angel?" Valentine asked. When I nodded, he continued. "I wouldn't mind keeping my distance. He seems a little unhinged. I don't think his focus is here, on whatever job that he and the little kite are pretending to work."

That worried me. I remembered what Jack said about witchy things coming in threes, which meant that another victim could fall from the sky any moment now. Not to mention the fact that the two agents had a certain amount of power over whether or not Spenser would get his job back.

Valentine's thumb dug pleasantly into a knot between my shoulder blades. "This makes you tense," he noted. "You still care about these people? Your job? This place?"

The question took me aback. "Why wouldn't I?"

Valentine made a little scoffing noise. "This is why I'm so certain you're much less than half-dragon."

I twisted around to try to look him in the eye, to gauge how serious he was. "Are you saying that if I were more dragon, I'd be heartless?"

His silver eyes narrowed. "I have a heart," he sniffed. "It's just not endlessly fascinated by all the nonsense that humans get up to."

I turned away from him, pulling forward a little.

His hands left my back, and I felt him shift to lean back on his arms. He let out a sigh. "We could fly away from this dreary place, go anywhere in the world, if you wanted."

"I can fly?"

"I don't know. Have you tried?"

"Do I have wings?"

"Can you shapeshift?"

I frowned. Obviously neither of us knew.

"Do you want to run away? I could take you away from here. We could go anywhere in the world."

Of course the idea appealed to me on a visceral level. Who didn't want to escape to a tropical island in the middle of nowhere, at least for a little while?

Obviously, however, what Valentine was offering was more than a temporary escape. He meant, did I want to leave this place forever.

The pelican was back, circling above us. Along the shore, sandpipers dashed in and out with the waves, pecking at whatever morsels washed up to the shore.

It was true that I only picked South Dakota because it was convenient to my needs at the time. I didn't entirely fit here. The energy of Pierre was very small town, insular, white bread, and nothing at all like my diverse, vibrant home-town of Chicago.

I felt woefully unprepared for my job.

Robert wanted us out.

When I listed things out like that, it wasn't as if I couldn't see the appeal of running away from it all. If Valentine really did have a hoard of banknotes somewhere, maybe I didn't need to have a job, after all. We could live like dragons, roaming the earth, like eternal tourists.

My mind, meanwhile, kept circling back to the idea of my life being noth-ing but nonsense. I knew Valentine had said that partly in response to my 'heartless' comment, but I also believed that he meant it on some level. He was virtually immortal, what did the concerns of a group of people really mean in comparison to the vastness of time?

It meant a lot to me, I was realizing.

It came as a surprise to me how bothered I was by the idea that Furfur and Tengu might not care if justice was being served.

I'd told Tengu that I wasn't a cop, and it was true. I never took an oath to protect and serve, but it didn't mean that I didn't enjoy being part of an inves-tigative team or fighting 'evildoers,' as it were. It frustrated me that with Spens-er sidelined and Furfur's weirdness, the team had never had the opportunity to do that thing we did—sitting in the conference room, eating donuts, tossing around theories, and musing over bits of evidence trying to make connections.

That wasn't nonsense. It was important. I wanted to get back to it.

Valentine's lips brushed my neck lightly, sending ticklish goose pimples racing down my arms. The way his teeth lightly grazed my skin made it hard to think.

"Will you come away with me, Alex?" His breath was warm against my skin.

Oh, how I wanted to say 'yes' at that moment, but instead, very painfully, the words eked out, "No, I don't think so."

"Because you're going to do the right thing?" came a vaguely familiar voice.

I turned around to see Furfur standing over us. Tengu stood a few paces behind him. They both looked ridiculous standing on a sunny beach in suits, ties, and sunglasses. It was weirdly creepy and impressive that they'd managed to arrive so silently, without even the crunch of sand or a 'bamf' and smell of sulfur.

In fact, I was about to accuse them of having materialized when I heard feet pounding down the pathway—along with all the various noises of brush and gravel and huffing of breath.

"Oi," Mac shouted to the agents. Behind him were Devon and Jett and the rest of the werewolf biker gang, "What the hell do you think you're doing?"

Tengu turned and pulled his sunglasses down to regard hair, ink, and leather. "We're taking these two back to precinct headquarters."

Mac stepped forward. His voice was a deep, threatening growl, "They're under my protection."

Valentine, meanwhile, hadn't stopped nibbling my neck. Into my ear, he whispered, "Cute. A wolf cub protecting the likes of us."

Us, because I counted as a dragon, too.

The wolves and the demons edged closer to a fight as the bikers jeered threats at the agents, "Just try to take 'em!" "Yeah, give us an excuse!"

Letting out a soft sigh into my ear, Valentine unwound himself from around my body and stood up slowly, deliberately. He was about to do something magical and take the decision away from me—a decision I'd just made. The decision to stay and see this thing through, with or without him.

Leaping to my own feet, I pushed him down with a little shove. "No."

It was a word.

Even though it wasn't even a swear, I created something, like a shockwave and, in a second, it wasn't just Valentine sprawling on his butt. Everyone stepped back. Some of the bikers even dropped to their knees or barreled into each other like a tattooed bowling ball Rube Goldberg machine.

"Seriously," I said when I had everyone's attention. "I'll go back with them. It's cool," I told the agents, "But not under arrest. We have a crime to solve and I want to solve it."

The ground trembled with my resolve.

If I was going to stay here, if I had any hope of belonging somewhere, then I needed to fix this. I was not guilty of anything and I was determined to have faith that Valentine wasn't either.

Everyone stared at me in stunned silence for several moments.

The werewolf biker gang continued to huddle together in a big pile of leather and hair at the end of the trail that led to the park. They hovered under the shade of the trees at the edge of the path, as though to step on the sand was to cross the Rubicon.

The two demon agents in their matching suits and sunglasses stood in the center of the hot sandy strip, like two dark spots on the sun. Their posture was loose, but ready. As always, they carried with them a sense of danger that was difficult to pin down, but yet very... present.

I was near the water's edge. Valentine stretched out on his back at my feet, propped up on his elbows.

The silence continued.

No one was more surprised than Valentine. I wasn't sure if my sudden display of power shocked him the most or if it was the fact that I'd decided to stay. His expression wavered between confusion and something else... betrayal?

Before I could assure him that just because I wanted to stay didn't mean that I wanted him to leave, Tengu lifted his sunglasses, perched them on the top of his head, and said, "Well, that seems reasonable." His partner looked ready to protest, so Tengu quickly added. "We'd had no intention of getting in the way of an on-going investigation. We are very sorry about the earlier... misunderstanding. Would you consent to ride back with us so that we can discuss the matter at hand?"

Things had gotten so tangled, I had to ask, "Which is?"

Tengu considered another moment and then said, "I suppose our main business is regarding Captain Jones and how the precinct is being run, and—" now he glanced at Valentine, who lay back on the beach like he was sunning himself. "The various... loyalties of the precinct members, yourself included."

"That's not the priority," I said. "I mean, we can deal with that, but we should be focusing on the drop victims."

"Does that mean you're prepared to turn over the dragon?" Furfur asked.

"Valentine didn't do it," I scoffed.

Tengu sounded genuinely hopeful, "You can prove that?"

Well, not yet.

The werewolves shifted restlessly at this strange standoff.

Mac glared between the agents and me. His thin lips curled into something very much resembling a snarl. With his hands crossed in front of his chest, he said, "Didn't she say she'd go with you? If the familiar is guilty, isn't the witch the one you want, anyway?"

"What?" I turned to give Mac a horrified look: "Are you helping?"

"As you wish," Tengu said, as though a deal had been struck.

Chapter Fifteen

Valentine stood up, slowly.

Everyone tensed at his movement. The werewolves looked ready to pounce or run, depending. The demons took a kind of fighting stance, like maybe they would draw whatever magical weapons they possessed.

Deliberately Valentine made a show of brushing the sand from his naked skin. Then, he yawned with a tongue-curling, muscle-popping stretch. Everyone watched him, holding their breaths, but he only looked at me. "This is what you want?"

"For the moment," I said. I turned to him and looked up into his face. I never grew tired of that sharp, predatory gaze in his stormy gray eyes, or the way his long hair hung like a black curtain in front of his pale, angular face. I didn't want to disappoint him, but this new knowledge he'd given me about myself was going to take time to digest. I supposed that was why he'd kept it from me for so long. "I need to... I don't know, figure out who I am, I guess. Plus, this dumb stuff? I finally realized that it's kind of important to me."

His smile was thin. "Your human nature is the dominant one, no doubt about it."

I gave him a teasing poke on his sand-encrusted shoulder. "Hey! That's an insult. I can tell."

I was trying to make the moment light, teasing, even loving, but Valentine crossed his arms in front of his chest. "I've never known a dragon who had to 'find' themselves. Humans, meanwhile, are perpetually uncertain of where they are."

"Indeed," said Tengu. He'd done that silent thing again and appeared at my elbow, making me jump. "Demons are the same. You are what you are. There is no changing your nature."

His partner made a noise in his nose like a snort. "Fuck fate, I say. Nothing wrong with a little soul-searching," Furfur said. He shoved his hands in his pockets. Unlike Tengu, he kept his sunglasses on, covering his eyes. "You have to know where you stand so you can take a stand."

Leaning into my ear, Valentine said, "As I told you, the war consumes that one. Be wary of his motives."

Furfur may or may not have pinned Valentine in his gaze—it was impossible to tell with those mirrored shades of his—and said, "You would have made an excellent ally."

Straightening up to his impressive height, Valentine snarled, "Ally? You mean slave."

I raised my hand to stave off the impending fight.

Raising myself up on my tiptoes, I gave Valentine's cheek a little kiss. "I'll be careful, I promise."

Valentine's expression was an unreadable mask. "I don't understand you right now. There is a wider world for creatures like us."

"I know," I said, letting my hands rest on the hard planes of his broad chest. I tried to feel for a heartbeat beneath my palms, but there was none. "I'm kind of surprised by it, too, but I like the small stuff."

"I will leave you to it, then," he said.

He stepped away from my touch, leaving me grasping at the air, as he turned his back and stalked towards the lake.

"You shouldn't leave the state," Tengu called after him. "You're still a suspect."

Valentine's only answer was to arc into a dive. As his body curved into the water, it transformed. Pale skin became glittery alabaster scales. Black hair shifted into ebony spikes that ran along a serpentine spine. Hands and feet shifted into powerful claws, tipped with wicked, jet-black talons. A long tail grew from Valentine's backside and slashed at the water like a fin, sending spray splashing to the shore.

As I watched him leave, I had to wonder. Despite what Valentine said, I thought, perhaps, my choice to stay had hurt him more than a little.

Over the werewolves' protest, I agreed to drive back to the precinct's headquarters in the agents' car.

On the walk up the pathway, Furfur kept stopping to kneel down to make a little mark with his finger in the dirt every few paces. Was he writing his name? Leaving a demonic trail of breadcrumbs?

Before I could ask, we'd arrived at their car. It looked like someone's idea of what government agents should drive—in the movies—from 1965. It was long, black, and shiny. The doors made solid noises when the slammed shut, and the backseat smelled of old leather and vinyl.

"You conjured this car, didn't you?" I asked them as I buckled in. "This isn't a real car. Does it even have a brand name?"

From the drivers' seat, Furfur gave his partner a stern look. "I told you it should be a Chevy or something."

"You're lucky the wheel is on that side," Tengu muttered. "We drive on the left in Japan."

Starting up the engine, Furfur grumbled. "I wanted a sports car."

"I was told we don't have the 'budget' for that," Tengu said. "Also, it's too ostentatious."

Mac rapped his knuckles against the window. Tengu cranked the window down by hand. "Yes?"

Mac ignored Tengu and peered back at me, "I'm going to be checking in later to make sure you're okay, got it?"

"Um, okay?" I mean, that was probably reasonable given that last time I was alone with these two, I'd ended up locked in a prison cell.

To the two agents, Mac sneered, "No funny business. I'm watching you."

"Yes, thank you," Tengu said as he proceeded to roll the window up in Mac's face, despite Mac doing the two fingers pointed at his eyes and then at them gesture.

Behind us, several Harleys started up and, as we pulled out of the parking lot, became a kind of motorcade or vehicular honor guard.

Furfur made a noise of disapproval and muttered, "Pack mentality."

Sitting back, I watched the scenery roll by outside the window. My thoughts circled back to everything that happened on the beach.

I could understand Valentine's frustration with me. I'd just discovered that I was dragonkind, and yet all I wanted to do with that information was to continue to live my mundane life.

I supposed other people would have taken the first opportunity to get out of Dodge—or Pierre, as the case might be.

We passed by a huge stand of oak trees. The sun was momentarily blocked, and in the shade of the huge trees I swore, for a split second, I saw an Asian guy with his thumb out. He had one of those old-fashioned, army green backpacks and looked very clean-cut; only when I turned to get a better look at him, he was gone.

"Oh! Hey, did you guys see that?" I asked. "That must have been the hitcher that Devon told me about!"

Tengu, who was driving, glanced at me in the rearview mirror. "Hitcher?"

"Yeah, go back—let's see if we can pick him up!" I said, still turned around in my seat to try to see the figure walking on the road.

Tengu didn't even slow down.

Furfur went back to looking at his phone. He'd pulled it out some time ago and seemed to be playing a game on it. The only other response he had was to say, "This town is a mess. I told you."

"Yes," Tengu said thoughtfully. "There are far too many phenomena for a town this size."

"You don't think it might be related?" I asked.

"To?" Tengu glanced at me in the mirror.

"The case?"

"Mmm, yes," Tengu said, turning his attention back to the road and not even trying to sound the remotest bit interested. "We should consider that, Furfur."

"Yeah, I'll take a note," he agreed, without ever looking up from his game.

It was becoming abundantly clear that these two agents, despite their insistence in taking the drop-victim case away from Spenser, had no interest at all in solving it. At least not beyond pinning it on Valentine.

"If you don't give a crap about the potential crimes happening in this town, what are you here for? The whole Spenser thing?"

After several strangely tense seconds and a glance or two at Furfur, Tengu cautiously admitted, "In a way."

"Well, what way? I mean I want to help," I said. "Seriously, if there's something I can tell you that can wrap this up, I'll do it."

Furfur chuckled darkly, "Want us gone that badly, huh?"

I didn't even pretend that wasn't true. "Yes, exactly. I mean, you tried to make my boyfriend into your slave solider... and after a nice pancake breakfast where I tried being friendly and everything. So, ask me the questions already, let's get this over with."

"I'm afraid it's more complicated than all that," Tengu said. "Spenser Jones has already admitted to all the 'crimes' he committed. He's on administrative leave. Those mundane things were dealt with immediately."

I didn't get it. "So why are you still here?"

133

"What we're investigating is..." Tengu gave another conspiratorial glance to his partner.

Furfur considered for a moment, and then nodded, and said, "We're investigating the level to which the town has been skewed."

"Skewed?" I asked for clarification, because, honestly? It sounded like 'screwed.'

"In the direction of unnatural," Tengu said.

Ah, this crap again. I sighed. "Why does it matter so much?"

Tengu frowned. With his droopy nose, his expression looked a little comical. "At its simplest, it's a matter of balance, I suppose. But you know the river analogy for magic? Natural magic flows with the current; Unnatural pushes against it. Well, think of it this way: too much pushing and the river is dammed up."

I thought about this for a second, but there was something not quite right. "That's not how it works—if the metaphor is literal, that is. Pushing against it all the time, that sounds to me more like a power generator, like, say, Hoover Dam. Because it's not that unnaturals stop the flow of the river, they just utilize it differently. At least, that's what I was told."

The uncomfortable silence that stretched said it all.

"Oh," I said, as it hit me. "I'm right. And, what you don't want is that much power in one group's hands."

There was another long silence. In fact, we'd pulled onto the street in front of the precinct's shop front before Tengu said, "Balance is important."

I wasn't sure I agreed, but I decided to play along. "Okay, let's say your investigation pans out. Turns out, the unnaturals have all the power. What then? What do you do about it?"

We'd arrived at the precinct, and they pulled into the small parking lot at the side of the building where Spenser normally kept our one official police car. I was surprised to see it there since he also tended to take it home with him.

"This is why we want to talk to the Queen of Faerie," Furfur said. "One solution would be to allow portions of the town to be annexed."

I had no idea what that meant, but it did not sound legal.

The sun began to sink into the Missouri River valley. Its fading light reflected off the yellowish brick of the old storefront that housed the precinct. The century-old advertisement for Coke painted on the side had peeled and cracked with age.

Tengu turned off the engine and unstrapped his seat belt. "Relocation would be the other solution."

Did that sound voluntary?

On the other hand, it wouldn't be the first time I was asked to move out recently. "So, you'd just randomly evict the unnatural elements?" It seemed unfair, especially since I didn't think it was the only solution. "If the issue is balance, wouldn't it also work to invite more naturals, you know, do a little tourist brochure or something?"

Tengu, who had come over to open the car door for me even though this wasn't the kind that locked people into the back, blinked. He opened his mouth and then closed it.

Furfur was the one who said, "It's not done that way. Anyway, think of the Tinkerbell Effect."

That sounded a little like the weak-ass argument of 'think of the children,' but I didn't know enough about how the Tinkerbell Effect worked to counter the argument. I did know that one of the concerns was a singularity of sorts that could happen if too many people believed in magic. I'd been told that such a thing could level forests like the Tunguska Event in Russia.

With Jack still out of commission, I noticed that the techno-magic of the precinct's mirage faltered around the edges. Ghosts of the busier office filtered through the 'soon to be open' empty storefront mirage. A blurred image of someone carrying a stack of paperwork flashed in my peripheral vision, only to disappear as I took a step closer to the door.

As always, when I stepped over the threshold a tiny electric shock like pin pricks ran up the length of my tattooed arm.

Hannah Stone stood in the doorway blocking our entrance like her namesake. Hard, sharp eyes met mine. I searched for a sign that she recognized me, but, if she did, Hannah's expression didn't change. To the agents, she gave a little nod as she shouldered past us on her way out.

"Where is Hannah off to?" I asked Tengu, because if anyone was still on the drop-victim case, it was Hannah.

Tengu shrugged noncommittally. "I think we have Stone directing traffic near that construction project."

There was so much to be offended by in what he just said, but I got hung up on that first pronoun. "We?"

He ignored me.

I tried a different tact, "You're having Hannah direct traffic?"

"It seemed a kindness to keep her busy," Furfur said.

Anger sucked all coherent thoughts from my head. "You... A kind... What?"

I'd been following the two agents without paying much attention. The office was otherwise mostly deserted, thanks to the fact that the power was still out. The place smelled like a wet towel, but the water seemed to have been shut off to the building. I only noticed that we'd come to the destroyed hallway when I had to pick my way around a collapsed ceiling beam.

Tengu dusted plaster bits off the table with the sleeve of his suit coat. Righting one of the chairs, he sat down. Sunlight streamed in through the hole Valentine had made in the ceiling. He gestured for me to sit across from him.

Furfur rested his shoulder against the wall behind Tengu, took out his phone, and started fiddling with it again.

"Since we can't properly record this interview," Tengu said, giving me a look that was clearly 'because you broke everything,' "My partner will be recording it."

I pulled a chair out from the wreckage. "Fine," I said as I swept my foot across the floor, clearing away broken bits of concrete. "So long as he doesn't randomly decide to activate a magic circle or something."

"Did we apologize for that?" Tengu asked.

"Yeah, sorry," Furfur said, sounding not at all sorry.

I glanced around the ruined room. I could still see faint chalk marks on the remaining walls. Everyone acted like Furfur had had a spontaneous break, but this looked awfully premeditated. I'd thought that coming back here would be a good chance to set the record straight about Valentine's guilt, but seeing the deliberate writing made me wonder if I'd made the right choice. After all, I'd learned in the car that they weren't really interested in working this case properly. I guessed that was the reason I should at least stick out the interview—if they were going to lazily try to pin it on Valentine, then I needed to be on record defending him, right?

Still. Sitting in this same room made me nervous even though the spell had clearly been broken by my curse. I decided to try out the power of naming again and, with as much conviction as I could muster, I said, "No spell can hold me."

I thought, maybe, I felt a small pulse of energy flow out from where I sat, like the ripple of a stone hitting the surface of the water.

Tengu must have felt it, too, because he shifted in his seat. "We're well aware of that fact, thank you."

"Let's get down to business," Furfur said, pointing his phone's camera at me.

"And what is that business again?" I asked, still miffed that they weren't at all interested in solving the crime.

"We need to know you won't actively work against us," Tengu said, opening his hands as though to indicate the damaged room, "Again."

Furfur followed suit and moved his phone in a steady arc, for a long panoramic shot of the room.

I tried not to blush or otherwise look guilty about the state the room was in. "It depends on what you're working on because we've established pretty clearly that it's not the drop-victim case."

"Your dragon is being careless with his food, that's all that is," Furfur said.

I held up a finger. "One, you need to prove that," and then I put up a second one, "Secondly, he told me he prefers cows."

"I would think there would be more meat on a cow," Tengu said.

"See," I nodded at Tengu to thank him for that contribution to my argument. Turning back to Furfur and the camera I said, "And, none of these people have bites missing, so no one is thinking of them as food."

My observation made Tengu take out his notebook and jot something down. "That's true. You would think a dragon would eat the whole catch, or at least taste it before spitting it out."

I gave him another nod. "Look, I know you guys don't care about who or what is dropping homeless people from the sky, but, as it happens, I do. I know you took over the case officially, Furfur, but why don't you let the precinct do what it does best, and you can just sign off on it?"

A loud caw interrupted whatever response Furfur might have had—as did the sudden rush of air and the sensation of bird claws digging lightly into my scalp. I tried to wriggle my head around to see what had landed on me. Some flapping, irritated bird chatter and a cold gooey string of bird poo later, Sarah Jane hopped off and settled on the debris covered table to preen herself.

"Consider us square," Jack said from the doorway.

Chapter Sixteen

"Jack!" I was so happy to see him that I forgot all about the poo in my hair. I almost tripped on some fallen plumbing in my rush to hug him.

Clearing his throat meaningfully, Tengu said, "Interviewing here."

"I kind of think we were done, anyway?" I waved goodbye to the camera that Fufur held. Looping my arm around Jack, I led him back to the main office.

Sarah Jane burst into the air again to follow us with a loud caw, leaving stunned and confused demons in her wake.

"Did I rescue you? Please tell me that I rescued you," Jack asked, "I've always wanted to be the rescuing sort."

"You totally rescued me," I assured him, stopping to wrap him in another huge bear hug.

Jack smelled good up close, a combination of shaving product, a warm soldering iron, and old leather. Longish hair tickled my nose and his shoulder blades felt too thin under his jacket. I pulled back to look deeply into his eyes. They were hazel today. Flecks of green sparkled like buried emeralds among the more prevalent ambers and browns.

I was pretty sure Jack's eye color changed with his mood, but maybe I was just that forgetful and they were new to me every time I stopped to really look at them.

"You okay? Really?" Before he could even answer me, I said, "I'm sorry. I forgot how close you'd be to the blast. I never meant to hurt you."

"It's okay," he said.

You couldn't tell he'd just gotten out of the hospital. I expected his arm to be in a sling, but it didn't seem to be.

"What happened?"

"Mild concussion, I guess? That and the dislocated shoulder, which, I will tell you, they really do just yank back into place."

I tended to think that if a person had a concussion they should have their head wrapped in bandages, like some kind of cheesy cartoon character, but apparently that was not a thing. He was dressed in his usual nerd-Emo-wizard style: hand-knitted Fourth Dr. Who scarf wrapped around his neck; broken-in soft black leather jacket with buckles and chains that would have made the werewolves salivate with envy; matching black jeans and Converse, and a black tee that had old timey block computer lettering that said, 'I'm here because you broke something.'

Sarah Jane hopped up onto his shoulder and plucked at the silver hoop in his ear, as though trying to steal it from him.

If her behavior bothered Jack, he didn't show it beyond a melancholy stare in the direction of Spenser's empty office and a deep sigh. "I heard you say something about the case. Is anyone still on it?"

Sarah had worked the earring catch open and hopped away to examine her prize.

Out of his pocket Jack pulled out an identical hoop and stuck it into his ear.

This must happen a lot.

"I don't know," I said in answer to his earlier question about the case. Hooking my thumb in the direction of the ruined interview room, I added, "Those two yahoos have Hannah doing traffic duty."

"Well then, it sounds like she needs rescuing, too."

"Oh my god, what a great idea."

But when we arrived at the construction site, we discovered Hannah wasn't there.

A new housing complex was going in across from a small park. The design was that 'ubiquitous luxury apartment' look, but they were carefully working around a piece of public art on the sidewalk. It was a rabbit, probably originally made as a cheerful, child-friendly piece, but moss had made the eyes look like they were wild-eyed. The design looked familiar, I asked Jack about it.

"Local artist, I guess," he said. "Same person who carved the eagle on the clocktower. Kaito Something or Something Kaito?"

I was surprised anyone had ever lived in this town that wasn't named Smith or Johnson.

There was no sign of Hannah anywhere, but I did see a cop stopping traffic so that a big digger could maneuver into the site. Jack drove us closer.

I hung my head out of the passenger side window of Jack's vintage Bug to ask the regular uniformed cop where he thought she might have gone.

The cop was a big, beefy Latino guy. "Something about a traffic accident out on the county highway, maybe something to do with roadkill."

We both wondered why a report like that had interested Stone and if it was the same county highway where our body had been discovered. The directions the cop gave us weren't familiar, but I pulled out a map anyway.

"Probably we should do that thing where we mark up the map, to see if there is a pattern to the body dropping," I said, as Jack thanked the guy and pulled back into the flow of traffic.

"Okay, Professor Holmes," he chuckled.

"I think it's just Sherlock," I muttered, digging around in his glove compartment for a Sharpie or a pencil. "Do you even read?"

"I watched the BBC show," he said. "The one with what's his name, the guy in everything."

"Martin Freeman," I said.

"Yeah, the hobbit."

I'd unfolded the map in my lap, only to discover that it was for the whole state of South Dakota. There wasn't even a smaller map of Pierre on the back, though there was one of Rapid City. "Aren't we the capitol? Is this town like nothing?"

"Pretty much," Jack said. "You could just circle the town. The other body was found outside of it, anyway."

The wind from the open window threatened to curl the map up as I tried to write on it. "This is so much cooler on TV."

"Chris Helmsworth."

"What?"

"That's who I want to play me in the movie." Jack stared straight ahead, nearly expressionless, except for a slight downward pull of his eyebrows. The radio was off inside his vintage VW Bug. The motherboard and circuitry magpie figurine swung from the rearview mirror.

I chuckled because sure, why not? I wanted to play along, but I felt so far out of the loop about who was cool. "Uh... can I be animated? Like in my war game?"

"Oh, if we're all animated, that's cool, too. Then, I want giant eyes and a rocking huge sword."

I smiled at Jack. "I'm really glad I didn't accidentally kill you today."

"Likewise."

I felt a wave of seriousness crash over me and I reached out to squeeze his knee. "No, I mean seriously. I've got to stop hurting the people I care about."

Jack let out a little breath and said, "Look, I'm not bothered, really. It was clear you were only doing what you needed to do to try to save Valentine.... Or, did you ever discover his real name?"

"Oh, well, we decided not to do the exchange thing," I said. "I guess, we're going as equals?"

"Darling, I love you lots, but he's a dragon and you're a human. There's no way you're equal to—" he stopped at my expression. "What?"

"I might not be entirely human?"

He pulled the car over. There were open grazing fields for cattle on either side of the road. Ahead, I could see Hannah in her uniform standing over something. She had a hand on her hip and the other holding on to her hat.

Once the car was completely stopped, Jack said, "Congratulations?"

"Or condolences," I admitted. "I'm not really sure."

"Fair," he nodded. "What's the other half, then?"

"Oh, I'm probably far less than half. But, dragon, too, I guess?"

"Right, of course," he said, sounding irritated.

"That makes you mad?"

"Ugh, it's just, he's already your familiar and so very much cooler than I am, and the one thing I had was that you and I were at least the same species. Now, I don't even have that going for me, do I?"

I leaned in to kiss him. "You've got plenty going for you."

His little frown told me I was going to have to do better than that. I could try more flattery, but with Jack the truth felt like the better option.

"I have no idea what to do with any of this. All I know is that when Valentine wanted me to fly off and abandon everything and do dragon-y things, I said 'no.' What I want," I pointed to the map and swept my hand to indicate the roadside where Hannah stood, "is here."

His eyebrows raised. "You said 'no' to flying away with Valentine?"

"Yeah," I said.

"To stay here?"

"Basically?"

He unbuckled himself and popped open the door. "You're an idiot."

Hannah had spotted our car and waved us over.

We walked over to what looked, from this angle, to be a deer carcass lying on the side of the road. Only, the closer we got the more obvious it became that it was a bit more than that...

"Is that what I think it is?" I asked.

"Yep," Jack said. "Centaur."

"Centaur roadkill," Hannah felt the need to add.

It was a male, though I might only have known that from the large, horse-like genitals obvious beneath the horse-tail backside and the lack of breasts on the naked torso. The centaur's body type was slim and ethereal, very classically 'fairy-like.' His hair flowed in fawn-colored waves from his head down along his spine until it melded with the short hairs of the horse. Beardless and with elven-sharp features, I'd have figured him to be no more than twelve—but I had no idea how centaurs aged.

Dead eyes stared open and glassy. A blue-black tongue stuck out of his mouth. His beautiful body was all impossible and broken angles.

It was horrible to see, but at the same time, the clinical part of me registered the fact that there were no flies. No ants covered his eyes, and none of the other usual bugs had made their way to the corpse. No crows had been scared off by our arrival, either

"Does he rot?" I asked, noticing that there were none of the other telltale signs of decay either.

"No," Jack said, taking a camera out of the pocket of his jacket. He started cataloging the scene.

"So, there's no way to know how long he's been here," I said, stepping out of the way so that Jack could photograph the corpse from all angles.

"Eventually they turn to crystal," Hannah said, as if that was one of those things people just knew about centaurs.

"Oh, right, sure," I muttered. "I guess we just check for the amount of crystal in his body... how am I even supposed to do that?"

"I suspect there must be a way," Hannah said again, sounding like most labs came standard with crystal-to-centaur test kits, "But we don't have to worry about that this time, because we've got the report from the accident. We know when it happened." She gestured toward the squad's radio, "About an hour ago the call came in. The real question is why. Why were the centaurs on the move?"

"Oh, do they usually... erm, herd around here?" I looked at the open grazing land thinking it'd be nice for horses, but didn't centaurs prefer people food? "I guess I thought centaurs were Greek?"

Jack took a few pictures of the fence and the surrounding farmland. "They've immigrated with the rest of us. Greek-Americans, I think they prefer now. Anyway, they're properly called Kentauroi, and I believe a group of them is an 'Eminence.'"

"Well, okay," I said, feeling a bit schooled despite the fact that I was pretty sure this hadn't been covered in any elementary class I ever went to. "Did we know there was an Eminence of Kentauroi around here?"

Hannah frowned at the farmhouse in the distance. "Normally, they stick to the big national parks like Yellowstone. I hadn't heard anything about it until the accident report came through. I wonder..." she looked at me then, "if something is spooking them. Something to do with whatever has been scooping things up and dropping them about."

I didn't want to know, but I asked anyway, "Are there are lot of big flying things that... hunt Kentauroi?"

"Rocs will, I think," Jack said.

Hannah gave me a meaningful look, "And dragons."

"But, to be fair," Jack said, still considering all the facts, "Werewolves hunt them too."

I tried to imagine Mac chasing after a centaur, his tongue lolling and tail wagging. It was far too easy. Only there was one problem, "Yeah, but it wasn't a full moon last night."

"If there's a werewolf pack nearby the Kentauroi could just be nervous. That could flush them out, perhaps. The motorist who struck this one was just a drunk ordinarium, or so the dispatcher thought. He did say something about a centaur, which is why I decided to come look. It's possible the motorist was a magician, hoping to collect tears and, well, overdid things."

"I thought mermaid tears were the valuable ones."

"Kentauroi tears are nearly as valuable," Jack said. "Anyway, it depends on the merperson. I'd not touch rusalkas' tears if you paid me a million dollars."

I didn't know what a rusalkas was, but Hannah nodded along, like she agreed. I decided that if I really wanted to know, I'd ask Jack later.

"You're planning to follow up with the motorist," Jack asked Hannah.

"Of course," she said.

We all nodded at each other for a few minutes. I felt like this was a very anticlimactic 'getting together of the team,' so I suggested, "Hey, let's all meet at Spenser's house tomorrow and go over the case."

"Not the precinct?" Hannah asked, looking at Jack for confirmation.

"Well, technically Spenser is not supposed to be working, but, if we end up talking about everything over lunch, that'd be okay, right?"

"Ah, I see," Hannah nodded. "A way to include him. I approve."

I hated to ask this, but I had to know, "Will you remember?"

She pulled out her phone. "I've been using the reminders. I'll write it up now."

I was impressed with her solution, so I gave her an approving nod. When Jack started to head towards the car, I started to follow him, but then looked at the centaur's body. "We're not going to leave him just lying there in the road, are we?"

Hannah looked down as well, "He is off to the side of the road."

They were treating the centaur like he was an animal, but he had a face. "Yes, but shouldn't we take him back to the morgue?"

"Oh, well, we could, I suppose. I'd like to put up a webcam to see if we can catch any poachers in the act," Jack said. Going the rest of the way to his car, he dug out a black bag from the trunk which was actually the hood on his VW.

"Doesn't he have next of kin?"

Hannah continued to stare at the body. "If he does, they do seem to have left him here."

Having gotten his equipment, Jack came over to join us. "I suppose I can leave my number in case someone wants to contact us."

"Centaurs have cell phones?" Were they animals or people? My head was starting to hurt with all this.

Jack laughed a little, "Don't be silly. I meant my glyph." He made a sign in the air with his finger. In the fading sun, his motions appeared to leave a trail, like a Fourth of July sparkler. He wrote it again in the gravel beside the body. It looked a little like the thing that Prince had changed his name to, only more... swoopy. "There," Jack said. "That should do it. If I've done things right, that should only be visible to grieving persons and none other. That way if we've got a magic-using poacher they shouldn't detect that we've been here. Now, I just need to find a place to hide the webcam...."

Several minutes later the camera was set up, nestled inside a knothole of the rickety fence. I made Hannah make a note in her phone to call for someone to transfer the body to my morgue by morning. Even so, I felt uneasy as we drove away, like we should have said a prayer or something over the body.

When I looked over my shoulder as we drove away, Hannah was doing just that.

☤

Chapter Seventeen

I had Jack drop me off at home. As we pulled up to the curb, I saw the "for rent" sign Robert had put up earlier.

"You think you could get Sarah Jane and her friends to poop all over that?" I asked, jerking my thumb in the direction of the posted notice.

Jack laughed, but in true nerd fashion felt he needed to explain, "Birds can't really control their sphincters, but I can ask her to perch on it for you."

"That'd do." I said. I figured that for the average ordinarium seeing a bunch of crow-like birds hanging around a property could be a deterrent. If nothing else maybe the place would look spooky and weird. God knows the bird crap would make Robert spare, as Jack might say.

I thanked Jack and got out of the car, feeling bone tired.

It'd been an insane couple of days. All I wanted now was a nice, long soak in the tub and a glass or two of wine.

I walked along the paved walk that went around the side of Robert's one-story ranch house. In the space between the house and the walk grew a garden full of cheerfully colored zinnias and Shasta daisies. Robert had such a green thumb. In the spring, I'd watched him take a big bowl of mixed seeds and toss handfuls of them onto prepared soil. He didn't do much beyond covering the seeds so they wouldn't blow away and watering, and this riot of beauty had sprung up.

It was its own kind of magic, for sure.

I wondered, would the two demon Internal Affairs agents categorize garden witchery as natural or unnatural? Being of the earth, one would assume natural, but gardening acted on the world. You didn't just leave things alone to do their own thing--you had to prepare soil, pull weeds, water, and kill pests. When you added that last one gardening was kind of nasty. Aphids were natural, right? So, who were you to spray the poor things with poison just because you liked the flowers better than the animals?

As I came to the back door, I decided that this was ultimately what I disliked about the natural/unnatural dichotomy. Gardening was a good thing. Without it, people would starve. Killing aphids in your garden meant that pretty things could thrive. To classify anything that 'pushed against the flow' as unnatural, cast it in this light that made it seem evil and wrong.

When, really, it was just another mode of being—a mode that people had been adopting since the first hunter and the first farmer. Thinking of it that way, unnatural was very 'natural' to humanity and, moreover, deeply powerful and spiritual.

Even though it was technically still my house, I knocked when I reached the back door. "Robert? Are you home?"

I was pretty sure he must be since the heavier storm door was propped wide and the screen window was down to let in fresh air.

Coming out of the living room in shorts and a t-shirt, Robert gave me a funny look as he opened the door for me, "Why didn't you just come in?"

"Because," I said, kicking off my shoes as I stepped into the cramped mudroom, "We've been fighting and I just—I don't know. I don't want to screw anything more up."

"Valentine packed up all the doo-dads," Robert said, pointing to the now starkly bare kitchen. Robert had obviously taken the time to polish all the surfaces and tidy up in general, but the kitchen was so white that it looked blank now, almost lifeless. Robert must have thought the same, because he added, "I hate to say this, but I kind of miss the clutter now."

I could have said 'I told you so,' but I'd been serious about not wanting any more fights today. I just nodded tiredly. "Yeah."

Robert went straight to the fridge and pulled out a beer. "You look like you had a shit day."

I laughed in that way that was nearly hysterical and could turn into tears in a second, if I wasn't careful. Taking the beer, I pulled myself together. "Yeah, it's... um. Wow. Let's see," I ticked off the crazy on my fingers, "I gave one of my best friends a concussion, almost lost Valentine, ended up in a weird prison full of gold, and found out that I'm not entirely human."

To his credit, Robert only snorted a little bit of his beer. "And here I was feeling bad because I took a half-day off work to wallow in self-pity and play World of Orc Quest."

I smiled at him, loving him kind of intensely at that moment for not making a big deal out of any of the weird shit I'd just said. "Yeah, how is the guild?"

"You should play with us," he offered. "It's been a long time."

"I played Monday!"

He gave me a sad look. Very puppy-dog. "Yeah, but not like we used to."

"You mean, like, for hours on end while drinking too much Mountain Dew and eating junk?" I teased him.

"Look," Robert sniffed. "Maybe that's how you rolled in your sad little Chicago apartment, but I've laid in canapés and beer."

"Canapés and beer?" I repeated. "Has anyone told you that you're awesome?"

"Not," he smiled, "often enough."

"Well," I said, following him into the living room where we had our game console, "You're awesome. Move over and give me a controller."

Robert and I spent several hours bonding over our mutual love of orc-killing. At some point a pizza got ordered because, despite the fact that Robert really did have canapés at the ready, I wanted something I could seriously sink my teeth into. As the night wore on, I kept expecting to hear the backdoor open and Valentine to come sniffing around for dinner or company.

It never happened.

I finally gave up on hope and the game somewhere after midnight. I could have kept playing, but Robert had to work in the morning. I didn't, not really, since my only plans were to connect with everyone at Spenser's house for lunch, but I should probably check in at my office to see if there was any news from the university about our first Jane Doe.

After helping Robert put away game consoles and recycle the pizza boxes, I crawled into my bed alone. Pulling a blanket over my head caused coins to shower the carpet.

I wondered if Valentine had gone off to his private, special place to look at the stars. Did he go there to think, I wondered? What was he thinking about right now?

Switching the light off, I lay in the dark, alone in my bed. Moonlight shone in through the window. Crickets chirped in that lazy, summer way. I stared up at the cracks in the plaster ceiling and tried to pretend I was okay.

Five minutes of that had me flicking on the lamp again, this time searching for my cell phone. I had a frantic five minutes before I remembered that I gave my phone to a gang of magpies. Intentionally.

With a frustrated grunt, I padded my way into the living room where Robert kept an old-fashioned telephone. Even though it sat in a recessed alcove like a centerpiece, I was pretty sure it was more than just a prop as I'd heard it ring. I picked up the receiver to check for a dial tone. Sure enough, it was there.

Now I just had to remember Valentine's number.

I stared at the rotary dial for several minutes. Nothing was coming to me. This was what was wrong with relying on technology, I thought. I'd offloaded my memories to some machine, and now, when I needed it most, the important stuff was gone.

A curse hovered at the edge of my consciousness, but I decided it wasn't worth accidentally leveling Robert's house by uttering it.

On impulse, I just started dialing randomly. I'm not even sure that what I started with was an actual US area code, but I kept plugging away confidently. I stopped when I thought maybe I'd rung enough digits. I might have put in seven, or it might have been a dozen.

The phone rang.

He'd pick up.

He always picked up.

My heart hammered through two more rings, I started to doubt. Was I even calling the right person? Would I get connected to Paraguay?

Finally, it clicked on, in answer. Valentine's voice was smooth and amused, "You remembered something else, it seems."

I almost asked 'what,' but instead, I said, "Your number is whatever I want it to be. Your cell phone isn't even a real thing, is it?"

He didn't bother answering what we both knew was true. "I'm staring up at the stars, Alex. Why have you intruded on my silence?"

Because I wanted to say 'I love you,' felt too mundane and human, so I gripped the old-fashioned receiver and said, "When I said I liked all the boring nonsense of existence, I meant that to include you."

There was a dark chuckle. "I feel a little insulted."

I wanted to say, 'now you know how I felt,' but I held my tongue because it was petulant and I didn't really want the argument it would start. I wasn't sure what to say instead, however. I'd thought we'd left things mostly in a good place, but he wasn't here. He was in his private place, instead of with me.

Maybe he just needed a little time?

I didn't want to give him time; I wanted him to be here, now.

I let out a sigh, wishing that the phone had a longer cord so that I could pace, "I find it so hard to believe I'm related to dragons," I said. "I have no patience whatsoever."

That brought out a real, genuine laugh. "You really don't. I've only been gone from your side for a few hours."

Why did it feel like forever, then?

It should be a comfort, knowing that all the times that I thought the only reason Valentine stayed by my side was because he was compelled to as my familiar was wrong. He was there, instead, out of choice, because he wanted to be.

Yet, I felt so much less sure of myself. What if he suddenly stopped loving me? What if he was distracted by something shiny? There was no way to <u>make</u> him stay by my side now.

I felt strange, wanting that.

Especially since I had Jack.

Polyamory had been so much easier when I thought that there was no possible way to lose Valentine.

"God, I'm selfish," I said.

"Now you sound like a dragon," he teased, warmly.

"You're coming back, eventually, though, right?"

The silence on the other end stretched longer than I would have liked. "I would like that moment to be when we can come together as equals."

"What does that mean?" I asked, even though I was afraid I knew. "I thought you scoffed at the idea of me finding myself."

"At the moment, you've chosen to embrace the mundane world. That's not necessarily a bad idea, though, it seems to me that you're still finding your way in it, finding your power. I think, sometimes, you mistake my presence for your power. I don't need to be standing by your side for you to be strong, Alex."

I frowned. "But I want you by my side."

He laughed a little at that. "I think you just proved to yourself that I'm never actually all that far away. I answered your call, did I not?"

I nodded, even though he couldn't see it through the phone. Or maybe his point was that he could.

I guess I felt a little reassured by that?

"Okay, I'll go out and be strong and stuff so you can hurry up and come home."

"I look forward to it."

I slept fitfully. It might have been the absence of Valentine's arms around me or the loss of his heavy, solid presence in the bed, but I think what really kept me awake half the night was an overwhelming sense of loser-ness.

That's what I decided at 3:17 am, after I'd rolled over for the hundredth time to stare angrily at the glowing red digits of the alarm clock on the nightstand on Valentine's side of the bed. It was a view that Valentine's hulking body usually blocked. Just seeing it reminded me he wasn't there. I swore the numbers flashed accusingly at me every time another minute blinked forward.

Wadding up the pillow that still smelled of him, I threw it at the clock. I'd hoped to knock the annoyance to the floor, but I only managed to tip the lamp and push the clock to a slightly crooked angle. Now it looked like it was giving me a mocking, sidelong glare.

My whole life in a nutshell, I thought ruefully.

I flung myself onto my back and let out a sigh. Frowning at the ceiling, I wished I were the sort who went for runs. I thought maybe if I could go for a long, pounding jog or something, I'd be able to physically work out what my brain couldn't.

A bright white light from the moon shone in through the curtains and I heard a strange, lonesome howl.

I sat up.

We had timber wolves in South Dakota. Sighting them was rare as they tended to stay in Wyoming and all the hunters told me we "had no breeding pair" which was apparently significant. Coyotes, on the other hand, we had in spades. They were the state animal, after all.

Somehow, I knew this wasn't a coyote.

I scrambled to the window and looked out. Silver light made Robert's backyard into an eerie photo negative of some Norman Rockwell tableau. The perfectly mowed grass appeared fringed in white, like a summer frost. The moon illuminated odd angles of the garage roof and the neighbor's shed.

An animal padded into view. I wasn't an expert, but this creature looked bigger than I expected a wolf or a coyote to be. Rangy and broad shouldered, its fur was the color of rust. When it turned and its yellow gaze captured mine, I saw a streak of white at the temple that reminded me of someone.

Of course. "Mac?"

Somehow, I expected werewolves to be scarier. Not that this wild animal didn't look capable of tearing the throat out of a deer or... a person, but, if that truly was Mac, he didn't look anything like anything I'd ever seen in movies or on TV.

In fact, he looked a little... cuddly.

I pushed opened the window, which had been closed for the air-conditioning. Mac-wolf watched me with his head cocked curiously, like a domesticated dog. He stood up on his haunches and sniffed the air, tasting my scent. He continued to stretch upward, gaining mass. His shape changed as well, fur growing thinner, some darkening until they became patterns of ink on skin.

In a minute, there was a naked tattooed man standing in my backyard.

Mac's usual topknot was gone, and his auburn-red hair hung in front of his face, like a ragged curtain. He flipped it back with a cheerful, "Hey, Alex. Feel like running with us?"

How weird that I'd just been thinking about an early morning jog. "Are you psychic?" I called back.

"Not normally?" he said, "But, you know, instincts. Why? Were you dreaming about running with wolves?"

He was chatting with me like it was normal to be naked in the backyard, but I couldn't quite stop my eyes from drifting down the scarred, hard planes of his taut body to that rusty patch between his legs. He walked toward my window confidently, with a swagger, as if he agreed that what he had was worth my open-mouthed stare.

"Uh..." I managed. "Kind of? I mean, I wasn't sleeping, and I could use a distraction. But, is it safe? I don't want to end up a werewolf, honestly. I'm having a hard enough time dealing with being part dragon."

He was close enough now to lean an elbow on my windowsill, "I'll only bite if you ask me to," he smiled, his long canine teeth flashing in the moonlight.

I'd been thinking about a jog, but running with wolves?

"I don't know, Mac. I mean, aren't you guys... dangerous?"

"Totally," he nodded, like the world's happiest dude-bro. "That's what makes it fun."

I thought about it for exactly two seconds, because you know what? I probably needed this.

"Yeah," I smiled. "Let me get my shoes."

Chapter Eighteen

I stood in front of my closet and wondered what one wore to "run with the werewolves."

Mac, meanwhile, continued to lean on my windowsill, his arms pressed up against the screen. He was, of course, completely naked, and, like so many of the men in my life, completely relaxed about it. His long auburn hair hung in front of his face. Usually, he wore a bit of it tied back, and I had to say that the whole 'muss in front' look was very alluring. Somehow, having the straggly locks falling in front of his face made him seem that much more... animalistic.

I could see more of the tattoos, too. Though the ink along his biceps reminded me of tiger stripes, I was now certain that they replicated darker swirls in his wolf-form fur.

As I debated which shoes to wear, Mac looked around my mess of a room. "Nice place," he said casually.

I shook my head at him as I sat down on the bed to lace up my tennis shoes. I'd turned off the lamp in order to see outside better, so I called bullshit. "You can't see anything."

Hell, I could barely see the shape of his face in the shadows. His ink was only so visible because the moonlight fell across his naked shoulders. Its silver light highlighted the contours of muscle and sinew.

"Actually, I can," he said. "I can see in the dark even when I'm not a wolf."

A howl echoed in the night.

The sound made me jump, and Mac turn his head. "They're wondering where I am," Mac said.

"You should go," I told him. "You know I won't be able to keep up with you anyway."

"I don't think you should let that stop you." Without another word, Mac turned from the window. He took off at a run. I stood up to see if I could catch sight of his transformation. In one moment, there was a beautiful, wildly tattooed naked man streaking across Robert's backyard and in the next, after he turned around the side of the garage, a red wolf with a white patch of fur just over his eye.

Standing by the window, I could feel the cool breeze. The air smelled fresh and like something farm-ish, the tang of manure, maybe, or skunk musk? Crickets sang. Above, the stars spread out in their glittering blanket.

I finished putting on my shoes, quietly tiptoed out the back door, and went out into the night.

It ended up more of a stroll with the wolves than a run, but, at several points during my wander through the neighborhood a wolf or two would snuffle up against my heels and trot along beside me.

Mac nudged the back of my knees until I consented to run a few paces. I was terribly out of shape, however. I only made it a few blocks with him bounding along at my side before I had to quit for lack of breath.

After an hour or two, I waved goodbye to my random wolf companions and limped home to collapse, hot and sweaty, onto the couch.

After all that exercise, however, I finally slept well. I woke up when Robert shuffled out into the living room in his pajamas on his way to the kitchen to get breakfast. We exchanged sleepy 'good mornings,' and I seriously contemplated returning to my own bed. I decided, however, that I should stick to the plan to check in at the coroner's office this morning before heading over to Spenser's place.

One quick shower and a change of clothes later, I felt refreshed.

I even busted out and made myself a couple of eggs for breakfast.

Everything was going really well until I stepped outside and realized I had no idea where I'd left my car. Was it still at the precinct headquarters?

At moments like this, I could see how easy it must have been for my stepmonster to convince me that I was insane. Because, seriously, how do you not know where your car is? Do normal people do that? I didn't think so.

Luckily, there was a bus stop not far from the house. Robert was the sort that when his house was in order (which it was again now that Valentine had removed most of his silver hoard) all the bus schedules were in a little organizer behind the takeout menus. Going back inside, I quickly perused the paper brochures and was able to figure out how to get from point "a" to point "b" with the least number of transfers. As I put them back in their place in the rack, I had to thank the powers that be that Robert was a bit of a Luddite. He must also be one of the last people on the planet in our age bracket who actually subscribed to the paper version of the newspaper, and I tossed it into the living room for him as I headed out to try this again.

As I walked to the bus stop, I tried to revel in the mundane. Look at me, world, I told myself as I strolled passed the ticky-tacky post-World War II ranch houses that were nearly indistinguishable from one another. Look at me, being all regular person, taking the bus.

I found the stop and stood waiting in front of the little sign. The day promised to be a little cooler than yesterday, at least. A strong wind chased fluffy, storybook clouds across a brilliant blue sky. The air smelled fresh, if a bit more 'farm-ish' than usual.

A few cars passed. We gave each other the small town nod of greeting, and I really wished that I'd brought a book or Robert's newspaper or something, because I was starting to feel weirdly conspicuous standing around without even a phone to look at.

Finally, the city bus came into sight. I got my change ready. When the bus stopped, I double-checked that it was going the right way. The driver gave me a look like I was a complete moron, but nodded in confirmation. Pierre buses were nothing like Chicago ones. As I slid into the first empty seat that wasn't right at the very front, I remarked to myself how clean and empty it was.

The only passengers were me, an old lady with several plastic grocery bags at her feet, and... Nana Spider.

She slipped into the seat beside me with a "Oh, hello, dearie."

As usual, Nana Spider always looked to me like a cotton ball on a stick. Despite the summer warmth, she had on a fluffy pink winter coat made round by several layers of down and the addition of the army backpack she always carried. Her skinny legs were wrapped in dark tights and her footwear was mismatched: one cowboy boot and one sneaker.

"You're not speaking in rhymes?" I asked her.

"Ah, but I am, and I'm growing quite weary," she sighed. Pulling her backpack off her shoulder, she began to rummage through it for something. She stopped to smell an apple she found. Apparently finding it acceptable, she took

155

a bite and held it in her mouth. Around a mouthful, she said, "One of my clan, the justice man."

"The guy on the road was for sure homeless?"

"Ah, it's no fun, when you guess it in one."

It might not be fun, but it was extremely useful to have confirmation that the other victim was, in fact, related to the previous Jane Doe.

The old woman with her plastic grocery bags at the front rang for her stop. Making a face at us, she gathered up her things.

I waved goodbye and she frowned at me, like she was quite affronted by or a little be scared of having had to share the bus with Nana Spider. I had a weird desire to point out that, despite her frizzy foof of unwashed steely gray hair and general unkemptness, Nana Spider was a good person—a powerful person, even.

"Never mind the insult, friend, we are avenged, in the end."

"By what?"

She pointed up at the sky. I wasn't sure if she meant that everything evened out in the afterlife, in heaven, or if she was referring to something literally above us.

Of course, she might mean whatever was dropping the bodies. I'd been thinking about this crime in terms of its magical components, but what if it were something simpler, baser? What it the reason all the victims had been homeless was because people generally disliked the homeless, found them to be a nuisance, an eyesore?

Obviously, something magical was still involved, but what if it was operating with a more... human attitude?

"Are there magical creatures who commit hate crimes?" I asked Nana.

Her bulbous eyes blinked at me for so long that I wondered if I should rephrase the question. Maybe Nana didn't know the term 'hate crime' or what I meant by it?

"Witches do," she said finally, "They're human, too."

True enough.

Apparently reaching her stop, Nana Spider ran the bell. She tottered off onto the street. I waved good-bye to Nana Spider as the bus pulled away.

Pierre's capitol building loomed before me. It was typical of a lot of state capitols in that it was built in a Federal style. Unlike the one in Washington, DC, Pierre's capitol had a copper dome that had burnished to a dull green. The dome was atop a tower, rather than capping the whole building, but it still managed that cold, impressive, forbidding feel that so many government institutions had. In fact, no matter how many times I walked up the marble steps, I still expected someone to tell me I didn't belong here.

I certainly didn't fit in terribly well with the various power suits that streamed in and out of the main doors. At least I wasn't the only one in jeans— pages, staff, reporters, and even some of the more hip, liberal state congress people and lobbyists dressed more casually. There were other elected officials like the Sheriff who had offices in the building that weren't the typical legislative types, too.

Even so, I normally preferred my basement morgue.

I was weird that way.

The interaction on the bus made me wonder. I'd been looking for a motive within the magical community, but could it be that someone was using a magical creature for a mundane hate crime? What if the reason those two people had been dropped from the sky had less to do with whether or not they were witches or gremlins or faerie or whatever, but because they were homeless?

It was a bit of a wild conjecture. I didn't even know if homelessness was a huge problem in Pierre. Sure, Nana Spider was around, but I didn't see a lot of people sleeping rough or under bridges. Was that just because I trained my eye not to notice them anymore, however? Had there been other crimes like this against the local homeless population recently?

I needed to find out a couple of things. First, was there someone local with a grudge against the homeless who might have 'stepped up their game' as it were? Someone who might have turned to someone in the magical world to make their job easier?

A second possibility that occurred to me was that maybe someone in social services might know if something like this might have been reported in the nearby towns. Could there be a magical killer moving through the US, taking out homeless people? It seemed likely that a flying creature had dropped the victims, and, if so, maybe that creature flew from town to town, too...?

I wasn't sure about that one, but I was beginning to really feel in my gut that these had been hate crimes.

Maybe the other thing I should check was to see if any other marginalized group had been targeted.

When I came into my office, Genevieve startled. She did some quick keystroke which I was very sure had just hidden a game of minesweeper or whatever porn she was reading. Plastering on a big smile, she cooed, "Ah, Alex! Good to see you. What can I do for you?"

By the way she held on thinly to that smile, I was sure she was worried I was going to ask her to deal with a dead cow carcass again. Instead, I asked, "So which would you rather do? Help me research some stuff or go fetch coffee?"

To her credit, she considered this for a few moments before saying, "Both."

She headed out to the cafeteria and I was left alone in my "big" office.

It was the sort of place that career politicians, like my predecessor, loved. Spacious and designed to impress, dark, hardwood bookshelves lined the walls. My sneakers scuffed the matching, highly polished floor. An oak desk dominated the space, so heavy and impressive that I felt like an interloper in my own office, like maybe I wasn't good enough to sit behind something so powerful.

The office smelled of a combination of fresh paint and red rot, the smell of old books. I liked the books. It was a collection of medical books, most of them outdated, but deeply fascinating—the kind that had the thin tissue paper over illustrations of blood vessels and organs. It surprised me that my predecessor had left them behind, but then I remembered he was even less qualified for the job than I had been. I'd at least started medical school, even if I never finished.

I snuck behind the desk and settled into the creaky swivel chair that had probably been rolled in some time during the 1940s and never replaced. At least the computer was new. I fired it up.

Genevieve would have to help me figure out how to search through county files, but I could at least do some basic research before she returned with my coffee.

I didn't actually expect Google to help me, but I started there, anyway.

I tried search terms like "Hate Crimes Pierre South Dakota" and "Homeless Death." I got a few hits, but nothing that pointed to any kind of trend. Most of them were clearly mundane, no magic involved in any obvious way. That prompted me to try, "Unexplained Deaths, Pierre."

To my shock, that worked.

One of the reasons I'd chosen to live in Pierre was because their murder rate was in the negative numbers. People died here, of course, but they didn't kill each other on anything that could be called a regular basis. Ideal conditions for a noob coroner like myself.

Of course, no one warned me that Pierre was a kind of vortex for the supernatural. According to Google, it always had been. I waded through several articles from recent years about isolated incidents of "wolf attacks" right around the time Mac's gang was probably riding through on their way to Sturgis; I bookmarked those. Apparently in the 1980s there was a spate of 'alien abductions' that I thought were more likely 'faerie abductions' since they occurred near the neighborhood of Spenser's mom's 'house,' which was actually a portal to the Faerie Realm.

Genevieve knocked on the door briefly before letting herself in. She had two large to-go cups of coffee. The smell gave me a bit of a caffeine rush as she set one beside me. She had her laptop tucked under one arm, and she pulled up one of the cushioned visitor chairs and opened it up opposite me. "So," she asked, "What are we after, Chief?"

I was pretty sure she was being a bit snotty with the 'chief' thing, but she seemed enthusiastic enough about the research. "I'm looking for...." I stopped. I wasn't exactly sure how to describe this, but I settled on, "...a pattern, I guess? Ideally, I'd love to find a trail of homeless deaths, from... er, dropping."

She glanced up over the familiar glowing Apple logo. "Homeless people dropping over dead?"

"More like dropping from the sky and dying," I said, feeling my face flush. Genevieve was an ordinarium, a regular person who, at least as far as I knew, had no sense of the magical underground or its inner workings.

Genevieve was also one of those women I could never be. She looked flawlessly put together, not unlike my demon stepmom. In fact, the similarity might be part of why I never quite warmed to her. Her hair was a kind of silvered-blonde. She was probably in her forties, which made her older than me, and she was the type who managed to look fashionably business-like in skirts and blouses and cute, kicky heels. Whenever I wore high heels, I always felt like I was a kid playing dress-up, pretending to be far more elegant than I could reasonably pull off.

She raised her perfectly sculpted, plucked eyebrows at me, but nodded and typed something into her computer. I went back to my own search.

For a long time, the only sounds in the office were the mechanical hum of central air, the occasional slurp of coffee, and the soft click of keys.

"Does it have to be homeless people that are dropped?"

I looked up. I'd been reading an article about 'strange, misshapen' roadkill that had been found near Yellowstone National Park and thinking about my poor dead centaur. "No," I said, getting up to come around to her side of the desk. "It can be any kind of dropping."

She gave me another quirked eyebrow at the word choice of 'dropping.'

"You know what I mean," I insisted.

"Look at this," she said. Somehow, she'd accessed the County Historical Society's photograph collection. There was the clock tower downtown. I recognized most of the buildings, too, though, of course, several stores weren't there yet. The cars looked like they might have been from the late 1960s. "Hippies," Genevieve said, sounding a little like she still didn't care for that sort. "Apparently, a bunch of them were dropped that summer." She switched screens with a swipe of her hand across the track pad. "I found a mention of an article about it in the microfilm collection. I can order a print for you, though the headline makes it sound like everyone was convinced it was bad acid. I guess several people died that summer, though."

"That's exactly what I was looking for," I said, though it didn't quite match up perfectly with homelessness.

I supposed that if I thought of homeless people as transient that could mean a lot of things in different time periods. Maybe these deaths were all kids hitchhiking their way to Haight-Ashbury or somewhere like that?

Genevieve seemed pleased to have found results. I began to feel bad that I didn't use her more often for jobs like this. I was about to say something, maybe apologize for not asking more of her, when she pointed to something that popped up on her screen, "Oh, here's another one... well, maybe."

I leaned over her shoulder to read: "AIDS suicide. Rescue Workers Contaminated?" I could see why she wasn't sure this was related, but there was the courthouse clock tower again.

"Did it used to be easier to get to the top of that clock?" I asked her, remembering that we'd had been pretty sure the first victim was a jumper, too.

Genevieve shrugged her delicate shoulder. Even though I was physically smaller than she was, all her features were sharper and more feminine. "I don't know," she said, "But there aren't a lot of other tall buildings to throw yourself off in town."

"Maybe I should look up suicides," I mused out loud, but I felt we were on the verge of something else. A pattern was emerging centered on the clock tower. I'd hoped for something more obviously related to homeless people, but maybe that wasn't the main connection. What did these people have in common? Was it 'hate crimes'?

I didn't normally think of hippies as the sort of people that were hated the same way as the homeless or AIDs victims, but maybe so? I glanced at Genevieve 's screen again and another pattern suddenly revealed itself. "Is it me, or is there a twenty year gap every time?"

She blinked and double-checked the dates. "How did I not notice? All of these articles are in the summer, July, even."

I frowned, peering at the tiny print. "Around the weeks of the 4th of July."

We exchanged a glance. The 4th was this weekend.

I picked up the heavy receiver of the ancient landline and dialed the number to the main Precinct 13 office. There were two rings before I heard Jack's crisp, British accent. "Hello, Bob's Pizzeria! Will this be takeout or delivery?"

"It's me," I said.

"Alex, what are you doing calling from this number? What even is this number?"

I smiled. My predecessor must have never interacted with Precinct 13 at all, and that was why Jack was pretending to be a pizza place. "I'm calling from the coroner's main office." I dropped my voice so that Genevieve couldn't hear me. "Your magpies still have my cell phone, I think."

"Oh boy," he said. "Was it shiny? It might be lining a nest right now."

"Great. I'm going to have to buy a new phone," I said.

"Oh! I can bring you one of the ones I have around."

"Is it going to be able to call the dead?"

"Do you need that feature?"

"Uh, not especially," I noted. "Look, do you want to hear what Genevieve and I discovered or what?"

"Not sure who that is, but I'm all ears," he said, and I could hear his warm smile through the receiver.

"Oh, did you not know that I had a secretary?"

"Fancy," he trilled.

"As if! Right, so get this..." I started, and then proceeded to lay out everything we'd discovered. There was a pattern of deaths involving various different groups: hippies, gays, homeless people. No one had much paid attention to them because it had always looked like suicide. The deaths always centered around the clock tower and the Fourth of July.

"It's some kind of American thing? An act of 'hate' patriotism?" Jack asked, sounding confused. "Because what does the Fourth have to do with any of this? I mean, I'm not a huge fan of all the flag waving and whatnot, but isn't America supposed to be the land of opportunity and all that?"

"Yeah, that part is weird," I admitted.

Genevieve had scooted her chair up so she could lean in and listen to my recitation of our theory. I could smell her expensive perfume. She twirled a bit of her hair around her carefully manicured finger. "Did it start in the Sixties?" she wondered. "I mean, people were arguing about what America was supposed to be back then, right?"

I wasn't sure about her line of thinking, but I shrugged. "Can you check? Also, since things seem to start there, when was the clock tower even built?"

She rolled her chair over to the other desk and the computer there.

"She's looking," I told Jack.

"Cool," he said. "I'll take this opportunity to tell you that the big excitement this morning at the precinct is scat gathering."

"Scat? Like, poop?"

"Apparently, the werewolves were running around in a residential area this morning."

"Oh." I said, feeling guilty. "That's maybe my fault. I went running with them."

"Wow, really?"

"It was more of a stroll."

Jack laughed. "Ah, yes, that famous book: _Strolling with Werewolves_. How do you manage to make things that should be cool so very, very uncool?"

"A gift?" I suggested.

All of a sudden Genevieve made a happy little choking sound and jumped up. I turned to look at her. She pointed at the computer screen, her mouth still working excitedly but not making any coherent sounds. I told Jack to hang on and set the receiver down to look at what was giving her apoplexy. It was a grainy picture from the County Historical Society. I recognized the diner in the picture, but where the clock tower should be was an office building. I couldn't quite see what this was so exciting at first, but then my eye focused on the stone figurine at the top. It was a kind of a gargoyle, except it was a giant American eagle, fierce and proud, looking judgmentally down on the street below. Like with the statue in the park, they must have saved the eagle and put it on the clock tower.

Those hawk-sharp eyes seemed to stare out of the photograph at me. The streaks of dark were under its talons—which, given that the statue should have been new, seemed like a clue.

I was pretty sure we were looking at our suspect.

I ran back to the phone and asked Jack, "How does a stone statue come to life? I mean, is it possible?"

"Of course, it's possible. Have you never heard of Pygmalion?"

I thought maybe I knew the story from my Greek mythology class in 6th Grade, something about a statue coming to life? It didn't really matter, so long as it was a possibility. "Are we still on for our lunch meeting? Because I can bring all this stuff."

"I'm not really doing anything here, anyway. I'll come to you."

Jack arrived bearing Starbucks.

As he handed me a mocha, however, he looked around and asked the question I'd been dreading, "Where's Valentine?"

Genevieve, who still sat at the wide oak coroner's desk collating our research, glanced up, clearly on the scent of relationship gossip.

I took a sip of the espresso to avoid having to answer right away, but they both continued to stare at me expectantly. "I'm being patient."

Jack nodded, like he understood. He perched on the corner of the big polished desk. His short curls were as disheveled as always. I wasn't sure I'd ever seen his hair looking anything other than 'slept on.' In fact, one side was a bit flattened, like he'd literally just been sleeping.

"Did you have a fight?" Genevieve asked. Jack had brought her coffee, too, and I could smell something pepperminty. I wondered how he knew what she liked or if he'd somehow used magic to guess right. "Did you guys break up?"

I didn't really want to talk about this, but they obviously wouldn't listen to anything about the case until I discussed my love life. "Sort of the opposite," I said, trying to figure out how to explain things to an ordinarium. "Something happened at work the other day that made us both realize that we... didn't owe each other anything? I'd been thinking that Valentine was staying with me for... reasons, but it turned out not to be true. This is a good thing, but it's a different thing? We're feeling our way into the new us."

Genevieve listened carefully, nodded as though she understood completely, but said, "You broke up."

Jack looked surprisingly hopeful at that news. I wanted to give him a kick in the shins for that. It wasn't like he didn't get to date me, either way.

"We really didn't," I insisted.

"Uh-huh," Genevieve said, giving me the eyebrow over the rim of her minty drink.

I sipped my mocha morosely and muttered, "Can we talk about the case now?"

"Oh, right." Jack said. Standing up, he ran his thin-boned fingers through his mess of curls. "Sorry."

"No worries," I said and then proceeded to lay out everything we'd discovered, starting with the conversation I'd had on the bus with Nana Spider than got me thinking about homeless people. Jack listened intently, studying the various newspaper clippings that Genevieve had printed out from the historical society's web page.

"There's definitely a pattern," Jack said. "I do think you might be right about the stone eagle, though it's very unusual for something inanimate to spontaneously gain sentience like this, particularly with malicious intent. A hex is more plausible. But, for it to continue... perhaps a curse? Even so, there's usually a triggering event. I don't see anything here that seems, well, 'big' enough, if you will."

I had settled into the guest chair and was swiveling back and forth thoughtfully. My mocha was gone, but I was still tapping the empty paper cup to my lip. "The thing that I keep thinking about is how the eagle is this symbol of America, right? But, it seems kind of... I don't know, un-American to go after homeless people, gays, and hippies."

"Maybe it's a Republican eagle," Genevieve suggested.

I nodded like it was a possibility, but I really didn't think it was that simple. "I don't know. I feel like something's missing."

"Agreed," Jack said. "Like the original curser. Who was it? What was their beef?"

We all sat in thoughtful silence for a long time. No one had the answer. We were out of ideas. The hum of the air conditioning was the only sound.

"Should we take this stuff to Spenser?" I asked Jack, gesturing at the pile of articles spread across the desk. "I mean, maybe he has a clue. He's lived here a long time, hasn't he? Or... at least his family."

"The good neighbors?"

Genevieve looked up at that, curious. Then she shook her head. "I don't want to know what you mean by that." With a stretch and a yawn, she stood up. "In fact, I'm going home and leaving you freaks to figure out your magical mystery. I need a stiff drink."

At ten in the morning?

Well, who was I to judge? She'd been a real trouper. She'd worked harder for me today than she probably had the whole time I'd employed her.

We said goodbye to her, and I thanked her for her help. She gave me an eye like she wasn't sure if I was being sincere or not, so I spontaneously hugged her. Which turned out to be very awkward, all stiff limbs and not-returning-the-hug-at-all. "Seriously, though, you've been a huge help, thanks," I muttered, but, as soon as I let go, she fled.

"Still marvelous with people, I see," Jack teased.

"It's a skill set," I said.

He laughed. Then, reaching into his jeans pocket, he pulled out a phone. "It doesn't call the dead, but you can connect to most data plans, including mystical ones, but watch out for the roaming charges in faerie, they'll kill you."

"Lovely," I said, tucking it gingerly into my pocket.

As I tossed my empty coffee container into the recycling bin under my desk, I noticed Jack hadn't bought himself any caffeine. By this time of the morning, he'd usually had two espresso drinks and was working on his third Mountain Dew. "Hey, did you need to stop by the vending machine?" At his blank look, I added, "For a pop or something?"

"Oh, I'm supposed to lay off caffeine because of the concussion." Scrunching up his face, he added, "I'm really not supposed to drive, either."

He'd been driving us around all day yesterday.

Seeing my look of concern, he said, "It's South Dakota, love. How am I supposed to get around?"

"I took a bus," I said, though it was true that it wasn't terribly convenient for anything outside of the city, which almost everything was. "You need to be careful, Jack. It's bad enough that I put you in the hospital. I feel guilty. Don't you dare die on me because you didn't listen to the doctor's orders."

"It was an accidental curse," Jack said. "You don't know your own strength."

"My swear was on purpose. I meant to flatten Furfur. And, I should know my own strength by now," I said. "I blinded Devon. I mean, thank god he's a vampire... or werewolf, whichever it is that gives him healing power."

We stood in awkward silence at the door. I felt like I should probably apologize more or something, but then the thought occurred to me, "You don't suppose that's how it happened with the eagle? An accident?"

"You mean an unfocused hex?"

"I don't know. Do I?" I asked, once again feeling like a numbskull for my vast lack of knowledge about magic.

"It's a possibility," Jack admitted. "If we could figure out what the actual curse was, we could probably counter it. Which would be good, if your calculations are correct. In the meantime, I hate to suggest this, but..." His bright eyes sought mine and held them, "...it would be helpful if we, say, had a flying ally on our side. You know, something that could battle the eagle in flight."

"You mean... like a dragon."

Jack glanced at where I'd tucked the new cell phone into my front pocket. "Just so."

That was great, except I was supposed to solve my own problems. Okay, Valentine hadn't exactly said that, but there was the whole conversation about how I was meant to start relying on my own power and not him.

"Okay," I said, "but we don't even know for sure we're going to need to have an aerial battle. Let's get everyone together over at Spenser's place and crack this thing."

Chapter Nineteen

Even though Jack hated it, I drove us in his VW to Spenser's place. It had been a long time since I'd used a manual, and Jack cringed any time I had to shift. I want it noted for the record, however, that I only ground the gears really badly one time, despite what he might have said.

Spenser met us at the door. As usual when he was out of uniform, Spenser looked deeply uncomfortable. It didn't help that he wore what could only be referred to as 'trousers' and a stiffly starched shirt. Who still starched or ironed shirts? The answer appeared to be Spenser, who might be secretly living in 1952. In fact, I had a feeling that if he pulled up the leg of his pants, he'd be wearing those weird sock garters my grandfather used to own.

He ushered us in. "Stone is already here. We're set up in the kitchen."

The last time I'd been at Spenser's I hadn't really had much time to appreciate his unique sense of interior decorating. If his clothes had stepped out of a period piece, then the interior of his house was cut and pasted from the pages of *Field and Stream*. The walls of his living room boasted not only a genuine mounted deer's head, but also a shellacked bass or other large fish.

"Wow," Jack said, his gaze lingered on the glass eyes of the taxidermy. "I love what you've done with the place."

Fortunately, Spenser seemed immune to sarcasm. "What's this about a big break?"

Before we'd left my office, I'd printed out all the relevant articles and put them into a manila folder. I laid everything out on Spenser's kitchen table and built my case, as I did.

While I talked, Spenser started pulling sandwich fixings out of the fridge.

When I was finished, Hannah carefully sifted through the papers. I noticed that her hair was shorter. It was still a bushy mess of tight corkscrews that she wore heavy over her forehead, but now it stopped just below her ears. It was a reminder that the rabbis hadn't been able to find all of her. She was missing pieces.

The missing pieces shouldn't matter to me. Spenser told me to think of Hannah as having suffered a brain injury. It happened to people all the time. It changed them. They were different after, but it didn't mean they weren't the same person.

I tried. I wanted to.

But I kept thinking that the Hannah I knew was dead, and this person was something incomplete.

An impostor.

Unconsciously, Hannah's hand reached up to the spot above her eyebrows, fingers tracing the Word there. It was a new quirk. The Hannah I'd known would never draw attention to the mark on her forehead, her vulnerability. And yet... the unconscious gesture gave me a weird kind of hope that the person I knew before was still inside somewhere, because this was a tic born of trauma. It was like she was checking to make sure the Word was still there.

She glanced up at me. "It's possible that your eagle is a golem of some kind," she said in her slow, measured way. "But if that's the case, someone must be controlling her. A golem can run independently, but someone made her— someone is her master."

Setting out a plate of turkey sandwiches, Spenser said, "We need to figure out who that is."

"They'd have to be pretty old," Jack said, looking up from a gadget he'd brought inside with him. He worked on it at a small table near a glass sliding door. The view looked out onto the backyard and a wooden deck festooned with containers filled with basil, tomatoes, and other herbs and vegetables. "I mean, if they're still controlling it. These cases go back quite far. At least to the Forties."

"That wasn't that long ago," Spenser said, helping himself to one of the sandwiches.

"How old are you?" I asked. "Maybe nearly a hundred years is like nothing to a guy who has been a cop since the Thirties."

Spenser raised a bushy eyebrow. He stared at me for a beat, but then shrugged taking a big bite of his sandwich. "Good point."

"What have you got there?" Hannah asked Jack, jerking her chin in the direction of the little machine in Jack's hand.

I recognized it from yesterday morning. "Your future GPS!"

"I'm plugging in the information of the previous 'suicides,'" Jack held it up proudly. "I'm hoping that it can make a best guess of where the next body will fall."

"Brilliant," I said.

He beamed.

Hannah crossed her arms in front of her chest. Her gravelly voice was slow and steady. "I've been thinking about the problem of the eagle's master. The earliest record you found was from the 1940s, correct?"

Jack had said so, but I dug through the papers to confirm. Finding our first article, I held it up. "Yeah, looks like it."

Hannah tugged at a curl that had fallen in front of her forehead. "So, a master could easily still be alive. If that's the case, why do the victims change? First, they were hippies, then gay men, and now homeless. It's not entirely consistent. Yes, they're all outsiders in some way, but it doesn't seem quite right. If a person had a grudge against one type of outsider, why doesn't that grudge continue exactly? Why does it shift to different groups?"

"They must have something in common," Spenser suggested.

I took one of the sandwiches and chewed on the soft bread as I thought about it. "They're all outsiders. Maybe if the stone eagle's master is still alive, he just hates on new people."

"Possible," Hannah agreed.

"Then why haven't we seen immigrants as victims?" I asked.

Spenser scratched his chin. His 'not on the job' stubble made an audible sound when he rubbed it. "Maybe the master is an immigrant?"

I didn't like that, but I supposed it was possible that you could be an immigrant and be a bigot.

We all sat in silence, considering. The only noises were the tick of a clock in Spenser's living room and the sound of Jack's thumbs tapping the screen. As I finished the sandwich, I flipped through the articles again.

"That's the last of them," Jack said, setting down his machine. "It's going to take some time to calibrate, but it should give us a best guess in a few minutes."

I set the article I was glancing through back on the kitchen table. "Did I tell you guys that the werewolves spotted a hitcher? I keep wanting it to be connected somehow. Thoughts?"

No one had any.

Spenser took a second sandwich from the plate with one hand and pulled a flip notebook out of his back pocket with the other. He used his thumb to flip through the pages. After swallowing a big bite of sandwich, he said, "What

I really want to connect up is the things that the dead said to you." Apparently finding what he was looking in his notebook, he set the sandwich down. "Here it is. First one said 'forgotten, but I flew.' The second said 'justice.'"

"Huh." I leaned back against the kitchen counter to think. "I guess I assumed the second one was just looking for vengeance, but that first one sounds almost joyful? Like, she was happy to not be forgotten?"

"But that's not the order of their deaths, remember," Jack said. "The body on the highway had been there much longer, so it goes justice first, then forgotten flying."

"What if the eagle isn't serving the master, but the victims?" Hannah said.

I thought about the autopsy that I was still waiting for results on. "We don't actually know what killed these people. Earlier today, I was thinking that there was something about going after the homeless that felt like a hate crime. What if the stone eagle isn't the one killing them? What if what she's trying to do is get people to notice their deaths?"

"If that's the case, we're looking at this the wrong way," Spenser said. "Is the eagle trying to expose a killer?"

"Maybe," I said, but something about that idea didn't feel right. I looked at the printouts on the table. "It seems weird that an active killer would stop at three and then wait a decade between each killing spree, doesn't it?"

"Three is a magic number," Jack said. "Maybe the killer is magical."

"It'd be nice if we knew what killed these two previous victims."

Jack's GPS beeped, making us all jump. He picked it up to scan the readout. Looking up at all of us, he said, "Especially since this predicts the next victim will fall on a county highway... sometime tonight. Probably."

Even with the uncertainty in Jack's prediction, we all sucked in a breath. Suddenly, we had a deadline. If we wanted to avoid another body dropping from the sky, we'd better crack this thing in a hurry.

Chapter Twenty

I regretted sending Jane Doe off to an expert. I was already calling Genevieve to see if she could light a fire under the University, but I had my doubts. It'd only been a day. The body might not even have arrived yet.

After connecting with Genevieve, I told her what I wanted. She hemmed and hawed about having to do extra work. I could hear shuffling of paper on the other end, as she looked for the University's number. "This is important," I snapped. "There's going to be another drop tonight."

"Okay, okay," she started, but then suddenly stopped and her tone shifted from irritated to guilty. "Oh! Uh… how angry would it make you to know that the body hasn't left the loading dock?"

"Not in the least," I said, excitedly. "Change of plans! Don't let them take it!"

Since she was planning on doing a shift at the precinct, I had Hannah drop me off at the morgue.

I spent most of the drive frantically Googling 'how to tell how long ago someone died' and other things I probably should have learned in medical school.

I'd planned to leap out of the car the second that Hannah pulled into a parking spot, but, when I reached for the handle, she put a hand on my thigh. She wasn't a toucher, so her move made me pause. "Thanks so much for the ride, really have to—" I looked at her hand, still unmoving and then up at her serious face. "What?"

"Can I give you some advice?"

I let go of the handle and sat back in my seat. I was anxious to get started, but now that I had told Genevieve to cancel the shipment, the body wasn't going anywhere on its own. "Sure."

The interior of the car was cool and so very quiet. I'd expected her to drive a big boat of a car, like a Buick, but we were jammed together in a Tesla. I suspected she'd had to go out of state to buy this thing, but it made sense in a way that she'd be environmentally conscious, being literally made from the earth.

She waited for me to focus on her again, and then said: "Don't worry so much about what you don't know."

My new cellphone was still in my hand. A tab was open to a medical blog. "But there's so much."

Hannah nodded slowly. "Trust me, I understand. I can also tell you from experience that if you try to fake it... it just feels fake. It doesn't work."

"But—" I looked at my phone again, helplessly.

Hannah gave my knee one last squeeze. "You have other strengths. Go with what you're actually good at."

I wasn't sure how anything she just said could apply to dealing with dead bodies, but I thanked her for her advice. Still cradling my phone in one hand, I waved goodbye to her from the curb.

Two hours and twenty minutes later, when I was ready to cry, Hannah's words finally made sense.

Jane Doe was back in my basement lab, laid out on the exam table. She looked much worse for having been unrefrigerated for a couple of days in high heat. I could barely tell that she had once been human, much less anything about a cause of death.

I was ready to bring the house down with swears.

Then the idea that I was too magical to be allowed to curse started to piss me off. Into the empty room, I shouted, "How is it that I'm so powerful and so useless all at the same time?"

That's when it hit me. Hannah was right. Why was I pretending to be good at the usual way to be a coroner? That was not my strength. I was being stupid thinking I could suddenly conjure a medical degree from the internet.

You know what I could conjure?

Magic.

Why was I trying to solve this mystery with forceps and scalpels, when I could just ask the corpse what killed her?

I pulled my office chair around from my desk, so that I could sit facing the body. It rolled noisily on squeaky wheels across the concrete.

Stripping off my latex gloves, I dropped them into the hazardous waste bin. I scrubbed my fingers through my short hair and gave the corpse a long hard stare.

I'd never tried to contact the dead on purpose. Normally, they would just spontaneously respond to my presence, say their piece, and that would be the last of it. Jane Doe had already talked to me once. Would she have more to say? Or was one shot all I had?

Closing my eyes, I tried to reach out—you know, mentally.

I wasn't sure how that was supposed to feel, however, so I mostly just thought about things I knew about this person. She'd had a nice sundress. She was happy not to have been forgotten.

Nana Spider had said she was 'the rhyming witch.'

I should have asked her name.

Ymir Rhymes.

My eyes snapped open at the sound of the voice in my head. "Your name is Rhymes? Ymir Rhymes?"

A thrill shivered down my spine. There was no direct answer from the corpse to my question, but I sensed it. This was working.

Taking a deep breath, I closed my eyes again and started talking. I told Ymir how sorry I was that she'd died. I explained how I ran into Nana Spider and how she'd picked up speaking in rhymes, and how funny I thought it was that her name was actually Rhymes, yet her first name didn't rhyme with it. I told her about how someone else had been dropped and about how I didn't know that guy's name either, but I suspected he might be homeless, though he'd had good shoes. "He'd wanted 'justice.'"

Yes. Justice.

"For what?" I'd opened my eyes at some point during my monologue and wasn't surprised that I couldn't see her lips move when she spoke. "Is someone killing you? Is the stone eagle making sure you're found?"

Yes.

I needed to remember to ask one question at a time. "Okay, let's try again. Were you murdered, yes or no?"

No.

No? I sat back in the office chair and contemplated the ruined corpse. My eye kept being drawn to one perfectly white rib bone that jutted up out of Ymir's otherwise collapsed chest. It was a grisly detail. "What killed you?"

Sick.

"You were sick?"

Yes.

I crossed my arms in front of my chest. Things were getting stranger. Ymir, my previous Jane Doe, the rhyming witch, had not been murdered, after all, but had died of an illness. Apparently, the stone eagle took her body from wherever it had been and dropped it from a great height to land in front of the clocktower.

Not only that, but this was a ritual that the eagle repeated every twenty years or so.

Why?

"You were happy to be found, to be seen, not forgotten," I said out loud. "The other guy talked about justice. Yet, the eagle keeps bringing these bodies into the light, to be seen, every twenty years, so something is still wrong, something—some forgotten body?—is still, what, hidden?"

Yes.

Since I told Spenser that Jack shouldn't drive himself, I had them both meet me at the Branding Iron Bistro on West Sioux Avenue. I was halfway through a chocolate cinnamon scone by the time they joined me at the table in the back.

"I think we're looking for a body." I said without preamble.

"Falling from the sky," Spenser said with a curious sort of nod. "I thought we knew this."

"No," I said, "I mean, like maybe someone that was killed in the forties. I was talking to the corpse, and I was thinking that maybe there's someone who hasn't been found. I think the eagle is trying to get us to find someone."

Jack sat down across from me. He'd bought a cream soda and sipped it through the straw. "Talking to the corpse?"

"Yeah, you know, my superpower," I said. "I decided to use it."

"Good idea." Spenser said. "Any idea who we're looking for?"

I ran my finger along the edge of my plate, scooping up the last of the crumbs. "I don't."

"So, we're back to square one? Not knowing anything?" Spenser asked.

I'd been feeling so good about my detective work, too.

"We do know a stone eagle is going to drop a body on some county high-way," Jack pointed out, showing us his future GPS app.

"Has it pinpointed the location yet?" I asked.

Jack studied the readout. "It keeps fluctuating along this area."

"Let me see that again," I said.

Jack handed over the phone. I looked at the stretch of highway highlighted on the map. "Isn't this about where the hitcher was spotted?"

"You think maybe a body is buried somewhere along the roadside?" Spenser asked.

"It's not too far from that farmhouse we stopped at, too," Jack pointed out.

Spenser stood up and straightened his shirt. "Let's start looking. Hopefully, we'll find something before the next one falls."

It turned out that if you want to see a ghost, they become harder to find. We were driving back and forth over a section of highway, hoping that the hitcher would show. Spenser and Hannah had split up the other likely spots. No one was having any luck.

"It's a real phenomenon," Jack said from the passenger seat. We'd had Spenser take us to my car, which I'd apparently left in the precinct parking lot. "It's the opposite of the Tinkerbell Effect. It's why ghost hunter TV shows are always such duds."

The mention of the Tinkerbell Effect prompted me to ask, "Did you know that the two demons are actually here to split up the town or something?"

Apparently, they hadn't been as forthcoming to the others, because Jack sat up straighter. "What?"

Swinging the car part way onto the very narrow shoulder, I paused to make a U-turn. We'd come to the end of our territory. It was time to make a pass in the other direction. "Yeah," I said, watching for traffic in the rearview. "If the unnatural energy of the town is too high, they'd send some of it into faerie, I think?"

The details of this were kind of murky to me. How did they even plan to do that? Would the realm of faerie just swallow up whole neighborhoods or what?

"Are you serious? They told you that?"

Jack's expression told me that this wasn't a standard operating procedure like the two agents had made it appear. "Yeah, it's the real reason they're here. Even though they took Spenser off the case, they don't care about it at all. You did notice I wasn't including them?"

"I guess I thought that was for Spenser's sake," Jack said, still sounding a little shell-shocked. "I figured we'd loop them in, eventually."

We could, I supposed, but, from what I'd seen, they wouldn't care. "So, this mission of theirs, it's not typical?"

"Dear gods, no," Jack said. "You're not supposed to send ordinary people into the goddamn twilight. What do you think happens to normal people who get taken to the Faerie Realm? They get caught between life and death. This is how you end up with things like the Bermuda Triangle and ghost ships!"

That sounded bad. "Is that bad?"

Jack nodded solemnly. "We can't let them do that. It would turn parts of Pierre into a literal ghost town."

"How do we stop them?"

"We can't let them negotiate with faerie, for one," Jack said.

Even though I doubted I'd see the hitcher, I kept scanning the landscape as we drove. "I don't know if that's going to happen. Spenser was pretty firm that his mom wasn't going to just open the doors to them."

"Well, that's something," Jack said.

We were lost in our own thoughts for a good stretch of highway. Out of the corner of my eye, I saw a blur. "I think I've spotted the hitchhiker!"

Chapter Twenty-One

Hitting the brakes, I pulled the car over.

Twisting in his seat, Jack looked behind us down the road. Gravel had kicked up dust. "I don't see anything."

"It was just a flicker," I told him. Reaching out, I turned on the radio.

"What are you doing?"

A song I'd never heard of before came on. The chorus was something about bluebirds over the white cliffs of Dover. The music had a little jazz to it, maybe swing, nothing at all modern or electronic sounding. I didn't know why, but I would have said without a doubt this song was coming from another era, big band or something like that.

"It's not the Andrew Sisters," Jack noted, "But, definitely Captain America music. Is this a regular station?"

I shook my head. There were AM stations devoted to big band, I was pretty sure, but I normally had the car tuned to NPR. The dial hadn't been shifted. "Do you think we need to open the door to him?"

The dust had cleared, and we both peered behind us. There wasn't anything more to see than that faint blurring that I'd noticed before.

"Is he still out there?" Jack asked. "I don't see what you do."

I kept watch in the rearview, keeping my head tilted so that I was looking out of the sides of my eyes. Something was there, I was sure of it, but it didn't move towards us like I would have expected a hitchhiker to do. "You know those road mirages? This looks something like that."

On hot, sunny days sometimes you can see a spot on the asphalt ahead that shines like a wet puddle. The humanoid image looked to me a little like that, except that instead of lying flat against the road, it stood upright. If I squinted just right, I could almost make out some of the details of the silhouette.

"He definitely has a backpack," I told Jack. "I think this is our guy."

"Why doesn't he come in? We're clearly waiting for him."

I squinted into the rearview mirror. There was something else odd about this shape. "Maybe because he doesn't have his thumb out. Did anyone report actually picking him up?"

"You're the one who talked to the werewolves," Jack reminded me.

I should really start carrying around one of those little notebooks like Spenser had or at least use my note app on my phone. "All I remember is that Devon said that they'd spotted a hitcher."

"When I saw him, we drove by so fast, I couldn't tell you if he had his thumb out or not," I said. I was getting tired of holding my head at such a funky angle, but I was afraid that if I blinked or turned away, the image would disappear. "Maybe he's not an actual hitcher. Maybe he's just a regular ghost."

"Which would explain why I can't see him," Jack said. "The only ghosts I can see are the ones in the machines."

I had to look to see if Jack was being serious or if this was one of his bad stretches of a pun. He seemed to be meaning that literally. When I looked back to the mirror, it was just as I had feared. The image had faded.

The radio cut back into national news.

I switched it off. I felt a little disheartened that we'd lost sight of the ghost, but I said, "Call Spenser. Tell him that I know approximately where we should start digging."

Spenser called professional exhumers to meet us on the roadside. In the meantime, I'd been talking to the dead.

Technically, I was just muttering to myself while walking back and forth in the approximate area where I'd seen the shimmering, but I would swear it was helping me triangulate the precise location. The ghost didn't exactly respond like corpses did for me, with actual words, but as I talked, I would feel this odd pull.

I felt the strongest when I asked certain questions. I'd been going on about how happy I was to have found him and sort of laying out the steps of how it had all came about, when I randomly mentioned that the other victims were, "...well, undesirables, I guess?"

Suddenly I felt a violent jerk, like an invisible hand reached out and grabbed mine.

Jack, who had been perched on the hood of my car doing something on his phone, slid down in concern. "Alex! Are you okay?"

The force of the pull had flung my arm out and twisted my body. I held the last position I'd ended up in. "I think the body is going to be over this way," I trampled a little deeper into the weeds of the ditch. "And he's very upset by—" I tried to decide what it was about what I'd said that had triggered the reaction. "I think, this is about belonging? Like, there's something about these people that the eagle is showing us, where they feel like—"

I love this place. My country. My home. Why? Why was it taken from me?

"Okay, that was creepy," Jack said. "Please never talk with all the voices again."

I hadn't realized I'd said anything out loud. My hand reached up to cover my mouth, but I let it drop. It was too late to hold back whatever weirdness had come out. "Sorry?"

Jack's heels crunched the gravel as he came to stand at the edge of the road. The drainage ditch I stood in was fairly deep. The highway maintenance people had trimmed the edges, but where I stood the grasses and weeds brushed my knees. I recognized some of them, things like shepherd's purse and knotweed. Not far from where I stood was a tiny patch of wild roses.

Wild roses look nothing like the commercial variety; they're closer in appearance to apple blossoms, with five flat, somewhat flimsy petals. These grew in a low mound on the ground.

There was nothing necessarily unusual about finding them growing alongside the road.

Yet.

"I bet he's there, under those," I said, pointing to the roses.

Jack nodded, like he agreed, "You think someone marked the grave."

I did, though I had no idea who. "There's something I don't get in the pattern," I said. "I know why homeless people feel kicked out of their homes. I mean, it's obvious, right? Something pushed them out—a domestic situation, poverty, mental illness, bad luck, anything really. I get, too, maybe why the hippies in the sixties might have felt like they weren't welcome in their own country, even though all the protests and civil rights marches and such were, in my opinion at least, to try to make America a better place. AIDs victims, too—I presume some of them were living quiet, closeted lives, when suddenly their whole world was turned upside down. But, what is it with this guy?"

"Don't you figure he was Jewish or something?" Coming partway down the ditch, Jack sat down so we could talk more eye to eye.

"Maybe?" It didn't feel quite right to me, though. "I know there were fascists in the U.S., but we spent so much time not joining the war and Jewish refugees were fleeing to here or trying to." I pulled on my lip, thinking. "I guess we did turn boats away, but I don't know."

"Did people say whether or not he looked Japanese?"

I shook my head. "That feels more right. I hate to assume that there wouldn't be any Japanese people in South Dakota in the 1940s, but do you think it's likely?"

"You wouldn't think there'd be a British immigrant, but here I am."

True, though the ghost hadn't reacted at all when we were talking about this. "Devon said that one of the people who'd spotted this ghost thought he was dressed like a soldier."

"Well, that would explain the eagle connection," Jack said.

I wasn't following. "How?"

"It's your symbol, isn't it? If this young man was off to be a soldier, but he got killed for being the wrong color, that's a tragedy, isn't it? Especially, if he was a patriot."

"Wait, what was the name of the sculptor guy? Kaito Something?"

"I can't believe we never thought to check before," Jack said, pulling out his phone. "I'll use my 'advanced search' function."

I didn't have to ask to know that was probably another one of Jack's non-standard magical apps.

The sun had begun to set. I watched the sky, holding my breath a little. I wasn't sure what I was hoping for, though. Was it a bad thing that the eagle was continuing to bring the forgotten deaths to light? Maybe we should be grateful for its grisly ritual. Perhaps it was okay to have a reminder, once every twenty years, of who we tended to forget in our society, whose deaths we should not consider invisible or unimportant.

"Solved," Jack said, pointing to a name on his phone. "At least, I'm 99.9% certain that Kaito Adachi is our man, especially since there's a note here about how he went missing and was presumed to have died in a Japanese internment camp."

I felt another pull, but it was less of a violent yank than a tug on my heart-strings, as it were. It was more like I was sent an overwhelming amount of feelings, most of them sad, but also validated. "It's him."

As we waited for the exhumers to get there, a dusty pick-up truck pulled up, probably assuming Jack's car had broken down. The guy who rolled down the window was the old man from the farmhouse we'd stopped at. "Well, if it isn't the police."

He seemed to find his jab funny, but Jack and I just stared at him blankly.

"You need help?" he asked, but he didn't wait for our answer as he pulled his truck in front of the VW. Climbing out, he seemed to suddenly realize we were standing some distance from the car. "Why are you standing way over—oh."

He'd come close enough to see that I was standing with my feet planted on either side of the rosebush.

"You found the poor sod, eh?"

Jack's hands curled into fists, like he might try to tackle the old duffer. "Did you kill him?"

"Me? Do I look to be a hundred years old?" He sort of did, but neither Jack nor I had the guts to say so. The old man continued, "Hell, no. It was my father. I've been tending the roses, though. Said he found some famous artist on the side of the road. I never knew who it was, but he made me promise to take care of the roses."

"Do you want to stay and see him off?" I asked. "We've called for someone to take him to be properly buried."

"That'd be nice."

Everything was confirmed once the body was exhumed.

Not that there was much 'body' left after all this time, but my magic came through for us again. Almost as soon as the skull was visible in the dirt, Kaito started talking to me.

He was a young patriot who wanted to do his part, but Japan was our enemy and his parents had come from there. He refused to believe he'd be turned away if he could just get to the recruitment center in Rapid City, he was a well-respected artist who'd lived in South Dakota his whole life with no problems. He might have been able to sign up, except that a group of roughnecks had waylaid him and beaten him to death. He'd been left to rot on the side of the road.

We all watched as the exhumers carefully removed his bones to be properly buried in the county cemetery. I guessed there would be some cost, but the old guy told them to spare no expense and send him the bill.

After the old guy gave the exhumers his information and drove off, I asked, "How do you suppose the eagle animated? Was it revenge?"

Jack nodded, "He might have been a witch."

"With an eagle familiar," Spenser offered. He and Hannah had joined us, bringing with them the exhumers, who were now reverently placing bones into a lined container.

A final feeling washed over me, and I said, "Yes, that feels right."

I would have suggested that we all go out to celebrate wrapping up the case, but there were still some things that needed doing. Not the least of which was waiting to see if the eagle was still going to drop a body.

"You know what would be cool," Jack said, as the four of us stood around anxiously scanning the darkening skies. "Is if anyone here knew a person who could fly around, you know, and let us know if they see anything."

True. I guessed that I could always ask.

I fished my phone out of my pocket. Now that the sun was setting, the air chilled somewhat. The mosquitos were coming out in droves. I dialed some numbers while thinking of Valentine, trusting my magic to connect us.

He picked up immediately. "Your new confidence is sexy. I'm on my way."

I wondered if he'd been waiting for an excuse, given that he was soaring overhead in a matter of minutes. Jack and I lay back against the hood of the car, watching Valentine's serpentine form sluicing through the darkening night sky. Moonlight glittered along his scales, like tiny flashes of comets streaking through the night.

"He really is quite gorgeous, isn't he?" Jack breathed.

He really was.

This was his true form—beautiful, majestic, and wild.

When it was clear that the eagle was a no-show, Valentine landed in the nearby field. The cattle had all been herded in for the night, but their lowing intensified when he touched ground. Tilting his v-shaped head in my direction, Valentine said, "No sign of this stone eagle. It seems to be at peace."

Again, I found myself unsure of how I felt about this. I made myself a promise that in the morning I'd go looking to see if any homeless person had died alone, forgotten.

"Do you think we need to do anything more to make sure the eagle has been released of its duty?" Jack wondered.

Without hesitation, I said, "Clean it."

Jack glanced at the dragon in the meadow, and then back at me. "Clean it?"

"I dunno, at least we should check to see if that creepy moss is still growing like blood streaks under its talons. I feel like if that's gone, we're good."

"Okay, but I'm also looking up rites of release," Jack said.

"Fair," I agreed.

Before sliding off the roof of the car, I gave Jack a little kiss. I tossed my keys in the direction of Hannah. "Drive Jack home, will you? I'm flying to the Badlands tonight."

He was a little terrifying with all those teeth, but Valentine smiled, as I hopped the little barbed wire fence and ran to him.

We made love under a field of stars.

Then, together, we slept on a pile of gold.

It was strange to wake up in a cave, however.

It was stranger still to be curled inside the crook of Valentine's dragon form, warm against his smooth scales. After sex, I'd asked him to turn back into his true self. I wanted to get used to who—to what—he really was. Besides, I could only imagine he slept better not having to maintain an illusion for my sake.

One eye cracked open, the liquid silver of it familiar. "Can't sleep?"

I'd slept well on the gold. The uneven surfaces should have bothered me, but they didn't. "We could live here, couldn't we?"

I wasn't sure how to read Valentine's expression in his dragon form, but his mouth hung open slightly in a way that made me think he was surprised. "You would consent to that?"

I looked around the dark lair as best I could in the feeble light that streamed in from the small hole many feet above us. "I'm going to need a bathroom, probably, and a dresser with some clothes in it, but isn't this more comfortable for you?"

"Infinitely."

"Well, I can certainly sleep here in the summer," I said. "I'll have to get camping gear and figure out the nearest working toilet, but we can make it work. Winter is going to be a problem, though."

"For me, as well," Valentine said. When I gave him a curious look, he added, "Cold-blooded."

"Oh, right." Sitting up, I used his enormous belly as a backrest.

"I've been thinking. I have a bank account somewhere. What if I used some of that money to buy us a ranch, somewhere between here and Pierre? You could keep your clothes and whatnot there and we could share it in the winter."

I liked that a lot.

"Jack is welcome, too, of course," Valentine said. "Particularly, when I feel like I need to roam."

Someday Jack would probably grow tired of coming in second to Valentine, but I thought we could all make it work for now. "Sounds amazing. Now turn back into a people so I can kiss you."

Somewhere around noon, I got a frantic call from Spenser. "Hell," he said, "That damned Furfur is commandeering parts of Pierre for Hell."

I made him start at the beginning. Apparently, Furfur and Tengu had sent in their report and had gotten the go-ahead from some head office in New York to "correct" the balance. They'd been out all night setting up runes, not unlike the ones Furfur had used to try to capture Valentine. Spenser wouldn't have known about it, except that some of the sections they'd marked were already claimed by his mother, who was royally—and I do mean royally—pissed off.

There was a fight between demons and faerie already in progress.

Valentine, who had been listening in to the phone call, his ear next to mine, said, "Now this is something I'd be more than happy to get mixed up in."

I smiled. "Just tell us where to meet you."

By the time we reached Steamboat Park, there was a stand-off.

The park was a grassy strip of land that ran alongside the Missouri river. The two demons stood near the stone base of an old-fashioned steel bridge, trying to protect the last of the glyphs with their bodies. I recognized the scrawling tags from the one that Furfur stopped to write in the dirt with his finger. These had been spray painted onto the bridge in bright red.

The werewolves had joined the fight. They stood in a circle around the two demon agents; some even had their motorcycles stopped on the bridge above.

Spenser stood with his mom. Maeve, Queen of Faeries, had chosen to look like an old woman in a pea-green coat and matching headscarf. Her hand was tucked into Spenser's arm, as though for support, but even from a distance I could feel the strength of her steely gaze underneath the Jackie O. sunglasses.

"We are only following orders," Tengu insisted. Something had chewed up the sleeve of his black jacket. The white from his shirt could be seen though the bite-sized holes.

"This town is too unnatural," Furfur insisted. "You refused to come to negotiations. I thought it best to solve the problem by sending parts of it to Hell."

"Always with the final solutions, you angels," Maeve said. "There is a far simpler one, you know."

Valentine and I came to stand next to Spenser who gave us a nod.

"We will simply add more natural citizens."

I leaned into Valentine to whisper, "What about the singularity?"

Queen Maeve arched a shushing eyebrow at me, but explained, "I was thinking very small people. Hardly noticeable, little pixies, just enough to restore balance."

Tengu looked like he might agree, but Furfur snarled. "Too late. I claim these lands for Hell."

He looked ready to do a magical snap of his finger, but Valentine crossed the distance inhumanly fast. It was as though he suddenly appeared behind Furfur, grabbing his wrist. He'd partially transformed his hands, and his claws dug deep into the flesh of Furfur's arm.

"Breathe one word of a spell and I eat you," Valentine hissed. "Stand down."

Maeve laughed a very joyful laugh. If she wasn't hanging on to her son, I thought she might burst into applause. To Spenser, she said, "Why didn't you tell me we had a dragon?"

I should be sharing Maeve's delight, but I couldn't tear my gaze away from the blood dripping down Furfur's arm. I'd made peace with so much about who Valentine was, but could I deal with this?

"You're bluffing," Furfur said to Valentine, though his voice was a little shaky.

Valentine's lips grazed Furfur's ears, whispering something.

"I surrender," Furfur said instantly.

Tengu worked out the details of balancing Pierre's natural/unnatural situation, while Furfur slunk off to sit dejectedly in their boxy government car. When Valentine came back to me, I asked him what he'd said.

"I reminded the Right Honorable Earl that if I pierced his body any more fully, he would discorporate and return to the place he came from."

I tried to figure out why that was bad and failed.

"Heaven," Valentine explained. "The Fallen are angels who changed sides. The last thing Furfur wants is a one-way ticket to the headquarters of the people he betrayed."

The werewolves decided that the peaceful resolution called for a celebration. Somehow a keg of beer appeared. Jack showed up with snacks. Someone ordered a bunch of pizzas delivered. Queen Maeve shifted into black leather and lace.

Jack cornered me to let me know that the moss had disappeared. "I'm going to do a little ritual, anyway," he added. "I was thinking it might be a good time to teach you a bit about how witch magic works. That is, if you'd want me for a teacher?"

"Oh, Jack, I'd love that!" I said, hugging his neck.

We consulted calendars, picking a time not only for the ritual, but also to do regular learning sessions. As we did this, Maeve sauntered by holding a plate of what looked like scrumptious appetizers.

"Don't eat anything she offers you," Devon was telling all the werewolves. "Trust me, it's a bad idea."

Seeing him reminded me of the promise we'd made Mac. I was considering doing my own version of a Furfur and running off to hide somewhere, when I ran into Nana Spider.

She handed me a pair of scissors and then walked off.

"Thanks?" I said as she wandered off into a stand of trees. To be fair, they were very nice scissors. I wasn't a big crafter, but I could tell they were the good kind. The sort of scissors that your mom told you never to use on paper.

Kind of a weird gift, though.

I'd missed my opportunity to escape from Mac, however. His arm fell around my shoulder heavily and he steered me back in the direction of the party. "Oh, hey, I see you're ready to break the Thrall, huh?" he said, nodding at the scissors.

"I am?"

He nodded. "Good timing, too, since we need to head out. Oi, Devon, come over here! The wi—practitioner is ready to do the thing!"

"You really can call me witch if you want," I said, wriggling out from under his somewhat sweaty armpit "Also, I don't know if I know what I'm do—" I stopped because as Devon approached, I could see that he was trailing something. Several somethings, actually, that looked like black threads.

I glanced at the scissors in my hand.

All of a sudden, I got an idea. "Hold still," I told Devon, and started snipping.

I thought Spenser might be mad at me, but, as I snipped the last of the threads from Devon, he came over and asked me to do the same to him. When the last of the threads had disappeared back into the aether, Spenser clapped Devon on the shoulder and asked, "So, is this a goodbye party?"

Devon nodded. "Yeah. At least for now."

At least for now was a sentiment I could understand. I would be living in a cave, at least for now. Valentine was here, at least for now. I had Jack, as well, at least for now.

Not everything had to be forever after. Sometimes it was okay to be happy, at least for now.

THE END

Acknowledgments

This book was a long time coming. I would like to thank the people who were especially helpful at reminding me that I was still a writer, even if I was having trouble writing. Particular gratitude goes to my son, Mason Rounds, without whose encouragement I would never have finished this book. Likewise, my lovely wife, Shawn Rounds, whose faith in me never wavered, even when I wasn't nearly so certain. I will always cherish the day we spent proofing this book together around the dining room table, laughing at my most egregious typos. I love you both more than words can express.

A similar note of gratefulness should be given to my writers' group, Wyrdsmiths: Eleanor Arnason, Kelly Barnhill, Naomi Kritzer, Theo Lorenz, and Adam Stemple. You were right, I couldn't just quit Wyrdsmiths because I felt like I wasn't producing enough. Thank you all for your faith in me.

Of course, this book would not be a book without Cheryl Morgan and her hardworking staff at Wizard Tower Press, or without Ben Baldwin's amazing cover. Thank you for taking a chance on me.

About the Author

Lyda Morehouse... leads a double life. By day she's a mild-mannered science fiction novelist. At night, she dons a leather cat suit and prowls the streets as vampire romance writer Tate Hallaway.

In her science fiction persona, Lyda is the award-winning author of the AngeLINK series. Her first novel, *Archangel Protocol*, was the 2001 Shamus Award winner for the best original paperback featuring a private investigator, and the winner of the Barnes & Noble Maiden Voyage Award for best debut science fiction/fantasy novel. It was a nominee for the *Romantic Times* Critic's Choice for best science fiction. *Apocalypse Array* was short-listed for the Philip K. Dick Award for distinguished mass-market paperback novels of science fiction.

Tate's books include the Garnet Lacey series, and the young adult series, Vampire Princess of St. Paul.

Lyda lives in St. Paul, Minnesota, with her partner, Shawn, their son Mason, three cats and a startling collection of wild dust bunnies.

Tate's whereabouts are currently unknown, though a good place to start looking is: www.lydamorehouse.com

Books by Lyda Morehouse

The AngeLINK series (Wizard's Tower)
   Archangel Protocol
   Fallen Host
   Messiah Node
   Apocalypse Array

Books by Tate Hallaway

The Garnet Lacey Series (Berkeley)
   Tall Dark & Dead
   Dead Sexy
   Romancing the Dead
   Dead if I Do
   Honeymoon of the Dead

The Vampire Princess of St. Paul series (New American Library)
    Almost to Die For
    Almost Final Curtain

The Alex Connor series
    Precinct 13 (Berkeley)

Lightning Source UK Ltd.
Milton Keynes UK
UKHW022104160223
417160UK00019B/901/J